The SHIP of SHADOWS

MARIA KUZNIAR

PUFFIN

PUFFIN BOOKS

UK | USA | Canada | Ireland | Australia
India | New Zealand | South Africa

Puffin Books is part of the Penguin Random House group of companies
whose addresses can be found at global.penguinrandomhouse.com.

www.penguin.co.uk
www.puffin.co.uk
www.ladybird.co.uk

First published 2020

001

Set in 11/16.5 pt Sabon LT Std
Typeset by Jouve (UK), Milton Keynes
Printed and bound in Great Britain by Clays Ltd, Elcograf S.p.A.

A CIP catalogue record for this book is available from the British Library

ISBN: 978-0-241-37291-3

All correspondence to:
Puffin Books
Penguin Random House Children's
One Embassy Gardens, 8 Viaduct Gardens
London SW11 7BW

For Dziadzio, for telling me stories.

For my dad, for surrounding me
with stories.

And for Michael, for making my life
my favourite story of all.

Voyage of the Ship of Shadows

Atlantic Ocean

SPAIN

Mediterranean Sea

Seville

Tangier

MOROCCO

Essaouira

Marrakesh

The Sahara Desert

The lost

PROLOGUE

Aleja was a girl so hungry for adventure that sometimes she found herself in strange places.

Tonight she was prowling the rooftops of Sevilla when she should have been sleeping, having stuffed a pillow under her bedsheets back home.

Scrambling from one roof to another, Aleja ventured deep into the oldest part of the city. Here the buildings loomed up, creating ramshackle paths. Crumbling stones tested Aleja's balance as she half climbed, half crawled along a narrow ledge. In the great domes and spires she imagined palaces, castles and cathedrals, and the stories their stones could tell, tales entrusted to kings and queens and explorers and scholars. Night was the best time for creeping along in the shadows, feeling the whisperings of the city in her blood.

Up here she could explore a whole new layer of her city and she loved it. Sweet Sevilla was scented with orange blossom and moored in history.

The darkness keeping her hidden from the ancient streets below, Aleja leaped across to another rooftop, and then ran across a flat white roof. Her little knapsack flapped against her back and she jumped as far as she could into the sky. Just for a moment it felt like she was flying. And then she hit the opposite wall with her arms outstretched and all the breath rushed out of her. As she scrambled to a safer position, Aleja grinned to herself. The city belonged to her.

She stared at the sails in the distance. Huge ships slunk in and out of the river port, full and heavy like gigantic sea beasts that had gorged themselves on riches. Sometimes, she knew, a ship would sail up the river with great chunks missing. Sailors would claim it had been attacked by monsters that lurked beneath the waves; giant kraken and leviathans and sirens with haunting songs were all waiting to take a bite out of passing ships. Sometimes the boats didn't come back at all.

With her back to a stubby tower, legs tucked beneath her, Aleja pulled out a book and opened it with a spine-cracking flourish. The Giralda – the tall, spindly bell tower that still carried ornate carvings from its time as a minaret – cast a soft glow on the pages, and she began to read.

Legendary Explorers told of Christopher Columbus's voyages from Sevilla and made Aleja thirsty for all the details of running expeditions and travelling across oceans. But those weren't her favourite stories.

More than anything else she loved reading about Thomas James, a British explorer who had travelled the world on his own ship and trekked through jungles and deserts and tundra. The book was written in English instead of Aleja's native Spanish, but she had taught herself to read English during long hours spent surrounded by books – the language had burrowed into her brain and stuck there. And she had read these words so many times they had clawed their way into her memory like familiar old friends.

A sudden noise snatched Aleja's attention. She stood up, peering down to the streets below. There, in one of the alleys, a man was scurrying along furtively with a large sack perched on his shoulder. She bit her lip, tempted to follow him, but he ducked out of sight and she lost him. She turned back to her book and soon lost herself in a world of adventure instead.

Sometime later, aware the night was slipping away from her, Aleja closed the book and whispered to herself,

'*Thomas James was the king of explorers, sailing under a disguise of merchant flags to hide his true intentions of uncovering the secrets of the world. His ship was marked with an old sigil . . .*'

These stories fed her dreams.

CHAPTER ONE

The Girl Who Dreamed

If she squinted her eyes just right, Aleja could almost pretend that the dust motes twinkling in the air were grains of sand thrown up from a desert storm. Or kicked up from a camel's hooves. She blinked, and now the motes were just the dust settling on the floor of El Puente, her family's tavern.

'More sweeping, less daydreaming, *cariño*,' her abuela said, shaking her head affectionately as she washed cups in a bucket of water. Pablo was helping – by steadily making everything wetter. A smaller, impish copy of their father except for the scar on his ear, Pablo was the younger of Aleja's two older brothers and had the clumsy touch of a toddler. He rushed through his chores until he exasperated their grandmother into letting him go.

Aleja resumed her sweeping. The shutters were closed to keep out the growing heat of the day and the only light came from the wooden doors open to the street beyond, where she could see her father setting up stools round the old wine barrels they used for tables. He turned to grin at Aleja. His short black hair was retreating with age, his face was tanned, and today his cheeks were pink with mirth.

It had taken him what had felt like years to smile again after Aleja's mother had died of a fever when Aleja was only six years old. Her memories of her mother were fuzzy round the edges. Sometimes Aleja worried she'd forget what her mother had looked like, but her abuela hugged her the fiercest on those days, wrapping her in stories of her mother until her face reappeared in Aleja's dreams.

Aleja's own face was petite and heart-shaped with dark-green eyes (striking up too many comments on how she resembled a porcelain doll). After two grandsons, her abuela had been thrilled about the birth of a granddaughter. But Aleja's brown hair didn't fall in a silky wave, nor did she allow it to be brushed and plaited like her grandmother wore hers. And her eyes were too stuffed with daydreams to be soft and pretty.

From where she stood, brushing the dust out of the stout wooden doors, her view stretched out to a wide square, and then, even further still, all the way to the sweeping Guadalquivir river and the Torre del Oro watchtower, which sparkled in the sunlight.

'Out with you if you're not going to be useful,' Aleja's grandmother was telling Pablo. 'It's going to be a busy day today and I don't want you under my feet.'

'Why? What's happening today?' Aleja instantly asked.

'There's a lot of activity down at the docks,' her father said, stepping back inside and wiping the sweat from his brow. 'The Flota de Indias is expected.'

Aleja shivered with anticipation; the Flota de Indias, the Spanish Treasure Fleet, was a large collection of ships that brought exotic goods and luxuries from the territories of the Spanish Empire across the Atlantic to the mainland. Aleja wasn't fussed about gold or sugar, but she *was* interested in the explorers who turned up on those ships.

Her grandmother noticed her fidgeting. 'You're not to go; I'll be needing your help in the kitchen today.'

Aleja slumped with disappointment.

'I'll tell you about it later!' Pablo said with a sneaky grin, darting out before Aleja could scowl at him.

'That's not fair,' Aleja said, gripping her broom tighter.

Abuela sighed. 'That's the way of the world, *cariño*. Pablo is older than you and too disastrous to be of use in the kitchen.'

'Poor Aleja, she'd captain a ship in a heartbeat if she could!' her father said, chortling.

Her grandmother's lips vanished into a thin line. 'Nice young girls don't go chasing after adventure,' she said, taking the broom off Aleja. She flung open the door to the kitchen. Aleja's oldest and favourite brother, Miguel, looked up with a start. Although he was fifteen, his doe-like eyes, floppy hair and dreamy expression made him look much younger. He had the same green eyes as Aleja, but his were often glazed over with dreams of the kitchen while hers were wild for the open sea. His face was dusted with flour and there was butter in his hair. 'You can bake the bread with Miguel,' their grandmother said, taking a damp cloth and scrubbing Miguel's face with it while making several loud tsking sounds.

Aleja hated baking every bit as much as Miguel adored it.

'Where's Pablo?' Miguel asked once their grandmother had bustled back to the front of the tavern to help their father open it for the day.

'He went out to the docks,' Aleja said, slamming the dough on to the counter.

'Ah.' Miguel rescued the dough from Aleja. 'You are the youngest; she's protective of you,' he added.

Aleja stared miserably at the dough. 'No, she's trying to mould me into the granddaughter she wants me to be.'

'Well, you're exactly the sister I want you to be,' Miguel said, nudging her with a smile.

The day grew hotter and hotter under a blue sky that stretched from horizon to horizon with not a puff of cloud in sight. Even the palm trees looked like they were suffocating. The tavern windows had been thrown open to catch the breeze, but it hadn't made the slightest difference. Stuck between sweat-stained shirts and the smell of too many people, their drinks and their tapas, Aleja quickly got bored. Sometimes the tavern talk was interesting, when it turned to rumours and stories of ghost ships or strange monsters or lost cities. Things that defied belief, that didn't fit into the everyday world Aleja knew. Things that whispered of magic.

Most people laughed and dismissed these stories – only the most sea-battered men, deep in their tankards, shared those kinds of tales. But that didn't stop Aleja fiercely believing in them all.

'– pirate attacks in the Mediterranean.'

'Two ships have gone down in flames from cannon fire.'

There were two sailors in the corner, talking rapidly in Spanish. Aleja looked up from the book she was sneakily reading.

'Worse than the actual pirates themselves half the time,' said one.

'If you ask me, pirate hunters interfere far more with port business, strutting around, filled with their own self-importance . . . and the Fury is the worst of the lot,' the first man grumbled. 'He'd decimate half the seas if he had the chance.'

'Hopefully he won't make port here,' the second one replied, wiping his hands on his trousers as he dropped a few gold coins on the table and made to stand up.

Aleja craned her neck to hear them as they made their way towards the door, gossiping about other ships.

'No, I hear it's crewed by women,' the first man was saying, while the other guffawed. '*Imagine.*'

'It's bad luck to have a woman on a ship, it is,' the other added seriously.

Aleja rolled her eyes.

'They say it's haunted by the shadows of all the sailors they've killed,' the first one whispered, his words trailing behind him like smoke. 'And that's why they call it the *Ship of –*'

Aleja slid her book into her knapsack, checked her abuela wasn't looking and then furtively followed them out of the tavern. But when she emerged into the bright sunlight, she was greeted by the sound of giggling. Two local girls her own age were lurking just outside the door, their dresses as pretty as their peals of laughter. She cast a look behind them. The two sailors were nowhere to be seen. Deflated, Aleja turned her attention back to the tavern, giving the girls a welcoming smile. One of them turned to whisper into the other's ear and they broke out in a fresh spurt of laughter.

Aleja's skin burned.

Ignore them, said Miguel's voice in her head.

She tried to forget the sick feeling in her stomach and return to El Puente, when suddenly she found herself face to face with someone even worse. Juan. He was Miguel's age and the son of a wealthy landlord, with a regal bone structure, deep grey eyes and words coated with venom.

She stepped back, her stomach tensing. Juan's best friend, Carlos, and his clingy twin, Pedro, fell back to stand behind her, their thin lips pulled in identical smiles. Aleja hated all three of them. Bullies were like wolves: they travelled in packs and would pick your bones clean. She tried to squeeze back into the tavern between Carlos and Pedro, but the twins moved quickly and closed the gap. Carlos pushed Aleja roughly back into the centre of the circle before crossing his arms, his grin displaying a mouthful of yellowing teeth. Juan snatched the books from Aleja's bag. She watched him try – and fail – to read the English titles, and instead look at the ships on the covers. He threw them on to the street one by one. Aleja resisted rushing over to pick them up; she didn't want to give Juan the satisfaction.

'You're not still waiting for some grand adventure to come along and sweep you away, are you?' Aleja watched the sneer crawl over Juan's face. He leaned in closer, dropping his voice to a whisper, as if he were going to share a jewel of a secret with her. 'Because I hate to tell you this, but girls can't be explorers. Female explorers don't exist. And even if they did . . .' He paused for effect and Aleja knew what followed would be especially vicious. 'They wouldn't want a scrawny runt like you in their ranks. You're pathetic,' he finished triumphantly, spitting at her.

Aleja closed her eyes, wishing she could disappear.

Juan stalked off with his friends amid a swirl of laughter. Aleja wiped the spit from her cheek, burning with anger and embarrassment, and scurried around in the dust, picking up her books.

Everybody knew her secret. Once she'd held it tight to herself, but she was too hot-headed to keep it private, and it had come bursting out in an argument with Pablo.

'You don't belong in the port; it's no place for a girl,' he had snarled.

'You're wrong!' Aleja had snapped back. 'You'll see. One day I'll be a famous explorer and I'll travel through all the biggest ports on a ship of my own.'

There was a beat. Then Pablo let out a howl of laughter, tears leaking from his eyes.

Mortified, Aleja had launched herself at him, turning his laughter into a scream. Their father had had to tear her away.

Two years later, Pablo's left ear still bore the crescent-shaped imprint of Aleja's teeth. These days, he pretended it was a wolf bite, but that hadn't stopped him telling half the city about her lonely dreams.

CHAPTER TWO

Books, Stars and Gunpowder

'Miguel told me what happened,' Aleja's grandmother said later that evening, easing a brush through Aleja's knotted hair. 'Still no luck making friends?'

Aleja shrugged, using her foot to nudge her book further beneath her bed. Her abuela had interrupted her in the middle of a novel in which the heroine had written a secret letter using lemon juice for invisible ink. Distracted by the thought of an ink that had to be heated to be revealed, she'd almost been caught reading the sneakily borrowed book and had to quickly toss it under the bed.

'They don't like me. I'm too different.'

Her grandmother began to tame another section of Aleja's hair. 'I think it's important to have friends, Aleja. Miguel can't be your only companion in life.'

'It's not that I don't *want* friends,' Aleja began, but found that she couldn't finish; a lump had wedged itself in her throat.

'I know, *cariño*. Perhaps you could try talking to other girls about their interests?' Her grandmother didn't voice the words Aleja heard in her head – the ones that said *instead of yours*.

They sat in silence for a few minutes.

'Here,' her grandmother said, finished. 'I saved this one just for you.' She handed Aleja a small coin that had been polished until it shone. 'Your mother used to collect these,' she added.

'Thank you,' Aleja said, watching it glint in the candlelight.

'Sleep well, *cariño*.' She lay a hand on Aleja's cheek before she left, closing the wooden door behind her.

But Aleja had no intention of sleeping.

The large courtyard of the university quarter was empty, cobblestones glowing in the moonlight, palm trees and stars Aleja's only witnesses as she scurried across it, hiding behind the trunks of the trees to ensure she wasn't spotted.

She gently lifted one of the heavy windows and climbed inside. The library was a long hall with marble flooring and tall wooden bookcases crammed everywhere, creating alleys of knowledge. As Aleja gazed around she noticed little spaces, secreted away to fit a handful of armchairs or a table and chairs. The sconces on the walls were lit for any scholars who might while away their nights in study, though the odd scholar Aleja came across was too immersed in their books to notice the girl who crept past them through the shadows.

She prowled in front of the shelves that reached to the ceiling and marvelled at their titles hinting at wonders around the world: *Unexplored Jungles of the Americas*; *Flora and Fauna of the Tundra*; *The Most Dangerous Pirates Who Sail the Seas*.

Aleja was in the mood for adventure after her eavesdropping. She lifted the last title from the shelf and took it to one of the old armchairs nestled between the shelves. The aged brown leather stuck to the back of her legs as she sat down. She flipped through the entries she knew well: Long Ben, also known as Henry Every, one of the richest and cruellest pirates to date. The *Ship of Shadows*, the legendary but barely documented pirate ship whose cut-throat crew inspired fear in the hearts of their foes. William Kidd, captain of the *Adventure Galley*, a savage pirate hunter turned pirate, and the Pirate Lord, an elusive but masterful treasure hunter.

Aleja skipped past many more accounts of murder and plunder, most of which she'd already heard in the tavern, before the book flopped shut. She glared at it. Juan's voice echoed in her thoughts: *Girls can't be explorers.*

Apparently they couldn't be pirates either.

Her frustration churned and bubbled inside her, ready to erupt like a volcano.

Aleja replaced the book with a sigh and picked up a volume of Herodotus's *The Histories* and slid it into her bag along with *Tales of Thomas James*. It was time to leave the library with its comforting smell of lingering pipe smoke and leather.

She didn't crawl back into bed. Instead Aleja tiptoed up to the roof. Up here, under the canopy of stars and a sliver of moon, listening to the lapping of the river on the ships' hulls, she breathed freely. She cracked open *Tales of Thomas James* and plummeted straight into an epic Thomas James adventure, written by one of his accompanying guides, Samuel Worthers. He commented that *Thomas was often seen scribbling away in his own journals*, and Aleja wished she could have read those, but according to her investigations they were long lost; no one had ever read them, though the passing references in books like these proved they had once existed.

She lay back, tracing the shapes of the constellations above her, picking out the harp that belonged to Lyra, the arcing wings of Cygnus, the swan, and the wingspan of Aquila, the eagle. As her eyes grew heavy she could have sworn one of them tumbled down from the sky, forming the shadow of a gigantic bird that swept over the roof, blotting out the moon's glow for a second. But before she had time to consider it, she was already melting into a dream of warm libraries and ancient books and old ships.

And then the smell of gunpowder tickled her nose.

CHAPTER THREE

The Sigil of Athena

Aleja sat bolt upright and stared out at the port.

Had she imagined it? She sniffed. No, there was definitely a charred scent floating in on the breeze. She squinted at the night, dark and thick around the ships. Nothing looked out of place.

Another flicker of moonlight. She looked up. A bird with an incredible wingspan was gliding over the port. It circled twice before flying away on silent wings to settle on the prow of an unfamiliar ship.

There.

The ship was sneaking into port.

It was a rather plain sloop with one great central mast. All the sails fanned out from there, though they were a little ragged from wear. The ship's slow speed must have been deliberate; Aleja knew that sloops were agile and fast, able to race past the heavier goods ships crossing the Atlantic and sailable by a small crew. But what really captured Aleja's attention, pressing her to the edge of the crumbling wall as she tracked the ship's progress into port with hungry eyes, was something else.

The ship was *smoking*.

Great slashes of the hull were blackened and stank of gunpowder from across the river. If she stared really hard, she could even see the outline of a hole left by a cannonball blast. This was a ship fresh from a battle. Aleja scanned it, curious. Stranger still, the ship didn't have gun decks.

She tried to make out the ship's flag. It had a white diagonal cross on a dark background: merchants. Why would someone attack a merchant's ship with no gun decks? Her fingers trembled with excitement. Maybe it had been attacked by pirates.

Aleja watched the sloop drop anchor at the far side of the port, away from the bigger ships, fading into the scenery and hiding its battered appearance in the dark. Everything was still for a few minutes but Aleja couldn't tear her attention away.

Then she spotted it.

At the prow something was glittering in the light of the ship's lantern. Aleja fumbled around for the piece of glass she kept on the roof and peered through it. Her view of the ship magnified, she now saw it was an etching of an owl with outstretched wings. Each wing bore a golden eye. Hard to spot and even harder to understand. But it niggled at Aleja; it was familiar somehow. Before she could muddle through it, a rickety gangplank was lowered and a couple of figures disembarked. They were walking towards Aleja's end of the docks. Aleja flew down the stairs and on to the street to investigate.

She hid behind the corner of the tavern wall and waited to see if the figures would pass her. A minute went by. Then another. And just when she couldn't resist any longer, she heard it. A hushed conversation heading towards her. She pressed her back harder into the wall, trying to pick out their words, when she realized what was striking about the voices. One of them was English – not unusual in itself as people sailed into Sevilla from all over the world – but it was, without a doubt, a woman's.

She peered out into the street.

The two figures had dark hoods pulled over their heads, but Aleja caught a splash of blonde hair spilling out of one and heard the second woman answer the first in English accented in a way she'd never heard before. 'Don't know where we'll find that amount of wood at this time.'

'We can't wait. The ship needs it now.'

'We'll have to steal someone else's supply.'

They walked out of earshot.

But instead of following them, Aleja rushed back in the opposite direction, away from the port. She knew exactly where she needed to be.

Dawn crested the horizon as Aleja raced against time, following the route she'd taken earlier that night – *yesterday?* – back to the university. She threaded through the courtyard, glancing up at the sky to see that it was already the colour of bruised oranges.

She clambered through the window and stole over to the stacks, slid *Legendary Explorers* out and sat on the floor. The book fell open to the page she'd read so often that she could almost summon the words from memory.

Thomas James was the king of explorers, sailing under a disguise of merchant flags to hide his true intentions, to uncover the secrets of the world. His ship was marked with an old sigil, that of Athena, heralding the knowledge he kept inside his ship. One that, rumour had it, could only be unlocked with his golden key. A shadow on the seas, Thomas James seems to have escaped the notice of his peers and history itself; little is known about his exploits, and his journals have long since been lost to the mists of time.

And there it was, at the bottom of the page: a tiny golden owl with outstretched wings bearing eyes.

Aleja checked the library indexes on ancient Greece until she found a tome called *Symbology of the Gods*. She flipped through the musty pages to the Greek goddess and read:

Known for her wisdom and strategic warfare, Athena's symbols included those related to battle, along with olive trees and, to represent wisdom, owls.

There was no mistaking such a distinctive symbol. It *had* to be Thomas James's ship. But if Thomas James had gone missing more than eighty years earlier, who were the women who now sailed his ship?

What had she heard earlier? *'I hear it's crewed by women ... They say it's haunted by the shadows of all the sailors they've killed and that's why they call it the* Ship of –'

Her heart thudding, Aleja grabbed the copy of *The Most Dangerous Pirates Who Sail the Seas* and found the entry she was looking for:

Ship of Shadows, *the*
    Legendary pirate ship. Tales often heard in taverns of the ferocious cut-throat crew. No known sightings.

Aleja felt certain that Thomas James's ship, the *Ship of Shadows*, and the merchant sloop were all separate stories of the *same* ship. She hugged the books to her, thinking of the women she'd overheard in the port.

She knew in her bones that somewhere, somehow, there had been other girls like her. Girls who yearned so badly, so deeply, for adventure and excitement that it churned inside them. And they had grown up to become *pirates*.

She *had* to get a closer look at that ship.

CHAPTER FOUR

The Start of a Story

Aleja slid the books back into place just as the first beams of sunlight peeped through the library windows. She stopped. Something was sparkling at her.

At the base of the bookcase there was another etching of a golden owl. This one was patchy, barely more than an indent. Whoever had marked it must have done so a very long time ago. Aleja kneeled on the floor and poked around the wooden base, looking for a weak spot. Tap, tap, *tap*. Aleja paused – the last tap had definitely sounded hollow. Breathing faster, she wedged her face as close as possible to the wood. There she found the smallest groove that she could *just* get her fingernail under . . . There was a low creak and a pop, and a section of the bookcase suddenly flew open, spouting dust and dead flies.

Inside there was a book.

The cover was golden with bronze letters stamped on to it, spelling out *Thomas James*. Aleja picked it up with trembling fingers. Could this be one of his lost journals? As soon as she felt how thin it was, she realized it couldn't be – there were only six pages of thick parchment inside. And they were blank. Disappointed, she studied each page, sure that she must have missed something. Nothing.

She sat back, her thoughts fast and ferocious. The book bore Thomas James's name. She'd found it in a secret compartment marked with the same symbol as his ship. And someone had gone to a lot of effort to squirrel it away in the library. Who would have bothered to do that for a blank book? No, it meant something, she was sure of it. She just didn't know *what*.

Tucking the mysterious book under her arm, Aleja climbed back out of the window and headed down to the river.

The port was rousing itself in the early hour, large wooden crates, everywhere Aleja looked, being lowered up and down by ropes as ships were packed and unpacked. The Guadalquivir was choppy with the volume of ships and boats manoeuvring round each other along the length of the river. It was one long, snaking port that curled round the city of Sevilla. Aleja stood on the eastern shore, where one of the largest wharfs ensured plenty of sailors tripped out of ships and straight into El Puente. Behind her the city unfurled into its narrow maze of the oldest streets and buildings. Gulls screeched and the air was thick and salted, reminding Aleja how close she was to the open ocean she'd never seen, though it was just half a day's sailing away. Aleja looked out across the port, the golden book clamped under her arm, working out how to get closer to the sloop. She *had* to see Thomas James's ship and the women who sailed it.

She rushed up the wharf, weaving in and out of wooden crates, scanning everything and everyone at the port. She didn't see any women who looked out of place. Aleja ignored the curses of two men carrying a barrel as she crossed their path and plunged deeper into the docks.

A makeshift market had been set up and stallholders were shouting their wares, holding up oranges and bottles of olive oil to tempt the new arrivals. Aleja had precious little time before her abuela would rise for the day to discover her missing. As she ran past the stalls, she bumped into another barrel-carrying pair. A fresh torrent of curses was aimed in her direction as the men scrambled to pick up the coins they'd dropped. She dodged their annoyance and heard something that made her pause. Someone at a nearby fruit stall was speaking fumbling Spanish with an unmistakably English accent. And she was a woman.

Aleja sidled up to the stall, a creature of eyes and ears and curiosity. She fixed her attention on the woman, who was bartering for a basket of oranges.

The woman wore loose trousers, supple leather boots that wrapped round her calves and a white shirt beneath a waistcoat that was laced shut. Her face was flushed pink but pale beneath, with a sprinkling of freckles over her cheeks and nose, and lines framing her eyes. Long chestnut hair was pulled off her neck and tied up with a leather strip. Her outfit was so peculiar – she was wearing trousers! – that Aleja couldn't help gaping, desperately hoping that she was staring at one of the crew members of the *Ship of Shadows*. One of the *pirates*. She was sure that she had stumbled upon a mystery that she didn't have quite enough clues to solve yet. But oh, how she wanted to solve it.

While she was deliberating whether or not to speak, the woman turned. She looked at Aleja like she was peeling away her skin to get at the secrets underneath. Aleja couldn't resist imagining what she would look like. Perhaps a whorl of thoughts patterning her body, all bright flecks of imagination and dreams. No sooner had Aleja had this flight of fancy than the woman had turned away, taken the oranges and reached out her hand to give the seller some coins. Aleja saw it all in slow motion. The tanned skin of her wrist, the calluses on her fingers, the shirt riding up the woman's forearm to reveal an inky design – an owl tattoo.

The woman turned and walked away. Aleja had a surge of panic. She couldn't lose her chance to speak to her.

At the very last moment Aleja found her voice. '*Espere. ¡Espere!* Wait.' She didn't know if she'd pronounced it right. She'd only ever whispered English words to herself by candlelight in midnight hours in the library, imagining herself leading expeditions across the polar ice caps, or down the Nile as a famous explorer, fluent in fifteen languages and knowledgeable on a wide variety of subjects. Never had she spoken the language to another person before now, when panic had propelled it out of her.

The woman halted. 'You speak English?' she demanded, frown lines between her eyebrows as she scanned Aleja up and down.

Aleja squirmed, wishing her dress wasn't so dirty. She didn't want to think about what her grandmother would say if she saw Aleja in this state.

She nodded, hoping the woman was looking for something other than cleanliness.

She was. For the tiniest second her eyes flicked down to the book Aleja was holding, and then whipped back to Aleja's face before she had time to blink. But Aleja had seen it: when the woman's eyes lit upon the embossed letters on the cover, her throat had bobbed up and down and her eyes had darkened. *She recognized the book.* More than that, she *wanted* it.

Aleja held on to it tighter, staring up at the woman. Did she know what secrets the mysterious book held?

The woman interrupted Aleja's puzzling. 'We're in need of a ship's linguist after our last one was . . .' She paused. 'Lost.' She flashed a brilliant smile that sent her frown lines scurrying away like mice. 'Interested?'

Aleja, a girl who had built herself out of words – Spanish words, French words, English words and even some Arabic – suddenly found herself lost for words. She stood there, clutching the book, while thoughts whirled around her head too quickly for her to catch. *Could* she go? She was tempted. A real adventure, at long last!

But something stopped her. She couldn't help thinking of how Miguel would feel if she suddenly disappeared from his life. Her energy slumped.

'I understand,' the woman said, her fierce eyes still fixed on Aleja.

Aleja glanced down, grappling for all the things she wanted to say, but when she opened her mouth the woman had already disappeared. Aleja spun round, frantic for one last glimpse of her, but the crowds at the marketplace were seamless, hiding any trace of her, trousers, owl tattoo and all. This time Aleja knew she wasn't coming back.

She'd always thought she'd leap at the chance for adventure, but she hadn't. She could still try to catch a glimpse of Thomas James's ship – she wanted to spy on the crew and see what they were up to, or find out where they'd been attacked. And she still had the book, which was a mystery all of its own. But her disappointment in herself didn't fade.

She kicked a nearby barrel. It rattled. Aleja frowned. Putting her eye to a hole in the lid, she saw something glimmering below. *Coins*. A mountain of doubloons was hidden inside the barrel. Looking up at the men carrying other barrels between them, occupied with loading them into a nearby ship, she recognized half of them – they were oafs in Juan's landlord father's employ. Money collectors. Ones who often visited El Puente. But what were they doing with entire barrels of gold coins in the port? Aleja picked up a few stray doubloons, glittering under the sun, and studied one while she pocketed the others. In a flash of comprehension she understood. They were forged copies.

A large hand closed over the scruff of her neck and hauled her away from the barrel. Aleja gasped for air, kicking her legs as hard as she could as a gruff voice snarled into her ear: '*¿Qué haces aquí?*' *What are you doing here?*

'*Nada*,' Aleja said, twisting to try to break his iron hold. He snatched the coin from her hand.

His grip on her tightened. He clearly wasn't planning on releasing her, so Aleja tried a different tack. 'I won't tell anyone,' she told him. 'For a price.'

His laugh rumbled out and his fingers relaxed slightly. Aleja seized her chance. Aiming a foot behind her, she kicked hard. The man's laugh morphed into a grunt of pain, and the fist round the back of her dress loosened, just enough for Aleja to twist once more and slip through his fingers.

Then she was off. She might not have been strong, but she was quick. Slippery like an eel, Aleja ran, winding her way lightning-fast through tiny streets in the maze of Sevilla's old quarter behind the port. She ended up on a wider avenue, the distinctive naves of the medieval shipyard before her.

Once, entire fleets of grand ships had been built here before being sent out to rule the ocean. Now the brick walls held only warehouses. All gothic arches and large stony spaces, with the occasional skeleton of a rotting ship to be found inside. It was said to be haunted, but Aleja had never seen a ghost. She ploughed deeper into the shipyard . . . where Juan liked to idle away his days.

When he spotted Aleja, Juan gave a predatory smile. Any other day it would have frozen the blood in her veins. He opened his mouth to speak, but before any more of his nastiness could spill out of it, Aleja tossed a coin to him.

'Look at it,' Aleja told him.

Juan looked at it with studied indifference. But Aleja was watching him hard enough to see some of the colour fade from his face.

'I suggest you stop taking such an interest in my life,' she told him, 'or I'll make sure the Port Authority takes a *very* close interest in your father's affairs. Beheading is the sentence for counterfeiting, isn't it?' She let the sunlight dance over the other coins before repocketing them. 'Evidence,' she said, patting her pocket.

Juan swaggered towards her. 'Are you threatening me?'

Aleja heard footsteps in the distance, running towards them. Strolling out of the shipyard, she flashed a smile at Juan. 'Yes.'

She forced herself to walk until she was out of sight. Then she ran. Juan didn't need to know she was being pursued by his father's henchmen. Let him sweat. After her thrill at having had the guts to threaten Juan, the echoing of boots pounding on cobblestones reminded her of the danger she was in. Darting up a narrow dead-end alley, she rested against the wall, trying to breathe as quietly as possible.

'It'll be fine,' she whispered to herself, squeezing her eyes shut. 'They won't catch me.'

A low laugh. 'Is that right?'

The man was watching her from the entrance to the alley, a slow smile spreading across his face. She now recognized him as the man she'd seen sneaking through the alleys the night before last. Behind him stood two other men.

Aleja swallowed thickly. 'I take it back – you don't need to pay me. I won't tell anyone what I saw.'

The first man stepped closer. 'Ah, but now I don't trust you, see? I don't particularly want to do this, but –' he shrugged – 'I need to know you won't talk.'

The sun bounced into Aleja's eyes, glinting off the metal blade of his dagger, raised and pointed towards her. Adrenalin torched her veins as she stared at its sharp, sharp edge, trying not to imagine what it could do to her. She shuffled backwards, dry dust wisping around the alley as she moved to its furthest point, all three men now brandishing daggers. She could feel the smugness radiating from them. They thought they had her.

She smiled.

CHAPTER FIVE

Pirates and Thieves

Before the three men could snatch enough air into their lungs to shout, Aleja shoved the book down the front of her dress, whirled round and dug her fingers into the stone in front of her, pushing up with the toes of her shoes until she was scrambling up the wall like one of the mountain goats in the Sierra Nevada.

Where others might have seen missing stones, jagged edges, or crumbled-away hollows in the wall, Aleja saw crevices for her fingertips and footholds to brace her feet against. Climbing was the closest she could get to flying, and Aleja liked to feel free.

Another few minutes and she was pulling herself up on to a roof terrace. Without pausing for rest, she ran across its length, dodging sheets hung out to dry, her heart racing as fast as her legs. When she reached the other side, and saw who was standing there, her shoes skidded on the sun-baked roof.

The woman in trousers was looking at Aleja with delight.

'And you climb too? *Excellent*,' she said in Spanish, stepping closer, until Aleja could make out the freckles under her wide-brimmed hat.

'I – were you following me?' Aleja asked, pushing the book further down the front of her dress.

The woman's eyes tracked it. 'I find we're in a unique situation here,' she said mildly as a chorus of shouts began to filter up from the surrounding streets.

'¡Ladrina!' Thief.

Aleja swallowed. She recognized the panicked voices of the men who had been chasing her in those shouts. Counterfeiting currency carried a severe penalty; if Aleja reported them, there would be an investigation. And then they would lose their heads. She knew they needed to find her. And if they claimed she was a thief, it would discredit whatever story she had, not to mention carry its own sentence. Aleja had no desire to be whipped in the street.

The woman nodded at the shouts. 'Exactly,' she continued as if they were sitting down to tea and not on a roof with an escalating manhunt unfolding around them. 'I'll give you a safe place to hide on board our ship, if you let me look at that book of yours.' Her eyes gleamed.

'Done,' Aleja said.

'Do you know the fastest way to the port?'

Aleja grinned. 'I know this city by heart.'

The woman spread her arms. 'Then take us there now. A back way, towards the eastern side, where our ship is anchored.'

Aleja knew the buildings in the oldest part of Sevilla were jumbled together like crooked teeth, and she leaped from one roof terrace to another, confidently forging their path. She heard the woman's footsteps behind her and was unable to stop a grin of delight as she stretched her arms out, her fingers seeming to scrape the endless blue sky. *She was going to see the ship.*

She climbed down a wall, searching for the path downwards with the toes of her shoes rather than her eyes. The shouts had multiplied. It sounded as if there were more men now, and they were spreading out. The grin dissolved from Aleja's lips. Neither she nor the woman spoke. They clung to the faint shadows and Aleja forced herself to keep running, keep moving. Zigzagging through the maze of Old Sevilla, she planned to loop round the backstreets, making her way to the port. Instead she tripped over an errant cobblestone and landed hard on her knees, scraping them with a hiss of frustration.

Before the woman could yank her up, Aleja felt a thick fist close over her elbow as she was getting to her feet again. 'Got you.'

Aleja tried to squirm free, but the man had learned his lesson and his other hand was faster than her, coming to rest his dagger against her neck. Aleja stilled instantly.

'Can't find anyone your own size to fight?' The woman was assessing the situation, her hand resting on her hip.

The dagger tightened against Aleja's throat and she gasped and gritted her teeth. She tried not to move a muscle, incensed that she couldn't bite and claw her way free.

'Why don't you let the girl go and you can fight me instead?' the woman continued in her awkward Spanish.

'This is a business affair,' the man finally answered her. 'The child is a thief and we don't tolerate thieves in this city.'

'What did she steal?'

No answer.

The woman nodded. 'I thought as much.' She stepped towards them, her boots making a smart clacking noise against the cobblestones. It made Aleja long for her own pair to strut around the city in. Another step closer, and the man loosened the dagger against Aleja's throat, instead pointing it at the woman. He kept his fingers wrapped like a vice round Aleja's elbow, pressing her to his side. She tried in vain to wriggle free.

The woman stepped closer again and he raised the dagger. Aleja thought the woman winked at her, but before she could give it another thought, the woman had reached down to her boot and sprung back up again with a curved knife. She spun round, knocking the dagger out of the unsuspecting man's hand with an echoing clang. Aleja sank her teeth into his arm before he could pick it up. Yelling, he let go of her and clamped his hand down on the bloodied gash she'd left behind.

'Nice,' the woman said approvingly before punching him in the face with a loud crack.

He slumped to the ground, howling over his broken nose.

'Now we run.' The woman kicked his dagger away, gesturing for Aleja to lead the way.

Footsteps echoed up and down the narrow clutter of streets as the manhunt for the *ladrina* grew in intensity.

'That was brilliant,' Aleja panted as the heat thickened around them. Bells rang out from the nearby cathedral. She wasn't sure how well the woman understood her – she seemed to be struggling with speaking in Spanish, as well as with finding her way around.

They ran through the centre of Sevilla, past the streets that swept along to the royal palace where the residents were richer. Horses and carriages were rushing past, and then Aleja could smell salted waters and hear the gulls. Aleja's blood sang with excitement – and not a small amount of nerves. She was going to see Thomas James's legendary vessel turned pirate ship, the *Ship of Shadows*, for herself! She couldn't help thinking that the captain of such a cut-throat crew must be terrifying in the flesh – scarred from battle, adorned with finery and weapons – a truly intimidating presence.

A fresh volley of shouts broke out behind them and the woman launched herself into a small rowing boat. 'Jump!' she shouted back to Aleja, untying the rope securing the boat.

Aleja jumped. The woman took up a pair of oars and steered them skilfully down the river, weaving in and out of bigger ships resting on the water and boats coming in to market day, until they were lost in the jumble of sails and people. Juan's voice slunk back into Aleja's thoughts. *They wouldn't want a scrawny runt like you . . .*

'Why did you help me?' Aleja blurted out.

The woman glanced at Aleja then, tearing away her concentration from rowing. 'You remind me of . . . someone. You're a feisty little thing. You wear your thirst for adventure on your face.'

It wasn't until they'd reached the far eastern reach of the port, where the hidden pirate sloop was resting in the water, that Aleja realized the woman had spoken in English, her native language. And Aleja had gobbled up every word.

CHAPTER SIX

Ship of Shadows

The sloop was far larger than it had looked from the port. Aleja sat in the rowing boat, thrumming with anticipation; she was close enough to touch the *Ship of Shadows*. The woman rapped smartly on the wood and two lengths of rope were immediately tossed down.

'Any good with knots?' the woman asked Aleja, still speaking in English.

'Mmm, I haven't tried before,' Aleja replied, the foreign words clumping together in her mouth. She hoped she was saying them right, but the woman nodded so Aleja guessed she'd been understood. She might only be hiding out on the pirate ship for a few hours, but she was determined to pass any test put to her. Especially after discovering her language abilities ran even deeper than she'd thought – perhaps she'd have another chance to take the woman up on her offer of becoming the ship's linguist.

Aleja watched her tie each rope in sure knots to each end of the rowing boat. Then she knocked on the side of the hulking ship again, and there was a swift jerk on the ropes that made Aleja cling to her seat. The rowing boat was slowly raised alongside the body of the ship. There were no cannon holes on this side, but the ship still stank of smoke. Nerves gnawed at Aleja's insides as she imagined meeting the crew. Images of murdering, bloodthirsty pirates stalked through Aleja's head. Perhaps she wouldn't even be allowed on the ship after all; maybe they'd throw her overboard. Aleja glanced at the choppy, dirty river water, thick with boats. Maybe she wouldn't be so nervous if she could swim, but then who'd want to swim in *that*? Biting her lip, she stole a look at the woman sitting opposite her; at least *she* didn't seem too murderous.

Once they were level with the deck, the woman stood, balancing effortlessly as they rocked. Gripping the taffrail, she vaulted over the side, leaving Aleja gaping in her wake. Aleja wasn't used to seeing women her father's age move like that. Determined to prove herself, Aleja jumped up and clung on to the side of the ship, her feet scrabbling against the damp wood, looking for anything to hold on to. It was harder than climbing up walls; the wood was smooth and her arms weren't strong enough to copy what the woman had done. Keeping the soles of her shoes flat against the ship, Aleja inched up like an awkward insect, reaching the taffrail and slipping over it. She fell straight down and the book dropped out of her dress. As soon as she hit the deck, a strange tremor shook the ship. The sails rippled, the wheel spun round by itself, and the wood creaked and moaned.

Aleja immediately scrambled to her feet, picked up the book and stared at the wheel, which slowly stopped spinning. She found herself in the presence of three curious women – the English woman and two strangers.

'What was that?' One of the women frowned.

Unlike the woman who had brought her aboard, the other two were very clearly pirates; their clothes were faded from the sea and sun, they were scarred from battle, and Aleja had never seen so many weapons on display.

'I have a theory . . .' The English woman trailed off as Aleja surveyed the pirates with the same once-over they were giving her. 'As I was telling you, she's a fierce little thing,' she said, amusement tickling the lines of her face.

One woman cocked her head as she looked at Aleja. Aleja held her chin high. This woman wore trousers and a shirt that were loose against her large frame. She had a wickedly curved cutlass strapped to her hip and was wearing a black hat perched on top of a cloud of curly dark-brown hair. Her face was rounded, with high cheekbones, long eyelashes and a bump in the bridge of her nose. The sleeves of her shirt were rolled up, affording Aleja a glimpse of a familiar owl tattoo inked on her dark-brown skin.

'Another port urchin?' The other woman raised an eyebrow, her accented English bearing the imprint of lands further south. She wore a headscarf and a matching long-sleeved gown in black and gold, the material tracing down to her single hand, the other sleeve pinned over an empty wrist. But it wasn't her missing hand or the two long scars that cruelly dissected her face that caught Aleja's attention. It was her unparalleled beauty. Aleja had never thought of beauty as dangerous before, but this woman wore it like a weapon. Her eyes glittered like the scimitar at her hip. Though she was younger than the other two, everything about her intimidated Aleja: her stance, the cold gleam in her expression, the opulence of her outfit. She looked like she was born to rule. This then was the captain.

'She uncovered something she wasn't supposed to, and half of the city are hunting for her now,' the English woman told the others. 'She needs a few hours of refuge until the search dies down.'

Why hasn't she mentioned the book? Aleja's fingers stiffened round its spine.

There was a flickering round the edges of the ship. Aleja gasped and almost dropped the book. They were surrounded by a legion of ghostly figures. Women and girls – all pirates by the look of them – had suddenly appeared, their dark-grey forms staring emptily out across the deck.

'Are they ghosts?' she asked, whirling round to take them all in.

'They're shadows of former crew members,' the English woman told her. 'Still alive and living around the world. You get used to them.'

'The *Ship of Shadows* is a ship like none other,' the captain said proudly as Aleja watched the shadows melt back into the deck. Aleja had always believed magic had to exist somewhere and here was undeniable proof.

'Thank you for letting me hide on board, Captain,' Aleja said to her, in awe.

The women exchanged a glance.

'Ah, perhaps my blundering about in Seville was too good an act,' said the English woman, amused.

'*You're* the captain?' Aleja stared at her, realizing she must have been testing Aleja since they'd met.

The woman arched an eyebrow at her. 'Captain Elizabeth Quint, at your service,' she said. 'This is my quartermaster, Olitiana.' She gestured towards the woman in trousers with the bared owl tattoo. 'And my first mate, Malika.' She nodded towards the woman with the glittering eyes and scimitar. Malika was now wearing a rather sinister smile at having been mistaken for the captain.

Olitiana passed the captain a large tri-cornered hat, which she set upon her head immediately, before pulling out a brown-leather wrist guard from her pocket and lacing it on. A flapping of large wings sounded, and an owl swooped down from behind the mast and settled on the captain's wrist, its talons curled round the leather. It was a white and tawny eagle owl, showing off its immense wingspan before it folded its wings and serenely stared at Aleja with bright orange eyes.

'Penumbra comes and goes as he likes,' the captain said, ruffling his stomach feathers affectionately. 'But he always finds his way back to me.'

Aleja thought back to the gigantic wings she'd seen the night before, skimming the moonlight, before she'd spotted the smoking ship.

'What's your name, child?' Olitiana asked.

Aleja tore her eyes away from the owl. 'Aleja.'

'What exactly did you find that set half of the city after you?' Malika asked.

Aleja met her eyes. Arrogance ran through this woman's face as deeply as her scars. She shrugged. 'I accidentally uncovered a counterfeiting ring.'

'Printing false coins is a big business,' the captain commented before turning to Malika. 'Come, we have things to discuss.'

'I should have kept more of them,' Aleja said ruefully.

Olitiana let out a laugh. 'Come with me, Aleja. It's best to get you below decks if people are looking for you. I'll introduce you to the others.'

'Have her brought to me later,' said Captain Quint, her eyes resting on Aleja for a beat before she jerked her head to Malika and the two of them stalked off in the opposite direction, already deep in conversation. Curiously only one shadow fell behind them as they walked – the captain's. Aleja's mouth fell open: Malika didn't have a shadow.

Olitiana strode off across the deck. Aleja rushed after her, wishing she could swivel her head all the way round like an owl; she wanted to memorize every detail. The quarterdeck was before them – a raised wooden deck that held the helm of the ship, the glossy wooden wheel that Aleja imagined the captain using to steer them towards distant horizons. There were two sets of steps up to it, one on either side of a small door.

'Captain's quarters,' said Olitiana, nodding towards it. 'You're not to go in there.'

Instead they stopped at a square hole cut from the deck, with a wooden ladder leading down. Behind them the furled sails flapped, straining to break free from their ropes and fill with air, and half of the planks gleamed under the sunlight, newly scrubbed and waxed. The other half were charred. Planks of fresh wood were stacked round the edges of the ship, ready for repairs. Further towards the bow, on the other side of the mast, was a curious structure. Raised from the deck on four stilts, it was a squat cabin with a single ladder beneath it and no doors or windows of any sort that Aleja could see.

'What's that?' She pointed at it.

Olitiana glanced up, already perched on the top of the ladder that led down into the ship. 'That's the navigator's room. It was built especially for Aada. Come on now.'

Aleja took one last look back. On the surface, the *Ship of Shadows* looked like any other merchant's ship. Rowing boats, barrels and ropes were secured along the sides and everything was neat and orderly and ordinary. The perfect disguise.

If it hadn't been half blackened and filled with pirates.

CHAPTER SEVEN

The Library

Aleja followed Olitiana down the rickety ladder that led into the belly of the ship. Her hands shook a little with excitement. Turning at the bottom, she was presented with a narrow wooden passageway, framed by gently swinging lanterns on each side. Down here it was near silent. It felt like stepping into a secret.

'The crew's quarters are back there. Though at this time, most of them will be in the galley in front of us.'

Aleja trotted obediently behind Olitiana, still clutching the book. The English words were sinking deeper into the grooves of her brain, becoming easier with each sentence she understood. She stumbled over the word *galley* until she remembered it meant the kitchen on a ship.

Thinking back to the English books she'd read about sailing, she tried to think in nautical terms. On a ship, walls were bulkheads, floors were decks, and left and right were port and starboard.

Trapdoors in the floor were chained shut, the padlocks rattling in the rusting links of the chains in time with the soft rocking of the ship. The ceiling was embedded with sapphires in clusters and patterns that seemed strange until Aleja recognized the shape of Orion. The constellations were mapped out on the entire ceiling in a fortune of jewels.

Whispers and deep clunking echoes ran up and down the passageway, and the longer Aleja narrowed her eyes at the shadows that puddled in the corners, the more they seemed to shift nervously beneath her stare. And then there were the silhouettes of owls carved into the walls of the ship, decorated with elegant swirls, with emeralds for eyes. Eyes that gleamed and watched Aleja as she made her way through the ship.

They descended another ladder into a darker segment of the ship. The air was murkier down here, the shadows thick as soup. Now and then the shadows lurched up and formed figures that ran down the passageway, spooking Aleja. Stepping away from a blank-eyed shadow that Olitiana stopped to flap away, Aleja noticed a door with an illuminated crack running down it. She couldn't resist taking a quick peek inside, edging her toes into the gap so it creaked open a little wider. Olitiana appeared behind her and she flushed.

'Sure you don't want to become a pirate?' Olitiana laughed again. 'You're well suited to it. We're going in here anyway.'

Aleja hid her puff of pride, trying her best to look guilty at getting caught out. But when she darted her eyes to the door and saw what lay inside the room, she gasped instead.

'You like books, I take it?'

'They're my favourite things in the world,' Aleja said emphatically. She wished she had longer aboard the ship to explore by herself and regretted turning down the captain's offer so fast. Especially when there were men hunting for her through the streets of Sevilla.

Aleja's family had probably discovered her absence by now and the thought of them finding her missing stung . . . But the *books*. She couldn't imagine what a pirate ship was doing with a fully stocked library, or what kind of books it held. Then again, this was no ordinary pirate ship.

'This is our library. Don't touch anything; some of these books are hundreds of years old,' Olitiana said, pushing the door open.

A girl of about fourteen and a woman around the same age as Malika were watching them from their seats at a long polished table. Two plump leather settees faced each other in the centre of the cavernous space. Rich Persian rugs added a touch more comfort, and shafts of light fell from a series of high portholes. Everywhere Aleja looked there were walls and walls of shelves, reaching into the shadowy edges of the room, curving round the portholes, towering far above them. Rolling ladders were fixed to a shiny railing that swept along the shelves to the uppermost books. Little tables perched at the ends of settees and armchairs, holding a collection of carved wooden owls, what looked like a human skull filled with coins, and a gilded globe. A large owl-shaped clock hung down one wall, its face cluttered with dials and hands that looked frozen in time. Heaps of books were spread across the polished table and Aleja spotted a map of the world peeking out from under them, engraved into the wood itself.

She was rendered wordless for the second time that day.

Glum lanterns perched on the table. Aleja had not missed the way the girl and the woman covered the pages with their hands as she'd stepped through the door. She itched to see what they were reading; it must be infused with secrets.

'Aada, Griete, meet Aleja,' Olitiana said, jerking her head towards Aleja with a bounce of her curls.

'A replacement for Raven?' the woman asked in a dreamlike voice. Aleja wondered if Raven was the lost linguist the captain had mentioned. Had she been killed in the battle that had left the ship battered and bruised?

'Aleja's not staying with us, Aada,' Olitiana said with a significant look.

'I see,' Aada murmured.

This then was the navigator. Aleja shot her a curious look. Aada was tall, with snow-blonde hair and luminous light-grey eyes, and she spoke in crisp, accented English that sounded familiar – in a burst of realization, Aleja knew she had been one of the hooded women she'd followed last night.

Griete sighed, slamming her book shut. 'It's useless,' she moaned. 'I can't find a single reference to –' A sharp glare from Olitiana cut off her words. She reddened, glancing at Aleja.

Aleja's intrigue deepened.

'Griete, why don't you find Aleja an empty cabin to wait in before the captain summons her? Aada can continue the research.'

The words washed over Aada, who had already fallen back into her own book.

Griete stood up, smoothing down a cream tunic that was thickly belted. There were interestingly shaped tools dangling from her waist. She wore thin grey trousers and a pair of battered brown boots with a salted crust. Diamonds shone from her ears and her arms gleamed with smeared grease. Before Aleja could follow her out of the library, the globe started rattling.

'Don't worry about that,' Olitiana said.

The globe continued to rattle, rocking on its axis as Griete ushered Aleja out of the library. She quickly closed the door, shutting the noise out.

'What was *that*?' Aleja asked.

'It's an old globe. It rattles with the movement of the ship,' Griete said.

Aleja knew she was lying. But she stood a better chance of getting information out of Griete if she didn't accuse her of it. Griete was tall and very rounded, with dark-blonde hair pinned up and speared with a spanner, sapphire eyes, and big dimples that she'd flashed once before her smile vanished. She was a few years older than Aleja, but there was something about Griete that eased Aleja's nerves.

'Why did you become a pirate?'

'I invent things,' Griete told her, twirling a peculiar twist of metal round her fingers as they walked through the ship. 'Back home in the Netherlands, I always dreamed of a place where I could be free to learn and work on my inventions, and the *Ship of Shadows* gives that to me.'

She didn't mention how or why she came to be living aboard the ship, but before Aleja could ask, a colossal bang rocked the passageway they were walking down and sent them crashing into one wall.

'What's happening?' Aleja asked, looking frantically around. Were they under attack?

Griete shook her head as she righted herself, tugging her belt straight as the ship steadied once more. 'That'll be either Farren or Velka; you'll meet them soon enough. Farren loves gunpowder about as much as Velka likes to play with chemicals. Everyone has their own talent on the *Ship of Shadows*.'

'The *Ship of Shadows*,' Aleja whispered to herself, watching another shadow flit by.

'That's right. And our ship is the shadow of the seas. It's like death – you don't see it coming. It stalks behind you, out of sight. Watching and waiting in the shadows.' Griete's smile took on a sinister light and Aleja shivered.

'Some of you don't seem so fearsome,' she said.

'Never underestimate anyone,' Griete told her seriously. 'The worst villains can be charming enough when they need to be.'

'What happened to the ship? And the first mate's missing shadow – how is *that* possible?' Aleja asked, bumping into a low door frame that Griete automatically ducked under.

'Pirate hunters happened to the ship,' she said shortly. 'And Malika's shadow was stolen by the same pirate hunter years ago. I suggest you don't discuss it with her.'

'And that other pirate, the linguist – Raven?'

Griete's face pinched together. 'She left. Up here.' She gestured to a steep ladder, bolted to the wall.

Aleja climbed up. Careful to keep the book clamped under her arm, she wondered what had happened. A brush with pirate hunters sounded awfully exciting – was it the same hunter who had been wreaking chaos near Sevilla? Aleja thought it must have been. She wondered how he had been able to steal a shadow. It was clear Griete didn't want to discuss it, though. Aleja wondered if she had been close to the pirate who'd left.

Emerging from the ladder, Aleja looked around. The ship was creaking gently, the lanterns swaying from the river current. The ever-present owl eyes dotted round the bulkheads glittered in the dancing light. Another wispy shadow rushed by.

'How long have you lived here?' Aleja asked, watching the shadows.

'Just two years,' Griete said, climbing up the final rungs. 'Some of the others have been here for much longer.' She walked Aleja up to a passageway that was framed by doors on either side. Two years felt like a lifetime to Aleja, who was imagining everything Griete must have seen and done in that time. Pushing open one of the doors with a loud screech, Griete whipped out a bottle of oil to douse the hinges with, blackening her wrists in the process, and left Aleja in the empty cabin to wait. Sitting on the narrow bunk, Aleja yawned; it was the middle of the day, but she'd been awake the entire night. The odd shout of '*ladrina*' still drifted along the river while the sun clambered higher in the sky. The bunk was built into the body of the ship and moved with it, inviting Aleja to sleep. She fought the lulling sway as long as she could, thinking about pirates, Thomas James's book and the curious ship filled with shadows, but she soon sank into a deep sleep and the hours slipped away beneath her.

Aleja woke with a start. The ship was filled with unfamiliar sounds and moonlight crept through the porthole. It was night.

Aleja leaped up, knocking into the lantern and leaving it swinging wildly in her wake as she snatched up Thomas James's book and fumbled to open the cabin door. The soft bobbing had shifted to a deeper rocking, and the moonlit ship looked more sinister by night. The wooden carvings of owls gouged into the walls stared creepily out at Aleja as she ran past them all, her bare feet slapping on the planks.

It must be a mistake, she told herself, trying to smother her panic and not think of her father and her abuela and

Miguel all looking for her now she'd been missing an entire day. She scurried up the ladder to the main deck, where the sight that greeted her stopped her in her tracks.

Water.

Reaching out to the very edges of the star-studded horizon.

'You're the new girl then,' a disembodied voice spoke in the darkness.

Aleja whirled round, but couldn't find the person who the voice belonged to. 'Show yourself,' she demanded.

'Up here,' the voice said, amusement curled round the words.

Aleja looked up. There was a girl clinging to the mast just below the crow's nest, her leg hooked round the pole, her arms on her hips. Aleja envied how effortless the girl made it look, even as the ship bucked on another strong wave. Aleja was used to scrambling about on rooftops and up walls, but this girl made climbing look like an art form.

'I'm Frances,' she said, sliding down the ropes until she was at eye level with Aleja, who instantly noticed two things. First, the girl looked about the same age as her, though she was a bit taller, and second, she possessed the brightest pair of amber-coloured eyes Aleja had ever seen.

'Aleja.' She was careful to say it slowly, *a-leh-ha*, knowing language was harder the faster it spilled out of someone's mouth. Then she shivered.

Frances noticed, her eyes tracking everything from behind the thick glasses she wore perched on top of her long nose. She had mousy hair the consistency of straw, sticking out in every direction.

'Aren't you cold out here?' Aleja asked, biting her teeth together to stop them from chattering. The air was cold and damp, and every now and then a fresh lurch from the sea sent sprays of salt water arcing on to the deck and splattering the two girls.

Frances shrugged. 'Reckon I'm used to it. It's colder in London than in Spain,' she added archly, her English accent a rougher echo of the captain's.

Londres. A smoke-filled city that was on Aleja's never-ending list of places to visit. 'I want to go there,' she said, wrapping her arms round herself.

'London? Why?' Frances looked at her. 'There are far more interesting places to visit.'

'Well, one day, I'm going to go everywhere. See everything in the world,' Aleja told her stubbornly.

Frances slowly nodded. 'That's a good dream to have. And it might come true sooner than you think.' She winked.

Aleja felt a flutter of panic. 'What do you mean?'

Frances gestured at the black water heaving the ship along. 'We left Spain hours ago.'

'*Dios.*' How would Aleja get off the ship now? She'd suspected as much, but it was still shocking to hear it spoken aloud. Plus she'd been completely robbed of the choice of whether to stay or to go. Aleja spun on her heel and strode across the deck. Frances suddenly appeared in front of her, blocking Aleja's way to the captain's quarters, her arms flung out to rest on either side of the door frame.

'I wouldn't if I were you,' she said mildly. 'Get some sleep. Things will look better in the morning.'

'I don't want sleep. I want answers,' Aleja said, ducking under Frances's arm and bursting into the captain's quarters without knocking.

The captain was standing in the dark, looking out of the wall of windows on the other side of her substantial quarters. One bulkhead held built-in bookcases and a curtained bed that was untouched; she hadn't yet been to sleep. A large mahogany table stood in the centre of the room, perched atop a Persian rug, with a collection of maps and fraying parchments spread across it. Through the clutter Aleja could see the silhouette of a large owl engraved in the table, studded with rubies. Penumbra was nowhere to be seen.

'You've noticed we're at sea, I take it?' Captain Quint said, stepping forward into the lantern's light. It was dim and shaky, swaying with the movements of the ship.

'You promised I could hide here for a few hours. A few hours *only*.' If Aleja's voice wobbled, she made up for it with her fierce glare.

'Have a seat.' The captain sat down on a plush armchair and swept her feet up to rest on the table with a thud. Aleja envied the trousers most of the women on board wore, affording them an ease of movement that was just plain impossible in skirts. She sat, placing the book on the table. At once, the captain slid it closer to herself, giving it a long look before returning her gaze to Aleja. 'As you know, I asked you to join my crew,' she began in a slow, measured voice.

Aleja prickled with irritation. 'You don't have to do that. I can understand you when you speak normally.'

'My apologies,' the captain said, arching an eyebrow. She reached forward for a dusty glass bottle and poured an inch into her glass. Swirling the contents around, she studied Aleja under the lantern-light. 'I select only the best and brightest for my crew, Aleja. The finest girls and women from around the world. Frances, for instance, is a thief of unparalleled skill. Griete astounds us all with her inventions, and no one can make a sword sing like Malika. Tell me, how did you come to speak English?'

'From books.' Aleja shuffled in her seat.

'And do you speak any other languages?'

'I've learned French and some Arabic.'

Captain Quint's eyes were fixed on Aleja, who saw the sudden flicker of excitement in them. The captain took a long drink. 'I do enjoy it when my suspicions are proved correct. I singled you out for your talent with languages, and because you wanted it; regardless of what made you hesitate, you wanted it badly enough to wear that wanting on your face.'

Aleja opened her mouth but the captain held a finger up. 'That said, I do not take girls prisoner. This is a free ship; my crew can leave whenever they like.' She drummed her fingers on the table. 'The problem lies with those counterfeited coins you stumbled upon. I underestimated how badly those men wanted to ensure they kept their heads.' Her laugh was sharp. 'When we needed to weigh anchor for our next port of call, the search for you was still ongoing. Tell me, what's the punishment for the thieving they were accusing you of?'

'Public whipping,' Aleja whispered.

Captain Quint nodded. 'I thought as much.' She took another long pull from her glass before slamming it down. Swinging her legs off the table, she leaned on her elbows to look Aleja hard in the eyes. 'I stay true to my promises, Aleja. I've protected you. I will return you to Seville, to your family. But first I must continue our quest. Which means, like it or not, I'm afraid you're going to come on a little adventure with us first.'

Aleja slumped back in her seat. Apparently she didn't have any say in the matter. But at the captain's words she couldn't help a new feeling blooming in her heart.

An adventure! Excitement was like the moment when a fire sparks to life: bright, powerful flames burning away Aleja's worries.

'Where are we going?'

CHAPTER NINE

The Captain of the Smiling Skull

'We'll be arriving at the Moroccan port of Tangier next. While on this ship you'll be expected to join in with the rest of the crew to keep the ship immaculate, as well as attend weapons training each morning with Malika. This is non-negotiable. All of our crew members, no matter how temporary, must be capable of defending themselves. In exchange you'll have your own cabin and cooked meals. And a fresh set of clothes,' Captain Quint added, eyeing Aleja's dirty dress. 'Additionally, there may be the odd . . . translation of texts you can do.' Her eyes slid to the side as she spoke, making Aleja wonder what she was hiding. 'I don't imagine you'll be on board longer than a month or two; though, as I mentioned before, if you wanted to become a more permanent crew member, your services would be welcomed. Are those terms agreeable to you?'

'Yes, Captain,' Aleja said, feeling half dazed. One or two *months*? Her family would be beside themselves. But an adventure in Morocco? It was the stuff of her dreams.

'Now, the book.' The captain's fingers shook when she picked it up, like it had taken every bit of strength she had to resist looking at it until she'd spoken to Aleja.

The captain opened it on the table. Aleja's mouth fell open. The pages were filled with ink. 'This . . . this was blank when I found it!'

Captain Quint slowly turned the pages for them both to drink in, pausing on the first, which was inscribed:

For my family, in case of emergency.

Thomas James

The captain's intake of breath was audible, hissing down into her throat. 'Do you realize what you've found, Aleja?'

Aleja stared at the book and shook her head. Other than the dedication, the writing was in no language Aleja could read. She wasn't even sure it was written in any language. Strange symbols, pictograms, a page covered in dots, and a map bare of any cities or landmarks. 'It's coded,' Aleja murmured eagerly, examining the thick parchment, the ink gleaming darker than night. She suddenly looked up at the captain. 'You knew this was going to happen, didn't you?' she asked.

Captain Quint looked thrilled. 'Oh, very good.' She leaned in closer. 'And how do you know that?'

'You said you had a theory when the ship shuddered as I came on board. When the *book* came on board.' Aleja ran her fingers over the golden book. 'But it's not the lost journals of Thomas James, is it? People saw him writing those, and this is encrypted.' Aleja frowned. And then she remembered something else. In *Legendary Explorers* she had read:

His ship was marked with an old sigil, that of Athena, heralding the knowledge he kept inside his ship. One that, rumour had it, could only be unlocked with his golden key.

'This is the key to the ship,' Aleja whispered, stunned.

Captain Quint raised her rum glass as if she was toasting her. 'I do believe it is.'

'But what does it unlock?' Aleja asked, frowning. 'And why was it in Sevilla, in that library?'

'I am afraid I have no idea why it was there. And as for what it unlocks, well – it's the key to some information I would very much like to acquire.' The captain was careful not to reveal her disappointment, but it was there all the same, like a brewing storm, in the whitening of her finger tracing the puzzles across the page and the tightening of her concentration – eyes narrowed, lips pursed.

Aleja watched her closely. 'I can't read it either,' she said. 'What information are you looking for?'

The captain looked up but it was clear she didn't really see Aleja. She was peering into her own thoughts. 'Nothing I can tell you at this moment.' She tapped her thumb against her lips.

Aleja frowned.

Captain Quint snapped out of her trance to slide the book across the table to Aleja. 'This doesn't leave the ship,' she ordered. 'But seeing as you were the one to find it, I'll be very interested to see if you can solve it too. Perhaps then I'll let you in on my secrets.' Her words gleamed with the challenge. 'I'll be instructing the rest of the crew to take turns in cracking it, along with myself, of course. Make sure you return it to the library whenever you're not working on it.'

Aleja nodded, determined to be the one to solve the mystery. Tracing the gilded letters that spelled out *Thomas James* on the leather cover, she imagined the captain trusting her with her secrets. 'This *is* Thomas James's ship, isn't it?'

The captain leaned back in her chair, kicking her boots back up on to the table with a dull thud. 'It is.'

Aleja waited for her to offer more information. She didn't. 'How did you come to be the captain of it?' she asked.

'Now *that* is a good story,' Captain Quint said. 'And a long one. The weapons room is next to the library. I trust you can find your own way there at first light.'

It wasn't a question. Aleja nodded. She was so consumed with the notion of sailing to Morocco that she couldn't worry about anything else. The captain had mentioned a quest – Aleja wondered if she'd get to see the desert, or if they'd be staying in port. She knew sailing the seas was a dangerous pastime, with storms and enemies preying on unsuspecting ships. But Aleja was too excited to think of those dangers, or what her family might think of her ploughing head first into a real adventure. It was all she could do not to skip back to her cabin, her heart soaring in delicious anticipation. She forced her feet to walk in a normal rhythm to the door.

'Oh, and, Aleja?' Aleja hesitated. 'Don't walk in here again without knocking,' Captain Quint said, turning back to stare out at the water.

Aleja shut the door quietly after herself, her face hot. She stood on the deck outside the captain's closed door for a moment, watching the gentle buck and sway of the water as they sailed down the North Atlantic Ocean, the ship creaking along. Left alone in the inky night, Aleja decided it was the perfect time to explore.

Taking a small lantern from one of the sconces, she went back down the wooden ladder and set off into the ship. The library was her first port of call – leaving Thomas James's book there would be the perfect opportunity to do a little snooping. She was desperate to see if the books that Aada and Griete had been poring over were still there, and perhaps find out what had caused that strange rattling noise from the globe. The door opened with an ominous creak. Excitement rippled through Aleja at the promise of the treasure that lay inside.

The table had been cleared, of course, but she ran a wondering finger over the chunky books nearest to her. The shelves towered all the way up to the high portholes in a variety of languages and subjects. Unable to resist, she pulled one out and opened it at the middle, diving into a glittering ball in the Palace of Versailles. She wasn't yet used to the strange wobbling of the ship floor and now and then reached to steady herself on the nearby shelves. When she reshelved the book, she arched her neck back to stare in wonder at the ceiling. Like the passageways, the wood above her was pierced with jewels. But here, instead of constellations, the entire ceiling had been painted with wings. Huge feathered creations that shone in brilliant whites, lustrous creams and sugared caramel. The edges of the majestic wings were encrusted with diamonds, capturing the spark of light from the flame Aleja was carrying. It felt like the entire library might take flight.

The globe rattled. Aleja turned to stare at it. It was perched on an end table next to a large armchair that towered with velvet cushions. Holding on tightly to her lantern, Aleja advanced towards it. The strange rattling was louder in the night's silence. Keeping her breathing quiet, she reached out to flip the globe open with her fingertips. She inched forward, braced to run away if something nasty was hidden inside. What could it be? Venomous snakes or poisonous insects from the tropics? Rare, deadly beasts found in the deepest jungles? Or perhaps a lethal curse that would ensnare her the second she let it free . . .

'I wouldn't do that if I were you,' came a voice from behind Aleja, making her jump and drop the lantern. Catching it, she spun round to find Frances propped up against the now-closed library door.

'You followed me?' Aleja gripped the lantern tighter. Setting the library alight wouldn't have been the best introduction to life on board the ship.

Frances grinned at her. 'Fancy a real tour? I'll show you all the best bits.'

'Sure.' Aleja walked back across the soft Persian rugs to where Frances stood before hesitating to throw a final glance back at the globe. 'What's in there?' she asked.

'Oh, that's just Geoffrey. He likes to hide in his globe whenever he's sulking. Which is basically all the time.' Frances rolled her eyes.

'Who's Geoffrey?'

'Want to see?' Frances's grin turned a little wicked at the edges.

Aleja suppressed a shudder at what Geoffrey might be. 'Go on then,' she said.

Frances pushed her glasses up her nose and rolled up her sleeves dramatically. 'Geoffrey! Someone wants to see you,' she sing-songed.

The globe fell still.

'Aw, come on, Geoffrey, you can't stay mad at poor Griete forever; she only wanted to look at the globe because . . . well, it's a globe. It's actually useful.' Frances gave a *what can you do* kind of shrug as Aleja stared at her, wondering if she'd lost her mind.

The next minute, she wondered if *she'd* lost her mind.

A wisp of silvery substance was twirling upwards from the globe's hinges – it appeared to be smoking. Aleja took an involuntary step backwards. Frances examined her nails as if she was bored. When the smoking grew more intense, the hinges popped open and the entire top half of the globe swung open. The silvery smoke gathered itself into a shape and solidified into a man before Aleja could blink. Or, to be precise, the top half of a man. He was standing inside the globe, the equator cutting him off at the waist.

'She positively spun me to distraction,' the ghostly figure grumbled.

'Like I said, she didn't mean it.' Frances waved her hand dismissively. 'Aleja, meet our resident ghost, Geoffrey. Geoffrey, this is Aleja. She's a stowaway.'

'I'm not a stowaway,' Aleja protested half-heartedly as she stared at the ghost. He had a curling moustache and wore a long white wig that flounced down round his shoulders in a multitude of curls. A gigantic captain's hat sat wonkily on top of the wig. His shirt was starched and ruffled, and stained with what looked like water – or worse – and he wore a smart jacket over the top of it, every inch of which was covered in buttons, medals and decorations.

Aleja had never seen a ghost before. People joked that some old places in Sevilla were haunted, but she knew they never expected to actually see a ghost, the same way they didn't truly believe in magic. She tried not to let her face betray her shock.

She thought of the stories she'd heard about the shadows of dead sailors haunting the ship . . . except that this ghost was pompous and moping around in a globe. Aleja suppressed a giggle.

'Indeed.' Geoffrey looked at her sceptically. 'Captain Edgerton, at your service.' He offered her a hand, bulky with golden rings that were now all vaguely transparent like the rest of him.

Frances snorted. Aleja reached out her hand to shake his, curious about what it would feel like. 'Pleased to meet you,' she said politely as they shook hands, his just firm enough to grasp. Instead of pulling away, Geoffrey passed his hand through hers, chilling Aleja's hand to the bone as she stared at it in amazement.

'That never ceases to amuse me!' He chortled. 'Many thanks for the entertainment,' he told Frances before dissolving into silver smoke and misting away.

'Congratulations, you didn't scream,' Frances said with another wicked grin.

Aleja ignored that. 'Are there more ghosts on the ship?' she asked, imagining bumping into spectres as she wandered the wooden passageways and ladders.

'Just the one,' Frances said cheerfully, beckoning Aleja to follow her as she walked out of the library. 'And he was accidentally brought on board by the captain.'

'Did he say he used to be a captain as well?' Aleja asked.

'Oh, yeah. He was the notorious pirate Geoffrey Edgerton, captain of the *Smiling Skull*.' Frances's whispers echoed up and down the dark passageway. The lantern was catching the odd gleam of the owls carved into the bulkheads, their jewelled eyes watching them. 'But that was a long time ago. He retired almost a hundred years ago now, and eventually was found dead, holding on to an empty bottle of rum and that old globe. Of course, he's been haunting the globe ever since, but the captain wasn't to know when she bought it. So he's been with us since then. Down here.'

Aleja followed Frances down another rickety ladder that shuddered beneath her feet. 'Now and then he likes to roam the ship, telling us all how he'd do it differently, how the *Smiling Skull* used to run things, et cetera, et cetera, but it usually doesn't take long for him to take offence at something and run off sulking to hide in his globe.'

'I've never heard of the *Smiling Skull* before,' Aleja mused, peering into the dark passageway before them.

Frances grabbed her arm. 'Will you tell Geoffrey that? Please?' She looked thrilled at the idea.

Aleja laughed. 'Sure. Where does this go?'

'Here,' Frances announced, halting and gesturing at a patch of floor.

Aleja frowned, lifting the lantern higher. 'What am I meant to be looking for?'

Frances felt around on the floor, her fingers shuffling through a layer of the salt residue that seemed to reach every corner of the ship. 'Ah, here it is!' She jabbed her hand into something invisible and a deep whirring struck up beneath their feet. Then a square of the floor simply fell away, leaving a gaping blackness in its place.

Chapter Ten

Secret Passageways and Cake

'After you,' Frances said, gesturing.

Aleja lowered her lantern to peer inside the hole. There was a wooden pole that ran down into gloom as thick as night, with short, stubby bits of wood nailed to it on each side. It didn't look particularly sturdy. Passing the lantern to Frances, Aleja sat on the edge of the hole, dangled her legs beneath her, then began climbing down the ramshackle pole. 'What's down here?' she asked, peering into the hazy shadows as Frances reached the bottom with the lantern.

Below sea level, it was dark and echoing. They were standing in the equivalent of the ship's cellar. Crates and tools were stacked up against the walls and a brig was secured in one corner, its bars thick and rusted. Frances grinned. 'This is where we lock our mutineers. There're bones in there if you look closer.' Aleja didn't.

Eerily silent, the shadows in the bottom of the brig clotted together and rose up, forming the bloodied figure of a murdered sailor, his chest punctured with throwing knives. Aleja shrieked and even Frances looked a little spooked. 'Stupid shadows,' Frances muttered under her breath, making shooing motions at it with her hand until it collapsed again. Aleja shuddered, feeling its blank grey eyes on them still.

'See that?' Frances pointed at something small on the wall.

Aleja traced the shallow lines. 'It's an owl.'

'Griete devised this whole system,' Frances explained. 'There were always secret passages running throughout the ship, but she found a way to better conceal the entrances. Push it,' she told Aleja enthusiastically. 'The secret passages are where the magic likes to hide.'

The *Ship of Shadows* seemed to run on magic and, eager to see more of it, Aleja pushed the little painted owl. Another rumble shook the wood under her hand, as if the ship was shaking its skin off, and then a portion of the bulkhead rolled open for them. Frances grinned, they both stepped through, and the bulkhead closed behind them once more.

'So how long have you been on this ship?' Aleja asked as they wandered through the hidden warren. It was dim and slightly musty, and Aleja soaked it all in. She was desperate to memorize everything so she could relive it in the future, like rereading a favourite book. Only this time it would be the most precious story of all – her very own adventure.

'Years now,' Frances said, leading the way. 'We've been all over the world several times.'

Aleja, listening intently, almost walked into the side of the passageway when it abruptly curved and hooked back round. 'Oh, yeah,' Frances continued, 'we've battled kraken and ridden camels in the desert – some of the beasts in those sands make kraken look like baby bunnies – and trekked through jungles. Once, I nearly got swallowed up by a snake in the Amazonian rainforest!'

'What happened?' Aleja asked, slowing to stare at Frances. She was enthralled at the mention of kraken and beasts – she'd been right to believe the sailors' rumours.

Frances grinned. 'I tried to strangle it with a vine but the thing got twisted round so I ended up jumping on its back and riding it through the rainforest instead.'

Aleja opened her mouth to say something when a deep rushing sound began to ripple through the passageway.

'What's happening?' Aleja asked, looking round, half expecting some beast to be racing through the narrow passage towards them. Instead there was gurgling and a luminous waterfall appeared, bubbling out of the wall and swirling around their feet. It sparkled bright blue with phosphorescence. Aleja leaped back, sure that water was rushing through a crack in the hull, but the puddle at the base of the passageway was kept small as if by –

'Magic,' Frances said, laughing at the expression on Aleja's face upon seeing the glowing waterfall. 'I told you it liked to hide down here. Something about secret passageways really captures the imagination,' she mused to herself. 'You never know what you're going to find!'

An entire wall of shadows descended from the passageway and became a group of rabbits that bounced through the waterfall with excited squeaks, turning their dark shadow-selves phosphorescent blue. The shining shadow-bunnies lit up the rest of the passage as they darted ahead, rousing other shadows that were slumbering in the ink-black corners.

When Aleja and Frances ran through the waterfall – Aleja feeling she must be dreaming – it turned their hair the same shade of glittering blue. Glowing brighter than the lantern and laughing at each other's hair, they slid into several hollows where other magical waterfalls had sprung up, attracting more mischievous shadows. After a steep climb, they emerged into the galley from a trapdoor hidden in the bottom of one of the cupboards.

'What are we doing in here?' Aleja asked, looking around the galley. It was large and burrowed back towards the stern. A gigantic table was bolted to the floor with wooden benches and the odd chair arranged round it. Along one bulkhead was the huge stove, with iron doors on the ovens and a chimney that funnelled all the smoke outside. Shelves and cupboards had brackets to stop the plates falling to the floor.

Frances turned to Aleja, her delighted face high-lighted by her bright blue hair. 'I thought you might be hungry,' she said. 'I know I am,' she added, rummaging around in another cupboard.

Aleja looked at her with amusement.

'What?'

'I thought you were going to show me some more magic,' Aleja admitted, her stomach still fluttering from the bewitching display in the passage.

Frances spread her arms wide. 'What could be more magical than food?' She stepped aside to reveal a cupboard crammed with cake, biscuits and more treats than Aleja had ever seen in one place. 'Ermtgen – our cook – keeps the best stuff in here,' Frances said, reaching in to grab a large tin.

The lid popped off with a sharp clang. Inside was an entire round of yellow cake with a thick, creamy top.

'Ooh,' Aleja said, her mouth beginning to water. 'Is there a knife or a plate or –'

'Nah.' Frances scooped a handful of cake out, passed it to Aleja, then reached back in for another handful. 'We'll just snag this bit and put the rest back.' She shoved her cake in her mouth with a little sigh. 'S'good.'

Aleja bit into her own piece. Soft and fluffy with a hint of vanilla, it was cake the way cake was meant to be: creamy and sweet. She wished she could save a slice for Miguel, but she was on an adventure and adventurers didn't stop to think about their brothers. She'd tell him about it when she got back home, she decided. In the meantime there was cake and a magic ship and more questions than she could fit in her mouth to ask.

Frances dug out two more handfuls of cake before she replaced the tin and showed Aleja back to her cabin, the two of them licking their fingers on the way. Frances asked a heap of questions of her own about Aleja and her life in the tavern and her brothers, which she seemed rather fascinated by. Aleja couldn't understand why. To her, nothing was more interesting than the *Ship of Shadows* and its pirate crew, and she couldn't stop wondering what the next day would bring.

CHAPTER ELEVEN

Weapons Training

A handful of hours later Aleja was standing on the polished deck of the weapons room as the first shy rays of dawn poked through the portholes. One wall was mirrored, reflecting Aleja's no-longer-blue hair back at her. She turned to marvel at the other three walls, all bursting with weapons from across the globe: Spanish-made pistols, English flintlocks, sabres from Eastern Europe, Persian shamshirs and many other blades that curved in shapes Aleja didn't know the names for. Large trunks of swords, cutlasses and daggers were dotted about and straw-filled mannequins hung from the beams.

Aleja counted two other girls besides herself and Griete before Frances scurried in, hair back to normal, cheeks bulging suspiciously. Aleja glanced over at her, filled with nerves in the unfamiliar room with girls who all looked older than her. Frances gave her a crumb-leaking grin and ambled over. She swallowed loudly.

Then Malika stalked in.

The room hushed. Aleja stood in-between Frances and Griete, who was in a world of her own, staring miserably at the floor. Aleja wondered what was the matter with her. The other two girls were behind them. They looked about sixteen, and Aleja stole curious peeks at them in the mirrors, wondering if she'd be introduced to them later. One of them had short emerald-green hair cropped close to her head, showcasing a long neck and full cheeks. She wore plain black trousers, a tunic and boots, but her sleeves were rolled up, uncovering a vibrant display on her sun-kissed arms. Exotic plants and flowers had been inked on to them. They delicately tumbled from vines that wrapped round both arms before creeping up her sleeves and vanishing from sight. Round her wrists were a jumble of silver bangles and chunky bracelets that clinked together every time she moved.

'Girls, this is Aleja, the accidental stowaway we picked up in Seville,' Malika said. Aleja resented being called that, but Malika had a no-nonsense, impatient tone that suggested she would not tolerate being challenged. 'Aleja, meet Velka –' Malika nodded to the green-haired girl whose arms Aleja had been admiring – 'and Farren,' she continued, gesturing to the other girl.

Farren shot Aleja a grin. She too had short hair, with shiny auburn locks that fell choppily around her tanned face. Her white shirt was tucked into high-waisted trousers, a black sash round her waist had two pistols stowed in it, and she'd finished off her ensemble with mauve pointy-toed ankle boots and black-leather gloves.

'I believe you've already met the others,' Malika said, losing interest in the introductions. 'Now. Grab a cutlass.'

Malika wore a bright purple headscarf and ornate tunic to match. She was swinging a cutlass while she waited for the girls to retrieve theirs from a trunk. As Aleja experimented with holding a cutlass, first in one hand, then the other, Malika tossed hers in the air. The blade whipped around as Aleja's heart thrummed, watching its track, before Malika caught it neatly by the handle again. She noticed Aleja gaping and her eyebrow quirked.

'My best friend is a sword. I can do more with my one hand than most could hope to do with both.'

'It's true,' Frances said, swishing her own cutlass out in front of her. 'This one time, we were in a forbidden city and there was this prince and –' She swung the cutlass violently to demonstrate her story and Aleja jumped out of the way.

Malika took a step back. 'Yes, well, thank you for that, Frances, but do be careful.'

Frances stopped swishing. And, rather unfortunately for Aleja, who had been eager to hear more, she also stopped talking.

'This is a cutlass.' Malika held her own up in the air for them all to inspect. 'It is not a sword. With a cutlass you'll need to fight at a closer range due to its smaller size. Who can tell me the other key difference?'

Velka's hand shot up into the air.

'Yes?'

'Cutlasses are for slashing motions,' she said, and Aleja noticed a crisp northern European bite to her words. English seemed to be the language the crew used as their common tongue, and Aleja wondered if there were simply more English people on board, or if the English people who were on board were too inept at other languages. The captain's bumbling Spanish came to mind. Twisting her lips trying not to smile at the memory, Aleja realized she'd missed something – the group was pairing up. Frances was staring at her hopefully so Aleja stepped towards her.

Farren and Velka paired up, as did Aleja and Frances, leaving Griete to fall in with Farren and Velka. Aleja felt awkward, like she was an unwelcome addition, but consoled herself with the thought that she wouldn't be intruding for long. But she wasn't quite ready to think of leaving just yet, not before she'd solved the mystery in the book – and especially not after what had turned up in her cabin that morning: a pair of her very own trousers. They were lightweight enough to run around in, with reinforced leather over the knees for climbing, and they'd come with a shirt that was small enough for her and a warm tunic to protect her against the frigid temperatures coasting in off the waves. Griete had tied Aleja's hair back with a leather strip so that the long strands wouldn't get in her eyes, and now Aleja was desperate to have a go at climbing up to the crow's nest.

In the meantime there were cutlasses. Aleja slashed hers through the air, brandishing it like she thought a pirate ought to. Frances brought her cutlass up to deflect Aleja's and the clash echoed throughout the room and juddered up Aleja's arm.

Aleja tried again, but this time, when Frances blocked her, her fingers trembled and the cutlass plunged to the floor. She bent to pick it up, red-faced. Malika's boots appeared in front of her.

'It takes time to build strength,' Malika said, studying Aleja's arms. 'Keep working at it. Expect to be sore tomorrow.' She moved off to the others.

Frances wiggled her eyebrows at Aleja. 'Want to try blocking me now?'

Aleja held her cutlass up, copying how Frances had blocked her. She suspected that Frances was attacking her slowly on purpose, giving her a chance to figure out where her hands and feet needed to be. Malika wandered by again to correct Aleja's stance, and Aleja began to understand how to move – fighting was like poetry; it followed patterns and rhythms.

An hour later, her arms shook as she put the cutlass back in the trunk.

Frances sighed happily as her cutlass clonked down on top of Aleja's. 'Now for my favourite part of the day . . . Breakfast!'

Griete tilted her face upwards. 'I can almost smell it already.'

'Frances,' Aleja began, lowering her voice as she checked they weren't being overheard by anyone. 'Why do you need daily fighting classes? What does this ship – what do you – *do*?'

Frances looked nervous. 'We're not supposed to say yet, not until you –'

'Frances!'

Aleja flinched along with everyone else at the anger in Malika's expression. Frances turned scarlet. 'I'm sorry, I forgot,' she said, unable to stop a glance in Aleja's direction.

'You're all dismissed,' Malika snapped. 'Except you.' She pointed a finger at Aleja.

Frances cast Aleja a worried look that did nothing to calm her churning nerves. The rest of the girls left, dispersing quickly and shutting the door behind them.

'Forget you heard that. If you were to be a permanent member of our crew, then you would understand what this ship does. But you're only here for a short while, isn't that right?' Malika's penetrating look rested on Aleja's face.

'That's right,' Aleja said. Perhaps if she was closer to Frances, then she might confide in her. Then again, the ship kept its secrets tightly locked up, so perhaps Aleja was better investigating for herself. And Malika ... Aleja stole a nervous glance at the woman. She was too scared to plague her with questions the way she had the other girls, but the first mate *had* been honest with her. 'What were you in Sevilla for?' she asked suddenly, the words tumbling from her lips before she could bite them back.

'You tell me,' Malika said, still watching her.

Aleja didn't know how to respond. She recognized avoidance when she saw it – she'd spent enough time around her brothers to know when someone wasn't being entirely honest. Or when they wanted something.

'What do you think we were doing?' Malika said slowly, perhaps thinking Aleja hadn't understood her.

'My English is just fine, thank you,' Aleja said. In fact, it was more than that: it was turning out to be immaculate. All those hours of reading had done more than entertain her; they had shaped her into the person she was, honed her memory and fed her with other languages. 'And I think you were fleeing an enemy. An enemy who took one of your own.'

Malika waited for her to continue, so Aleja ventured further into her own thoughts. 'Your ship was smoking, so you needed to stop and stock up on wood to make repairs. You'd probably made a long journey, possibly across the Atlantic, so you would have needed to replenish your food and water stores. And . . .' She hesitated, thinking of Malika snapping at Frances.

Sometimes she wished she knew when to keep quiet, instead of having her tongue charging forward before her brain could catch up. Like now, when she found herself prolonging the conversation with the most terrifying pirate on board, instead of taking the opportunity to catch Frances up for breakfast. No wonder chaos shadowed her footsteps.

'And?'

'And you were . . . looking for something. To do with Thomas James. But I'm not sure what. Or why.' She doubted that the captain had been looking for Thomas James's book, not when she had been surprised both by the appearance of the book and its contents. No, they had been after something else. 'What *were* you looking for?' she asked, frowning.

Malika smiled, her scars stretching across her face. 'Anything can be bought for the right price,' she said, her voice slinking down to a whisper. 'Even secrets.'

Chapter Twelve

Secrets

Secrets. What kind of secrets did the *Ship of Shadows* deal in? Aleja told herself that she didn't like secrets, but that wasn't true. What she disliked was being excluded from a secret. *Knowing* secrets made her feel superior – the little gem of information tucked safely away, the delicious thrill of knowing something that others didn't. Being the only one on board the ship who didn't know something made her petulant.

'I wish you'd tell me,' she told Frances once she'd joined the other girls in the galley. Guilt swept across Frances's expression as she dug into her plate of griddle cakes.

Ermtgen, the cook, was a thin, older Dutch woman with a severe grey bun, who had professed her love of flipping griddle cakes to Aleja while stacking her plate perilously high with the thin rounds of fried batter. Now sitting opposite Frances, Aleja poked one dubiously; she'd never tasted a griddle cake before.

'It goes in your mouth,' Frances said, forking another generous bite in before she'd finished chewing the first.

Aleja scrunched her nose at the half-eaten mulch inside Frances's mouth. Still, she understood. She'd achieved a whole new level of hunger after waving around a heavy cutlass for an hour before breakfast. She decided to follow Frances's example and took a large bite. Sweet hot batter and a sprinkle of sugar had never tasted so good. She shovelled the rest into her mouth as well, gleeful that there was no one on the ship to remind her of her manners. She couldn't wait to tell Miguel about the griddle cakes, and hoped he'd recreate them for her when she got home.

'And I can't tell you, you know that,' Frances was saying, speaking with her mouth full. 'Unless . . .'

'Unless what?'

'Unless you've decided you're staying after all?' Frances looked at her hopefully. 'We all know you were offered a place on board if you wanted it, else you wouldn't have been allowed on in the first place.'

Aleja felt a flush of pleasure. Back home she was always left out of the boys' games because she was a girl, and rejected by the girls for being a bit wild. Aleja was just Aleja and she wanted to do what she wanted, without being told otherwise. But here ... here there were girls just like her. Girls who fought with one hand, girls who climbed and invented things and sailed across oceans to get what they wanted. It was tempting. But the thought of never being able to tell Miguel about Ermtgen's cooking, or never seeing the look on Pablo's face when she boasted about her adventures on board ... it stung.

'I can't,' Aleja whispered, staring down at her fork. 'My family ...' She felt guilty enough as it was for enjoying her time away from them.

Frances looked sad for a moment until she shoved another forkful of griddle cake into her mouth and sighed in pleasure. Aleja wanted to ask where Frances's own family were, or what had happened in her life that had led to her living aboard a pirate ship, but for once she didn't dare. Some secrets were precious.

Aleja slipped her hand into her trouser pocket. Missing her grandmother, she'd moved her lucky coin there, where she could wrap her fingers round the metal and imagine it soothing her worries away. Squeezing the hidden coin with one hand, she peered around the galley.

The rest of the crew sat on benches and chairs round the massive table. Farren and Velka were playing chess, Velka leaning forward to study the board with a frown, Farren muttering in French and chewing on the end of her fork. She sat back, her mauve boots propped up on the table until Ermtgen gave her a fierce look and she removed them. In the other corner Griete was sitting by herself, sadly nibbling a griddle cake. 'She'll be OK,' Frances said when she saw who Aleja was looking at. 'She just needs some time.'

Ermtgen zoomed up and down the entire galley as she mixed and fried, shooing away anyone who came too close. Above them the distant sounds of sawing and hammering carried on as the *Ship of Shadows* was pieced back together again.

Everyone on the ship knew their place. Aleja thought it must be nice to fit together like clockwork, each member of the crew a cog or gear that the ship couldn't do without. And the longer she spent on board, the more delighted she grew with everything.

The *Ship of Shadows* dawdled along the water, stuck in the headwinds off the coast of Spain. Aleja was secretly delighted about this and spent most of her time exploring. The lower decks of the ship were thick with enchantment and each time Aleja went down there, she could feel the magic tingling against her skin. The shadows were more active there, their silhouettes darker, their movements faster.

She found hidden rooms that were empty apart from the spiced smells that spilled out of them. She found a loose plank in one of the passageways, which she pulled up to reveal a hidden mountain of gold ingots. Geoffrey occasionally skulked into sight, his silvery figure appearing to deliver enthusiastic historical lectures or attempting to make her jump, depending on which mood he was in at the time.

It never took long for Frances to appear by her side, and with her Aleja learned even more about the ship. It was a puzzle box of secret rooms and hidden parts that gleamed with magic, all waiting to be discovered, like buried treasure. The things that Frances showed Aleja twisted her perception of what was possible, sending her into a dreamlike amazement. Shadows sometimes dislodged themselves from the ship's many corners and latched on to her ankles, so that more than once she discovered an extra silhouette stalking her footfalls. The weapons room often echoed with the clashes of ancient battles.

'And the owl carvings are linked!' Frances told Aleja excitedly one day, as captivated by her role as tour guide as Aleja was to be on board. She suspected Frances hadn't had any crew mates her own age in a while and was perhaps a little lonely too. Frances left Aleja standing beside one jewel-studded owl and ran up the passage to another, cupped her hands round her mouth and whispered into it.

'Can you hear me?' The whisper of Frances's voice spilled out of the other owls, an echo rustling throughout the ship.

The secret passages that zigzagged through the deepest parts of the ship continued to harbour strange magic that shifted each day, from phosphorescent waterfalls to glittering mists, a jungle that sprouted up overnight to bubbles that floated down and gave Aleja and Frances mad fits of involuntary laughter.

'This ship was crafted with the fabric of legends,' Captain Quint had told her when Aleja had asked how it was all possible. She'd patted the side of the ship in satisfaction. 'When something is immortalized in stories, it gives it an air of enchantment, I find.' She peered closer at Aleja then, a nearby lantern flashing light on to her face in odd patterns. 'Every legend you hear about the *Ship of Shadows* is true. Its magic is fed by them . . .'

And running through those passageways, side by side with Frances, Aleja could feel that magic in the owl eyes watching them pass by and in the shadows running after them for brief spells.

The library had a series of tiny hidden doors cut into the shelving, which swung open of their own accord each time Frances stepped confidently towards them. Aleja stared, her gaping mouth mirroring the dark hollows behind.

'Magic,' Frances said smugly.

Inside the hollows were rare books. Sitting on reading podiums and encased in glass for protection, their pages were crisped with age, the covers old and peculiar. 'This one's especially interesting,' Frances said, pulling a book off a podium to hand it to Aleja. She looked through the pages, noting that it was written in an archaic English scrawl she had to squint to read.

'How old is it?' Aleja asked. The cover felt strange to the touch, and it definitely looked as if it belonged in a museum.

'A few hundred years.' Frances's grin leaked mischief. 'But it's bound in human skin.'

'Yeugh!' Aleja dropped it.

Frances howled with laughter.

During an evening meal of bread, cheese and fruit that Farren, Velka, Frances and Aleja had decided to eat on a patch of clear deck near the bow – Griete had declined to join them – Aleja figured out that not *everything* was as magical as Frances had led her to believe.

'The rare-book section doors run on a weighted mechanism,' Farren explained. 'I'm not quite sure how it works – it was one of Griete's inventions – but there is a mechanism under the wood that triggers the doors to open themselves. Half the doors on the ship have them.'

'Your cabin is further along than ours – she didn't reach that far,' Velka added. The silver bangles she was wearing shimmered under the sun as she reached for another hunk of bread.

Farren grinned. 'Griete spent weeks tearing up the ship floors trying to get it to work. It was during a particularly rough crossing on the Atlantic when we were all exhausted and bored out of our minds. You should have seen Malika's face each time she had to jump over the splintered floorboards.'

'That was nothing to how *you* reacted,' Velka said with a laugh, turning to Farren, who Aleja now knew was the boatswain – responsible for maintaining and fixing the ship. 'She followed Griete around, cringing every time she dug into the wood,' Velka told Aleja.

'I thought I'd have to repair it all at sea!' Farren said defensively.

'What happened?' Aleja asked, looking between the two of them.

'Eventually Farren couldn't bear the sight of that much damage and pretended to ignore it like the rest of us,' Velka said.

'And then Griete figured out how to make the mechanism work and now we're all slightly lazier,' Farren finished.

Frances sighed. 'Magic was a better story.'

But Aleja was equally fascinated by the inner workings of the ship and its crew. 'So what's the ship's mission?' she asked as casually as she could, popping a few grapes into her mouth.

Farren grinned at her. 'Nice try,' she said.

'Pirates don't tell,' Velka said, her grey eyes twinkling.

'So you're pillaging and sacking towns?' Aleja raised her eyebrows.

'Nah,' Frances said, taking the last chunk of bread and smushing cheese on top of it. 'The captain's got a strong moral compass. We're more . . .' She munched on her bread, thinking. 'More like Robin Hood. Stealing from the rich to help the poor and all that. And lining our own pockets as well, of course.' Frances and Farren knocked their pieces of bread together as if they were clinking glasses while Velka shook her head at them in amusement.

This was interesting, but it didn't stop Aleja wanting to discover what the ship's mission *really* was. What was this quest that Captain Quint had mentioned, and why was no one else talking about it? She'd seen different crew members take turns with Thomas James's book, but none of them mentioned it when she was around. Answers to Aleja's questions were carefully crafted, smoothing over any cracks where the truth might seep out.

'We research the trends in trading, and which new lands we should visit next,' Olitiana had told her.

Frances had taken to saying, 'Eh, it's just boring stuff. The politics of piracy and all that' after Aleja had spotted the captain speaking to her in hushed tones.

'Aada works with the captain to plan where we'll be travelling next, or which treasure fleet makes an easy target,' Velka told her, her expression earnest enough that Aleja found herself almost believing her.

'We're looking for the pieces of the last girl who asked too many questions.' Malika's smile showed too many teeth.

Throughout each of these encounters Aleja was busy thinking hard. If no one would answer her questions, then she needed to dig deeper.

That evening she sat on her bunk with Thomas James's book on her lap, staring at the map of the world on the final page. No cities were marked on it, just a rough outline of land and sea. She couldn't say why it had attracted her attention, not when so much of the book contained coded puzzles and odd shapes that looked far more impressive and secretive. Maybe it was because she'd thought the map would be first to give up its secrets.

'. . . wind is ridiculous. We're getting nowhere, though we've been sailing since we left Spain, and now Aada is telling me a storm is headed our way,' Aleja heard Captain Quint complain to someone as two sets of boots ambled past her closed cabin door.

Aleja put the book, still open, at the foot of her bunk to go and look out of the porthole. It was a shadowed world outside, night falling thicker every second, the sky filled with aggressive clouds clumping together on the horizon. The waves were dull grey and choppy, lunging at the ship. Aleja shivered and pulled a blanket round her shoulders, still not used to the colder sea air. A loud bang came from further up the passageway, followed by Velka's shriek and Malika's curse. Smiling to herself, Aleja flopped on to the bunk on her stomach, the book open in front of her nose.

And then she realized.

The book smelled of lemon.

CHAPTER THIRTEEN

Puzzles, Storms and Iguanas

Scrambling to unhook the lantern from where it was hanging on her cabin wall, Aleja's hand shook a little. One wrong move and she would set the whole book alight. Carefully, she inched the lantern closer to the map, until she could feel the page warming up. Nothing happened. But still Aleja edged the lantern closer, staring at the page and hoping and hoping . . .

A tiny brown fleck appeared. Close on its tail another appeared. And then another. Then yet another. And as Aleja watched, her fingers trembling, they grew into letters.

Suye wepa thek aosk

It wasn't any language she knew.

So Aleja did what she always did when faced with a puzzle: she went to the library.

Aside from Penumbra, perched on the edge of one of the settees, the library was empty. When she opened the door, the ship bucked up on a strong wave, rousing Penumbra, who glided out over Aleja's head and swept up the dark passageway. Aleja turned her attention to the strange words she'd uncovered.

Perhaps they were Latin? She was flicking through a guide to translating Latin into English when she happened to glance up and notice a higher shelf that snatched her attention. Aleja had already scoured the library for mentions of Thomas James, of which there were none. She guessed the captain had any such titles in her quarters and even Aleja wasn't foolish enough to try to sneak in there. She climbed up a few more rungs, at the top of the thin ladder now. Running a finger over the spines in front of her nose, she found the one that had tempted her away from the puzzle. *Secrets of the World*. Now *this* was her kind of book. Balancing on the ladder, Aleja began to rifle through the pages. A temple of sacrifices under some unnamed lake in Tibet; ancient forgotten civilizations in the jungles in the Americas; the mythical lost city of Zerzura, somewhere in the Sahara Desert; and tiny underground churches and forts with hidden treasure spattered across Europe. It was all fascinating. Aleja had just reached a part that claimed there was an ancient map that could pinpoint all the world's secret places, when the library door opened again and Farren called cheerfully up, 'There you are! I've been looking for you!'

Startled, Aleja almost dropped the book.

'I've been sent by Frances to fetch you and Velka – she's found a new room on the ship!' Farren continued.

'A new room?' Aleja shelved the book and started to climb back down the ladder. The ship gave another lurch, sending the ladder rolling along the bookcase. Farren quickly grabbed it and Aleja hopped down.

'Yep, they appear now and then,' Farren said, leading the way past the weapons room and up a ladder, past the galley and into the passageway where the cabins were. 'We'll just grab Velka.'

Aleja knew that the legends about the *Ship of Shadows* fed the magic of the ship, but a new room popping into existence? She hadn't realized that could happen.

'Oh, of course,' Farren said when she noticed Aleja's amazement. 'It's how we got most of our hidden rooms and treasure chambers beneath the deck. The shadows are the heart of the magic on board,' she added, eyeing a splodge of darkness that was plodding along in her wake. 'But the legends are its blood. And it's always fun to see what people believe about the ship.' She grinned and stepped up to Velka's door, which swung open on

Griete's mechanism, releasing a burst of humid air. The splodge squeaked and scurried away into a larger glob of shadows at the end of the passageway.

Aleja looked curiously inside. She hadn't seen any of the crew's cabins before – in her time at sea she'd preferred to run wild around the magic of the ship, but now she found herself pondering what Frances's might look like. Judging by its occupier, it would definitely have cake, she thought, smiling to herself. Velka's cabin was a riot of colour as vibrant as the greenery tumbling down her arms. Large vines and tropical trees filled the space, a gentle mist weaving round their rubbery leaves. Bright butterflies in reds, pinks and oranges fluttered about in a huge glass enclosure at the foot of Velka's bunk, where an iguana the same shade of green as Velka's hair was sitting on her pillow. A collection of glass vials, beakers and test tubes was spread out across her desk, secured by bolts in the wood. There was smoking moss-green liquid in one that sloshed around with each wave they hit.

'Shut the door,' Velka said, blowing out a small purple flame beneath one of the vials. She added a few droplets of something to the smoking beaker. 'And don't mind Peridot – he's harmless.'

Aleja looked at Peridot the iguana with great interest. 'Where did he come from?'

'I found him a few years ago in a rainforest in the Americas. It wasn't until we returned to the ship that I realized he'd climbed inside my bag. I've tried to return him to the wild a few times but he's too taken with my cabin – he always comes straight back.' She pulled another beaker towards her and stirred a bright sapphire liquid into it.

'What made you want to be a pirate?' Aleja asked, picturing Velka in the jungle.

Farren laughed at this. 'She accidentally blew up half the dock in her hometown in Sweden messing around with those chemicals.'

Alarmed, Aleja took a step backwards.

'That was years ago,' Velka protested. 'But Farren's right, I was running away from the explosion I'd caused when I ran straight into the captain and she hired me on the spot, interested in what else I could do. Much like she was with you when you left your family's tavern. *Temporarily* left,' she amended. 'Though we're all certain you'll change your mind and accept the captain's offer.'

'I've got a bet riding on it.' Farren winked at Aleja.

'Why do you think I'll stay?' Aleja found herself unable to resist asking.

'This ship has a way of seeping in under your skin. Once you're on board the *Ship of Shadows*, you're home,' Farren said simply, her eyes on Velka.

'Now, just give me a minute and I'll be with you . . .' Velka's voice trailed off into the depths of concentration as she poured the sapphire liquid into the smoking moss-green beaker. It hissed and began to mist.

Aleja went to watch the butterflies, wondering at how Velka maintained this bright garden. A small bang sent Velka leaping backwards with singed eyebrows. Aleja suppressed a giggle.

'Frances found a new room,' Farren said, leaning against the door, ignoring the mini explosion. 'Do you want to come and see it?'

Velka stood up and stretched her back. 'Sure. Should we fetch Griete?'

'I already asked but she wants to be alone,' Farren said quietly.

'Is she OK?' Aleja asked.

Velka and Farren exchanged a look.

'What?'

'She's still struggling with Raven defecting to another ship,' Velka said, her silver bangles clinking as she opened the door. 'They were best friends.'

'Oh,' Aleja said, feeling a stab of sympathy for Griete. She hadn't realized Raven had left to join another crew. 'What was Raven like?'

'She was good with languages, like you, but not with spoken ones. She read ancient languages. She was very quiet and she'd had a hard life before Farren rescued her,' Velka replied, leading the way out into the passage.

'That doesn't excuse what she did,' Farren said, shutting the door harder than was necessary and cutting off their conversation before Aleja could ask any more questions.

Farren led them up on to the main deck. A dark, seething mass of water surrounded the ship. Captain Quint stood at the helm, guiding the ship through the swelling waves. Malika and Olitiana were adjusting the rigging, reefing the mainsail and hoisting the smaller storm sails up the mast instead.

Aleja paused. 'Do they need help?'

Velka shook her head. 'This one's a small storm. It's only the serious storms that need all hands on deck, but you rarely get those in these parts. They're just in a hurry to reach harbour before we're attacked again.'

'Are we in danger?' Aleja asked, meeting Velka's eyes.

'We have a powerful enemy, one who has the power to be our undoing,' Velka began before Farren shot her a warning look and she fell silent, leaving Aleja frustrated once more.

By the time they'd reached the bow of the ship, Aleja's trousers were plastered to her legs with salt water. They were under the navigator's room, and Aleja glimpsed Aada high above them, staring at a map.

'Here we are,' Farren shouted as the ship ploughed through another wave.

'What are we looking at?' Velka yelled back over the crash and pound of water against the hull.

They were standing at the tip of the boat, a narrow triangle of empty decking that met to form the bow. Aleja couldn't see any trace of Frances, nor where any secret room could possibly be.

Seconds later, a curved panel on the side of the ship, just below the taffrail, popped up and Frances's head emerged, looking very self-satisfied. 'It's in here!' she called, disappearing once more.

After another wave sent them clinging on to the taffrail and coated them with sprays of cold water, Aleja ran across to the open panel. Inside, there was a sheer vertical slide. With another freezing wave looming, Aleja jumped down on to it.

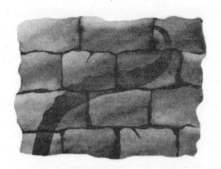

Chapter Fourteen
The Cave of Shadows

Aleja coasted down the slippery wood, the slide hugging the curve of the ship's hull. Waves smashed against the wood next to her head as she plummeted deeper into the belly of the ship. All of a sudden, the chute ended and Aleja was spat out into a small dark cave.

She barely had time to scramble out of the way before Farren zoomed down, then Velka, all of them in a rush to escape the freezing water slipping down the back of their necks and gluing their clothes to their skin.

'Welcome,' Frances said dramatically, holding up an antique silver-plated lantern, 'to the cave of shadows!'

Finding a large smooth rock to sit on, Aleja stared around her. They were sitting in a rocky chamber that might have been carved out of a mountain or been deep below the earth if she hadn't known they were sitting in a ship. Charcoal-grey stone jutted out around and above them, threaded through with marbled veins. A collection of old silver lanterns dangled haphazardly around the cave, and everywhere Aleja looked shadows rustled.

'Brings new meaning to the name *Ship of Shadows*, doesn't it?' Farren said, looking around.

'The name definitely inspires the most rumours,' Velka mused, running her fingers through her emerald hair, which was plastered to her head and now looked black.

Aleja gathered her own hair in her hands to squeeze the water out. Farren was wringing her shirt out at the same time, until Frances pulled a face at them both. 'You're soaking the cave,' she complained good-naturedly.

'The cave-ave-ave,' the cave whispered back at them.

Velka gave a start. 'What was that?'

'It seems to have a selective echo,' Frances said, setting the lantern down on the rock she was sitting cross-legged on. 'I haven't figured out everything yet, but the shadows are even more active in here.'

Aleja caught sight of a tail whisking round the back of the cave and spun on her rock to follow it. It was a shadow-mouse. 'They have more physical forms, like in the secret passageways,' Aleja said, looking up to where shadows clotted together beneath an overhanging rock. 'Look, something's forming there.' She pointed.

Farren, Frances and Velka craned their necks to look under the rock. A shadowed face stared back at them. Velka squealed and laughed. 'That's too creepy.'

''eepy-eepy-eepy,' the cave whispered.

'Speaking of creepy.' Frances blew her lantern out, plunging her own face into shadow, her amber eyes and glasses glinting in the swaying light from the other lanterns. 'I have a story for you.' Her grin sent a shiver down Aleja's spine.

'Let's hear it,' Farren said, leaning back and propping her boots against a rock.

'Wait, I want my cake first,' Velka said. Aleja and Farren looked at her. 'What? Frances never takes us anywhere without cake,' Velka said defensively.

Frances slid a tin across the rocky floor towards Velka, who passed round slices of thick apple cake. Aleja curled her legs up and munched on the sweet crumbly cake, waiting for Frances to begin.

Frances cleared her throat. 'It was on a stormy night, not unlike this very one we find ourselves sailing into tonight –' she began in a deep, ominous voice. Farren, trying not to laugh, choked on her cake and Velka had to whack her on the back. Frances glared at Farren before continuing in the same dramatic vein – 'that the crew of the *Scourge of the Seas* found themselves sailing into a patch of rough water, where the seabed was coated in broken ships and the skeletons of sailors who had gone before them.'

The shadows of a group of skeletons appeared on the cave walls. Aleja jumped, finding a staring skull right next to her. Velka gasped and Farren shifted away from a bony shadow-hand that skittered around near her boots. Frances looked delighted, continuing her story with a devilish grin. 'And then things took a turn for the worse,' she said, widening her eyes. 'Long slithering tentacles emerged from the heaving water and wrapped themselves round the ship! They'd sailed into kraken territory.'

'Half her stories involve kraken even though we've never seen one,' Farren whispered loudly to Aleja, receiving another of Frances's glares in response.

A small shapeless shadow inched closer to Aleja, nestling next to her boot.

'The kraken was a relentless beast, impaling sailors on its massive teeth and chomping through wood like it was cake. The crew fought and fought but it was no use; the captain knew they would soon die.'

Aleja found herself engrossed, watching the shadowed tentacles rippling along the cave walls, the shadows sucked in by Frances's words.

Suddenly a figure shot up from the rocky cave floor.

Aleja jumped and Velka shrieked.

'Ah, you've found the –' he said before stopping and staring at them in bewilderment.

By the time Aleja had realized it was just Geoffrey her heart was already pounding and the ghost wore a disgruntled expression. 'Oh, really,' he said, puffing his chest out so that his ghostly medals bounced against his ruffles. 'It is not as if you are not accustomed to my presence on this excuse for a ship.'

'Geoffrey, you *are* a ghost,' Farren said impatiently.

'I have never known such rudeness in my entire life,' he muttered to himself, fading back into mist and disappearing in a huff.

'And then the kraken spoke!' Frances said loudly, leaning forward to reclaim her story, the shadows surging around her. 'It told them the price of their lives. A sacrifice. Something precious. They offered gold and jewels and the crew members they liked the least, but the kraken didn't want any of those. It wanted something irreplaceable. Something rich with meaning.' Frances flipped something small, which glittered in the lantern light as it spiralled up, up and then down, tumbling through the air and on to Frances's palm. She held it up for them all to see. 'Only *that* could buy them safe passage.'

She was holding Aleja's lucky coin.

'How did you do that?' Aleja asked, thrusting her hands into her pockets to check that it wasn't an illusion.

Frances flicked the coin back to Aleja, who caught it neatly. 'Slippery fingers,' Frances said, wiggling her fingers.

Farren let out a guffaw as she stood up. 'Come on, we've been here a while; we don't want the room to vanish on us.'

Aleja looked up from her coin. 'Can it do that?' she asked, her mouth hanging open a little.

Frances's eyes gleamed wickedly. 'We've lost more than a few crew members that way.'

'*Honestly*,' Velka said as Farren laughed again, 'the stories you tell!' She turned to Aleja. 'Considering the new rooms are conjured to life by legends, they can be a bit temperamental,' she admitted, 'but they fade out slowly. No one's ever gone with them.'

There were iron handholds above the slide, but it was still a slow climb back up the chute. A couple of shadows trickled up on to the deck with them, including the small one that had sat next to Aleja's boot.

It wasn't until they'd run back down to their cabins that the thought struck Aleja. 'Could I dream up a new room for the ship?'

The others laughed.

'A lot of people have to really *believe* that it's true before we get a new room,' Farren explained, a twinkle in her hazel eyes. 'Our shadows – former crew members – help to keep the legends alive around the world, but even they can't dream up new rooms for us.'

'That hasn't stopped Griete from trying to get a bath, though.' Frances laughed again. 'She's been trying for years but she still hasn't given up!'

Yawning, Aleja went into her cabin. To her bemusement, before she could shut the door, the small shadow rushed in after her.

The storm dragged on for days, blowing the ship off course, further into the Atlantic Ocean until they lost sight of the coast. When it finally cleared, Captain Quint had stalked into Aada's cabin, where the navigator was busy re-plotting their course. Aleja, Frances, Velka and Farren were put to work scrubbing the decks after an hour of waving cutlasses around under Malika's supervision. Griete hadn't left her cabin yet. High above them Penumbra whirled round the puffy traces of clouds; there was still no sight of land. The little shadow that had spent the night in Aleja's cabin, wrapped round her ankles, hadn't left her alone yet and was now flitting in an owl shape round her brush. Aleja watched it morph to a brush and then back to an owl, amused by its playful antics.

'How did this come to be Captain Quint's ship?' Aleja asked Frances, her arms aching from scrubbing at the frothing seawater. The two of them were on the starboard side, clearing away the salt that had dried on deck after the storm and keeping the deck moist so it wouldn't crack in the warmer weather they were sailing towards. Velka and Farren were on the port side, out of earshot.

'After information again?' Frances sounded amused. She sat back on her heels to tip another bucket of seawater on to the deck.

'Well, you don't have to tell me anything secret,' Aleja persisted. 'Just how she came to sail it. You love a good story,' she added slyly.

Frances chewed her lip. 'All right,' she said, leaning in closer, a gleam in her eyes. 'She stole the ship. Her family once were rich, years and years ago, but they'd fallen on hard times and the captain had no way to buy the *Ship of Shadows*.'

'Why did she want it?' Aleja asked in a whisper.

'I can't tell you that,' Frances whispered back. 'But she stole this ship years ago and sailed it single-handedly away on to the ocean to get away from the owners. Absolute madness, of course, but they say madness and genius go together, don't they? Anyway, the storms almost took back the ship that night, but she survived. She tied herself to the mast and just waited. Waited until the waves got bored and gave up. She turned pirate that night, making her own rules, mastering the seas as a free woman.'

There was a moment of reverent silence as they both pictured Captain Quint forging her own destiny that stormy night alone on the ocean.

'You missed a spot.' Malika appeared above them, startling them both back into scrubbing the deck. Aleja studied the woman under a curtain of hair, as she followed the captain down into the ship. Aleja waited and, like clockwork, Aada emerged from the navigator's room and went down after them.

'Why do the three of them keep meeting in the library?' she asked Frances.

Frances looked pained and said nothing.

Aleja sighed. 'Fine. But will you at least tell me how Malika got her scars?'

Frances jerked as if Malika was still standing behind them. 'We don't talk about that,' she said quickly. 'That's Malika's business.'

It seemed the more answers Aleja tried to find, the more mysteries she stumbled upon.

She wondered if any of the answers would be inside the navigator's room.

The next time Captain Quint, Malika and Aada vanished for another secret meeting in the library, Aleja was ready.

No one saw her scurry across the deck, tailed by the little shadow.

Hiding behind one of the posts that held the navigator's room high above the ship, she double-checked no one was looking. Olitiana was at the helm across the deck. Aleja glanced up at Penumbra screeching above and climbed the ladder. It led to a square trapdoor. Pushing it open, Aleja emerged into the navigator's room, looking around with deep curiosity.

Huge windows were positioned at the bow of the ship, meeting in a sharp point. Under the windows cubbyholes were built into the wood, filled with rolled maps, navigational tools, odd little teacups and a huge chunk of charcoal-grey rock with purplish veins shot through it. A round table with mismatched chairs was nestled in the triangular part of the room and covered with more maps, nautical charts and silver mathematical instruments. Aleja went to poke around at them, noticing an incredibly old map of Morocco had been left out on top. Unfortunately it showed the entire country and after looking for clues of the ship's destination and examining the little numbers written round the edges to mark the longitude, Aleja gave up and investigated the rest of the room instead.

A huge telescope was anchored to the floor in the middle of the room, with a squishy purple armchair positioned next to it. Looking up, Aleja gasped when she realized that the entire roof was made of glass. Being in the navigator's room was like being perched in the sky itself, surrounded by clouds and waves and the circlings of Penumbra high above. Thomas James's book was on the armchair. Aada must have been taking a turn at cracking it. Yet more maps and diagrams of the stars littered the solid wooden walls surrounding the rest of the navigator's room, and a hammock swung gently in one corner over a massive snowy fur stretched across the floor. A trunk filled with Norwegian battleaxes sat next to it. Aleja was just about to pick one up when the trapdoor thudded open.

Aada had returned.

CHAPTER FIFTEEN

The Navigator

Aleja didn't have time to hide.

'Ah, I wondered when I might find you in here,' Aada said in her soft voice.

'I was looking for the book,' Aleja said, glad she'd spotted it.

'Please, have a seat.' Aada gestured towards the table and chairs.

Aleja sat, enjoying the dip and soar of the ship through the water, each foam-topped wave visible through the glass along with the pistol-grey sky above. Aada poured something thick and strong-smelling into two cups, passing one to Aleja and curling her fingers round her own. She perched on a chair opposite.

'This book,' Aleja said, flicking through the pages to the map, 'there's a message here but I can't work out what language it's in. Is it Norwegian? Or any language you know?'

Aada studied it. 'No,' she said, strands of her white-blonde hair slipping over her face. 'This is what I've been studying.' She turned a few pages back to a series of strange shapes. 'They look like Norse runes, but not quite.'

'Can you read them?' Aleja asked eagerly.

Aada gave a shake of her head. 'This book is truly a puzzle to me.'

'What's it like in Norway?' Aleja asked instead, fascinated by both Aada and her cabin perched above the ship. Aada kept odd hours and Aleja had often seen her wandering about the deck in a dreamy haze, lifting her face to the star-studded sky. Aleja, deeply intrigued by the ice-covered north, had been waiting for the perfect opportunity to ask about it.

'My country is beautiful,' Aada said, finishing her drink and setting it down. 'I come from the very north, from the Arctic.' Aleja's interest perked up at this, her imagination tumbling into ice-flecked seas and snow. 'And I would love to tell you all about it – when your friends aren't below, trying to pretend you haven't been caught spying again.'

Aleja tried to disguise her guilt and disappointment by taking a swig of her drink. It was hot, thick and bitter. Spluttering with surprise, she looked up at Aada, who gave her a pleasant smile. 'Ah, coffee's not for everyone,' she said.

Over the next few days life on the ship began to take on a pleasant rhythm of its own. In weapons training Aleja learned how to fight with cutlasses and swords and daggers and, during one particularly chaotic session, bows and arrows. Farren had turned out to be an excellent shot despite claiming she'd never forsake her pistols for a bow, but Griete had accidentally speared Velka's hair in an ill-timed moment, and Aleja and Frances struggled to hit the targets. Olitiana was teaching Aleja the basics of seafaring, instructing her in the names of the different ropes and sails and what each did. Aleja had even stopped jumping each time Geoffrey glided through the walls to spook her, gleeful every time she dropped a book on his account.

She still sneaked around the ship by night with Frances, exploring the other rooms that had been rumoured into creation. The fireplace in the galley had a secret false back that led into a tiny room at the rear of the ship, which was walled with glass. Suddenly finding herself looking underwater, Aleja gasped at the mass of water frothing around them. She lifted a lantern to look deeper into the watery dimness. Attracted by the light, a porpoise suddenly appeared, frolicking on the other side of the glass. Aleja and Frances had stayed and played with it, waving the lantern around until it swam away and Frances got hungry.

And then there were the temporary rooms that oozed with magic and had Aleja dragging her feet each time they left, careful never to outstay the room. There had been a pantry stocked with jars instead of food, each one containing an entire storm, complete with glowing purple-black clouds and tiny zaps of lightning, ready to be unleashed on unsuspecting foes. Aleja had stuffed a couple in her pockets and had taken to reading by storm-light in her cabin. The cavernous room stretching out between the cabins and Olitiana's quarters, defying the rules of space itself, was filled with suits of armour that marched around by themselves and a wall of disguises, including masks and wigs that were eerily lifelike. 'In case you feel like assassinating anyone,' Frances told her brightly. Once put on, they'd seal themselves to your skin for the next hour, trapping you in an image that wasn't your own, as Aleja found out the hard way, Frances cackling at her frustrated efforts to peel off the man's face stuck to her own.

Once there had been a thin room walled with windows that looked out into other lands. Aleja had lingered in that one, watching snow coat a forest of firs in a sparkling white blanket until Frances had impatiently yanked her out.

But Aleja's favourite nights remained the ones of pinching cake and sliding down into the cave of shadows, where Frances relished telling stories that spurred the shadows into action. Aleja had been curious about whether her little shadow would stay down there, but it happily tailed her out each time, melting along in her wake and spending the night tucked round her ankles. She was getting used to its constant presence and often found herself talking aloud to it.

Aleja had also learned to recognize Frances's mischievous grins, as well as not to take *everything* she said as truth. This came after an especially long-winded story Frances had told her about a time when she'd been caught stealing a priceless ruby from a sultan.

'And then he sentenced me to be his royal poison taster!' she said, while Aleja looked at her shrewdly, asking, 'Sultan of where?'

To which Frances had promptly answered, 'Japan', which, as Aleja knew, didn't even *have* sultans.

So she'd paid her back.

Aleja had borrowed Velka's iguana, Peridot, and popped him into an empty cake tin, carefully leaving the lid a little ajar, and stashed him in the cupboard just before Frances ambled into the galley looking for a snack. Frances waited to open the cake tin until the two of them were up on deck, Griete, Velka and Farren with them. After jumping and almost dropping the cake tin, Frances had shrieked with laughter and Aleja couldn't stop her lips twitching every time she remembered it.

The little shadow still tailed her footsteps and Aleja felt attached to its shapeshifting form, the others looking on bemusedly as Farren pointed out, 'It's curious, I've never seen a shadow attach itself to one person for so long.'

It felt different to her usual shadow, which was as insubstantial as ever. Sometimes Aleja could have sworn she could feel it when she petted its whispery form, the air beneath it slightly thicker, stickier than usual. 'But that can't be possible, can it?' she murmured to the preening shadow-kitten. 'You're just hungry for attention,' she said, her fingers trailing through the shadow and on to the blanket below.

Her one frustration was that she couldn't work out what the phrase in the book meant: *Suye wepa thek aosk*.

She scoured the library, becoming a permanent fixture among the books and firmly establishing herself in her own role on board the ship, but she was still at a loss. And she wasn't closer to solving any of the other puzzles in the book either. None of them were.

Aleja's attention began to drift on to other things. As they heaved along the waves she heard a sharp ring that dragged her focus on to something she hadn't noticed before, a pair of mounted steel bells.

'The magic etched into the metal senses whenever you cross paths with a kraken,' Frances told her excitedly. Any kraken was far beneath the surface of the grey water, though, and, despite Aleja running to look over the side each time the bells struck, she hadn't been able to glimpse so much as a tentacle.

'You'd better pray to whatever gods you believe in that you don't see one,' Farren said to Aleja one day. 'Kraken are a nasty business. Never seen one myself but I've salvaged the odd wreck.' She rubbed an old scar on her forearm, staring out to the clouds bunching together on the horizon. Penumbra was flying alongside the ship, melting in and out of the gloom as they watched. It was a cold day, with most of the crew below decks, but Aleja had just finished a session with Olitiana teaching her how to trim the sails. She knew she'd never forget standing at the centre of the ship, adjusting the sails to help the ship cut through the waves.

'Is that how Malika lost her hand?' Aleja whispered, her curiosity spiking as the bells let out a steady stream of peals.

'No,' Farren said shortly. 'That was a different kind of evil,' she added after a long pause, slamming a door shut on their conversation.

'Oh.' Aleja looked at the bells. 'They're still ringing. Do they only ring when kraken are close?'

Farren nodded, glancing down at the water. Aleja looked down too, thinking about how deep the water plummeted beneath them: deep enough to hold monsters and the ships they'd wrecked. From the stories that Frances relished telling Aleja on the stormier nights, it seemed that the seabed was littered with skeletons. Aleja's fingers tightened round the taffrail as she peered further over the side.

'The bells are engraved with a tip dipped in kraken blood and old magic,' Farren explained. 'Left on their own, they'll ring when they sense kraken nearby. The louder they ring, the closer we are. And if you were to ring that bell yourself, you'd summon the nearest kraken to the surface. Which I do not recommend.'

'What about in rough water? What happens then?' Aleja asked, trying to remember if she'd heard the bells ring during the storm they'd recently sailed through.

'Ah, the bells are magic. The greatest storm in the world couldn't make those bells ring.'

Aleja stared at them. They looked like normal, slightly rusty bells to her. Apart from the engravings. In a symbolic language, long since lost to time as deep as the oceans, it spelled out words no one could read. Small and spiky, the deep etchings had been roughly scratched into the metal, looping round the bells, which were enclosed in glass and mounted on an old door. They were nailed upright in the centre of the upper decks, preventing anyone from knocking into them and accidentally summoning a kraken. Aleja shuddered at the thought, her fingers finding her way to her pocket to squeeze her lucky coin.

'What have you got in your pocket?' Farren asked, looking at Aleja's hand still dug into her pocket.

'It's nothing. My coin.' Aleja pulled it out, flashing it in the lantern light before tucking it away again.

Farren looked at her curiously. 'Why are you always touching it?'

'For luck. My grandmother gave it to me before I left.' Aleja's cheeks reddened.

'Ah. I wasn't one of the crew members who the captain rescued either; I also left my family.' Farren shrugged. 'Then again, loneliness can be hard, even in a good home. Was that what it was like for you too?'

Aleja nodded. Her little shadow crept closer to her, folding itself into a small fox that sat next to her boot.

'Then it's a good thing you've found your way on board. It doesn't matter how long you choose to stay; once the captain's invited you on, you'll always have a place on this ship, always be one of our shadows around the world. The rest of the crew know that; that's why they've accepted you as one of their own. Because you are. That shadow trailing you around proves it.' Farren seemed to sense that Aleja was struggling for words and changed the conversation, nodding at the coin. 'You should wear it round your neck.' She couldn't help grinning. 'Then Frances will have a harder time getting it off you.'

'How?'

'I'll make a small hole in it for you. You can thread a string or chain through it and tie it round your neck. That way you'll never lose it.'

Aleja handed the coin over. Farren carefully selected a pointed tool from her nearby chest and twizzled it into the coin. Next she pulled on a thick leather glove and strode over to the nearest lantern. Its light was brightening the dim, clouded day the ship was cutting through. Opening the glass door, she held the coin over the flame, before attacking it once more with the tool, chiselling straight through the hot metal. When she'd finished there was a neat little hole in the coin.

'Thank you,' Aleja said, marvelling at Farren's craftsmanship as she turned it this way and that.

Farren gave her a length of string. 'I don't have anything fancier than this, but you can replace it when you get your wages.'

Aleja, tying it round her neck, looked up with interest. 'Wages?'

'Of course. We each get a wage at the end of the month – why do you think you've been scrubbing the deck?' Farren looked amused, but it hadn't occurred to Aleja before. 'Sometimes it's higher or lower, depending on the needs of the ship. And sometimes it isn't in money. One month last year we got paid in raw-cut emeralds and rubies as big as your fist. That was a good month.' Her eyes glazed over.

Aleja left Farren to her memories. After the lack of wind, then the storm, they were now further delayed due to more storms brewing in the ocean ahead, but they were inching closer to northern Africa each hour, according to Aada. Which didn't leave Aleja much time to figure out what they were doing.

The captain, Malika and Aada were meeting more regularly in the library. Aleja hadn't solved anything in Thomas James's book, and, worse, she had no idea where in Morocco they were going or why. And she was tired of not knowing things. Just rummaging around the library wasn't getting her any information, nor had her hunt through Aada's cabin. No, it was time to take a bigger risk.

Starting tonight, she'd have to spy on the captain.

CHAPTER SIXTEEN
Thomas James

'And have you decided about the girl? Can we trust her?' Aada asked.

They were talking about her. Aleja craned her neck to hear what Captain Quint would say, ignoring the protest in her knees as she kneeled on the hard wood, her face rammed against a thin crack in the library door, the passageway lit by a single storm-jar. If the others refused to tell her what secrets they were harbouring, what they were sailing to the northern tip of Africa to find, then she would just have to seek the answers herself.

Listening hard, Aleja frowned at the series of bangs emanating from the weapons room next door – a volley of gunpowder, undoubtedly from Farren. It had just fallen quiet, and Captain Quint had started to speak, when to Aleja's immense frustration a silhouette covered the crack in the door and Aleja had to scoot backwards. She pocketed her storm-jar and hid behind a barrel, her little shadow zooming back with her. She waited for the door to close once more. It didn't.

'Believe it or not, you're not as stealthy as you seem to think you are,' Malika said from behind Aleja, her soft voice filled with danger.

Aleja dragged herself out. 'Sorry.'

'Get in there.' Malika used the toe of her boot to open the door.

Aleja trudged into the library, scarlet-faced.

'Spying again, Aleja?' Captain Quint asked casually as Malika stalked in behind her. Aada ignored them all, lost in her own thoughts.

Aleja's cheeks burned. 'I didn't mean –'

Captain Quint waved her hand. 'What do you make of this text?' she asked instead.

Aada glanced up, her pale-grey eyes fixing on Aleja.

'Captain, is it wise ...' Malika left the question dangling in the air.

Captain Quint gave Malika a long look.

Aleja padded across the library floor, the Persian rugs springy beneath her boots, the swinging lanterns chasing shadows round the bookcases like a mad cat. The diamond-encrusted feathers painted on the ceiling gently glinted and Penumbra was softly dozing on one of the rolling ladders, a forgotten rat's tail still clutched in one of his talons. Malika sat down at the captain's right-hand side, pushing aside the dusty tome she'd been scouring before catching Aleja. Taking one of the cushioned chairs, Aleja sat and folded her legs beneath her. Captain Quint pushed the book in front of Aleja, her index finger tapping the start of the third paragraph. It was handwritten in Spanish and almost impossible to read. She scrunched up her nose in concentration, tracing the letters curling across the whisper-thin page.

And so I followed Thomas James's explorations, even into his darkest moments as the illness progressed to his mind, for we had become great friends and I mourned the thought of a world without him. My greatest adventure, however, took place without him in an exotic city in the north of Africa as he disappeared for weeks without me.

Thomas James. Whatever book she had just read from, Aleja was certain she hadn't seen it in the library before. The captain was speaking and Aleja ignored the excitement fizzing inside her to listen.

'The last of Thomas James's travels are only documented through his companions' journals,' Captain

Quint told Malika and Aada, 'which means we can only work on what they imply – what might be happening between the lines.'

'And what are the chances of Thomas James disappearing for weeks from Marrakesh without running an expedition?' Aada said, her gaze drifting away.

'He was *definitely* running an expedition. And to . . . the place we're heading to next,' Captain Quint said, carefully skipping over the name, much to Aleja's annoyance. 'But it's a great shame he never covered the last of these expeditions in his own journals. I can't even guess which direction he would have headed in, and searching through the whole region of northern Africa would take a lifetime.'

What were they looking for? There was definitely a connection between Thomas James and Captain Quint – in fact, her entire mysterious quest was connected to him. But how? Aleja stared at the map of the world engraved on the library table and racked her brains to think back over the books she'd read about him.

'Does it say anything else?' Malika asked Aleja, who had stuck her finger in the book to keep her place and was reading the title: *The Lost Explorers*.

'Erm.' She hurriedly flipped back to the short paragraph she'd read before. '*As you can see, the focus of Alejandro Cabello's journals was not on Thomas James, but rather his own expeditions that he was planning at the time.*

Therefore, until Thomas James's lost journals can be uncovered, he will remain forevermore one of the Lost Explorers.'

No one spoke; the three women were quiet with thought.

Aleja seized the opportunity. 'You said Thomas James never covered the last of his expeditions in his own journals,' she said, turning to Captain Quint.

Captain Quint studied Aleja. 'That's right.'

'But there's no way of knowing that – his journals have been lost for years,' Aleja said. 'And I've never known of anyone ever reading them.'

Captain Quint leaned back in her chair. Aleja felt her attention like a second skin. 'I've read his journals.'

Aleja almost stopped breathing. What she wouldn't give to read them. 'Then what you're after, your quest, it's got something to do with Thomas James,' Aleja said, watching the captain exchange an unreadable glance with Malika. 'This ship wasn't just his – your entire ship's mission revolves around him too.'

Aada had been silent throughout this exchange, but Aleja was willing to bet she hadn't missed a single word or glance.

'You're right,' Captain Quint said. She leaned forward, strands of chestnut hair escaping their tie. 'I told you it was a great story.'

Aleja waited. 'Are you still waiting for me to prove myself?' she asked eventually. 'What do you want me to do to show I can be trusted?'

'I'm not sure.' Captain Quint's eyes twinkled. 'But I'll know it when I see it.'

'That's not –' Aleja began, but she was destined to be left hanging as a deafening noise broke out on the deck above them.

Penumbra's eyes snapped open. He rustled his feathers and shrieked.

'What the . . .?' Captain Quint frowned, a hand on her sword as she strode towards the library door. She threw it open and ran up the ladder. Penumbra flew smoothly over her. Malika fled after them, leaving Aleja and Aada staring at each other.

'Is that –' Aada started to ask.

'The kraken bells,' Aleja whispered.

CHAPTER SEVENTEEN

The Kraken Bells

Aada looked steadily at Aleja. 'Have you ever fought a kraken?'

'No.' Aleja swallowed. 'Have you?'

'Once, many years ago. Though never on this ship. They are not common in these waters; they prefer the colder climes. Stay here if you wish – there is no need for you to be on deck.'

Aleja shook her head. 'I'm coming with you.'

'Very good,' Aada murmured.

There was a rough splintering sound, and the ship that Aleja had come to think of as a solid thing beneath her feet suddenly shifted, flinging her and Aada to the floor. Frances's stories about kraken had been like hearing a good ghost story – you felt cosy even as you shivered at the spooky tale. But now, as she thought of one in the flesh, effortlessly shoving their ship aside, Aleja's legs trembled with fear.

Aada was already back on her feet. 'Come on,' she said, her dreamy expression banished. She whipped a hand behind her, freeing the battleaxe strapped to her back.

They rushed up the ladder to the galley, which was deserted even of shadows. Aleja grabbed two of the sharpest kitchen knives she could see and tucked them in her belt. When they climbed the next ladder they were left hanging on with legs and arms wrapped round the rungs as the ship skipped another wave, crashing sideways for a heart-rending moment before righting itself. With an *eep!* of alarm the little shadow fled inside Aleja's boot. Comforted by its presence, Aleja breathed deeply before scurrying up the final rungs into the salted air, which was thick with shouts, shrill ringing, the crack of Farren's pistols and a low bestial keening.

A fat tentacle was slithering over the wet deck, while several more reared in the air high above the ship's mast, poised to strike. Aleja stared up at them in horror. Each tentacle was wider than a door and pale grey, with rows of pink suction caps that oozed and stuck to the ship, leaving strands of saliva-like residue behind. Aleja saw Malika deftly knot her headscarf tighter with one hand, kick her boots off, put her cutlass between her teeth and jump into the water.

'Malika, no!' the captain roared, spinning with her sword above her, braced for the tentacles above to make impact.

Waves rolled over the deck as the kraken played with the ship, the wooden frame shuddering under the weight of those enormous tentacles. Aleja grabbed a rope, narrowly avoiding being swept into the water. She was clutching one of her knives but unsure what to do. The kraken was bigger than she could have imagined, and the very real threat of it snapping the ship in half and killing them all filled her with fear. Struggling back to her feet, Aleja spotted Frances sneaking towards the nearest tentacle and ran towards her. Noticing Aleja, Frances gestured towards the tentacle. She raised her cutlass in a silent question and Aleja nodded. The two of them attacked, Aleja biting back her fear and sinking her knife into the tentacle. It was spongy.

'Yeugh.' Frances shot it a look of disgust as it leaked a black substance.

Aleja leaped back as the tentacle shot out from under them and disappeared into the water, taking her knife with it.

Olitiana was trying to steer away from the kraken, the large wheel of the ship trembling in her hands. Velka and Aada were adjusting the rigging and sails according to Olitiana's shouted instructions. The captain and Griete had attacked another tentacle, which was wrapped round the mast, until Farren shot it with a pistol and it whipped back into the water, leaving ropes of stringy goo behind. Their relief was short-lived as the ship's hull let out a creaking protest and the body of the kraken appeared in the water, its large mouth open, revealing endless rings of razor-sharp teeth, each tooth longer than one of Aleja's legs. She gulped. The kraken screeched, blasting them all with a wave of its rotting breath.

Noticing yet another tentacle snaking on to the deck, Aleja ran towards where Olitiana was trying to control the ship, grabbing Frances on the way. She sank her second knife into the tentacle just before it could entwine itself round the wheel. A spurt of black goo splashed over them and the kraken screeched again, whipping its wounded tentacle back into the water.

Aleja wiped the gunge off her face. It stank of rotting seafood.

She held out her hands, her legs wide apart and bent at the knees to stabilize herself on the slippery deck, which kept slanting in odd directions. Frances held the same stance next to her, her cutlass also raised against the threat of teeth and tentacles.

'Where's your weapon?' Frances shouted across to her.

'I lost it in the kraken!'

Frances tossed a dagger across to Aleja, who gratefully snatched it out of the air.

As the kraken opened its terrible mouth, the beginnings of another screech trembling in its throat, the blade of a cutlass suddenly appeared through the back of its mouth. It thrashed its tentacles wildly, and the crew all ducked as a few slapped the deck, splintering the wood.

'If your purpose was to make it angry, you've certainly succeeded,' Captain Quint yelled to Malika, who had reappeared on the kraken, her dress dragging half the ocean with it. The captain didn't seem at all surprised.

Frances sighed in relief. 'Finally.'

Aleja looked at her incredulously. 'Isn't it a bit early to say that?' she shouted as another tentacle whipped round the ship, the kraken ignoring the cutlass jutting out of its mouth and deciding it would rather toy around with the ship instead.

'Not at all.' Frances was grinning now, gesturing back at the kraken, to where Malika had reached the summit of the beast and was preparing to plunge a second sword straight through its bulbous head.

Aleja gagged and turned away not a second too soon. She heard a wet splatter hit the deck accompanied by another sigh from Frances, a cheer from Farren and a screech from Penumbra, who had been anxiously whirling above. The ship rocked on a large wave. Looking back, Aleja watched the sea reclaim the kraken. Its huge mass slid down, slipping away from the ship, buried by the water. The last tips of its tentacles sank down under the waves. Captain Quint wasted no time in throwing a length of rope into the water. Aleja and Frances rushed to the side of the ship. There was no sign of Malika. She'd plummeted deep into the ocean with the body of the beast and there was a moment of silence as everyone scanned the water for a glimpse of her bright sky-blue dress and headscarf.

'There,' Aleja shouted, pointing at a spot of colour coming up from under the water.

Malika shattered the surface with a deep gasp. Captain Quint swept the rope over the water for her to grab. After the captain and Olitiana pulled her up and on to the ship, Malika half fell on to the deck, a cold smile lingering on her lips.

Penumbra let out a piercing shriek. Looking up, Aleja saw something that chilled her bones.

The kraken was looming up out of the water.

Malika must have only wounded it, and its bright yellow eyes were staring, fixed on the ship, rivulets of black slime trailing from its bulging head, its mouth leaking more of the stuff. It opened its mouth, but it couldn't screech any longer. Aleja gasped, staring up at it.

'Prepare for attack!' Captain Quint shouted, leaping up the netting that led to the crow's nest, her sword in one hand to get to a better position opposite the huge beast.

Malika growled, unsheathing her cutlass with another terrifying smile as the kraken rose from the water. It was as big as ten ships.

Aleja clutched the dagger, braced for the tentacles to smash down on to the deck. But the attack never came. Penumbra arrowed through the air, sharp talons extended, and shot straight for one of the kraken's eyes. He pierced it with a soft popping sound. The kraken flailed, its tentacles churning the ocean into a frothing cauldron. Penumbra whirled round into a second attack. Before he could strike again, the kraken began to flee, reaching out with its tentacles to claw its way back into the water, as far away from the eagle owl as possible.

'Well, I've never seen anything like *that* before,' Frances said, as awed as Aleja felt.

Captain Quint, still on the netting, held her arm out and whistled. Penumbra sailed back on to her arm. The captain climbed down, effortlessly bearing the weight of the enormous owl on one wrist, and jumped on to the deck. 'Let's hope it doesn't return,' she said grimly, watching the squirming tentacles.

Aleja suddenly remembered the storm-jar in her pocket. She threw it as hard as she could at the kraken.

There was a deep rumble. The water turned the same ominous shade of purple-black as the clouds rolling in from the horizon. Bolts of jagged lightning ripped through the sky. It was the fiercest storm Aleja had ever seen, with all of its might concentrated on the patch of water around the kraken. Waves reared up and seemed to devour the last of the tentacles, and the kraken vanished from sight.

'Woah,' Frances said, shooting Aleja an admiring look.

'Nicely done, Aleja,' Captain Quint said as the thunder and lightning faded away. Aleja grinned.

'Now, take care of this, Olitiana,' Captain Quint commanded, strolling into her quarters with Penumbra and stroking his feathers.

'Right.' Olitiana clapped her hands. 'Get to work, people. We need this deck scrubbed tonight.' She glared to ward off the grumbling. 'We make port tomorrow, and I will not have us reaching Morocco on a ship that is falling apart and stinking of kraken guts.'

It was true – the upper deck was smashed in places, revealing glimpses of the galley and cabins below. A steady dripping of black ooze down into the lower decks had Aleja's stomach clenching. What wasn't broken into pieces was covered in black slime, and there seemed to be an endless amount of it. Aleja had no idea how they would manage to clear it all by morning; it seemed too impossible a task.

'Here.' Griete appeared, her arms laden down with brooms and buckets. She passed a broom to Aleja, who stared at it bleakly.

Frances accepted another, wearing the same expression on her face, along with streaks of kraken ooze. 'The glamorous life of a pirate never ends.'

'Here's your dagger back,' Aleja said, holding out the dagger to Frances hilt first.

'Keep it,' Frances said.

'What?' Aleja looked at it. The dagger was light and easy to wield, devilishly sharp and engraved with a ring of tiny owls round the hilt.

Frances grinned then. 'I said keep it. Consider it a present from me. Besides, you're probably going to need it sooner than you think.'

CHAPTER EIGHTEEN

The Aftermath

Hours later, the deck still smelled faintly of kraken gunge.

'At least it's not black any more,' Griete said with a bright smile as Frances turned to look incredulously at her. 'What? It isn't,' she said defensively, crossing her arms over her ink-stained broom.

The splintered planks had been sawn off, the remaining deck sanded down. Farren was waiting to make port before fresh wood could be patched over the ship's wounds. Luckily they'd passed over the deepest waters and were heading into the calmer seas that lapped round the harbour city of Tangier.

'That's the best we're going to get it,' Olitiana said, swiping a hand across her sweaty forehead and looking out across the horizon to the shadowy outline of land. 'It's dawn. Get a few hours' sleep before it's all hands on deck. No weapons training today.'

Malika looked disappointed, but Aleja felt the relief echo through her muscles. Muscles she hadn't even known existed before Malika had gleefully got her hands on them. Not to mention before she'd fought off kraken tentacles and scrubbed an entire ship.

'Clean first or sleep first?' Frances yawned as they made their way back to the cabins. The ladder descending to the lower decks was still coated in viscous slime and salt water, but Frances managed to float down it, her limbs working in ways that Aleja deeply envied; hers were jellied after the night of cleaning. 'Someone should clear that up,' Frances commented, looking at the ladder. They all ignored it.

'Clean. Definitely clean,' Griete said, looking at the dirty grey smudges on her arms with disgust. 'I stink worse than a whale carcass.'

Frances snorted, polishing her glasses on her equally dirty shirt. Then she elbowed Aleja. 'Told you being a pirate was glamorous.' With that she walked into her cabin and shut the door behind her. Seconds later, they heard the thud of her boots being kicked on to the floor.

The first rays of sunlight filtered down the ripped wood, illuminating corners of the ship that hadn't seen the sun in a long time. The shadows had shrunk down and fled, the sapphires that traced out Orion had fallen down, Geoffrey was nowhere to be seen, and Aleja's little shadow was still hiding in her boot. The *Ship of Shadows* would be limping into port. And Aleja was too tired to care. Dragging her feet along the dirty, broken pirate ship, she touched the coin strung round her neck, realizing with a guilty start that she hadn't thought of her family in days. It had been a few weeks since she'd left them now. 'Sorry,' she whispered to the coin as she wandered towards her cabin, the eerily bright owl eyes tracking her path in the dawn glow.

She closed her cabin door behind her, pulled off her boots and set them aside. 'You can come out now,' she said to them. Nothing. Peering inside, Aleja saw a midnight wisp lurking inside the toe of her boot. It was quivering. 'I promise it's safe,' she told it softly, reaching in and tickling it with her finger. She had no idea if it could feel her, but it seemed to like the attention. The shadow hopped out in the form of a frog and sat next to her. Pouring water from the jug into a bucket and wetting an old cloth, Aleja started scrubbing away the dirt imprinted on to her skin. 'I'm going to have to think of a name for you if you keep sticking around,' she told the shadow-frog.

By the time she'd finished she was pinker and the sun had risen over the horizon. That great sea beast looming over the ship had terrified her, but she was proud she'd managed to fight. Fight with the confidence that her new friends were standing with her.

Curling up, she closed her eyes against the sunlight peeking in through the porthole. The chill of the open ocean was curiously absent, replaced by a dry heat that was more familiar to Aleja, sending her tumbling into dreams of palm-tree-flecked cities, groves of olive trees and the sweet smell of orange blossom.

Captain Quint hadn't slept, Aleja was sure of it. Her eyes sagged in her face, underscored by deep violet shadows. Now that the kraken slime had been scrubbed from the ship, Aleja was impatient to revisit their previous conversation. What could she do to prove herself worthy of the captain's trust? She shuffled on her feet, the frustration gobbling up her attention. Aleja barely heard what Captain Quint was saying as she addressed the crew on deck, until she plucked her own name from the orders.

'Frances and Aleja,' the captain said, 'the youngest but the slyest. You two will have a short walk through the harbour and market. Aleja, keep your eyes and ears to the ground and report back to me any mention of our ship. Anyone noticing us in harbour, anyone asking questions about the *Ship of Shadows*, I want you to unearth it first. Frances knows the city; she'll be your guide. Stay together. And no thieving – not this time,' she added as an afterthought, fixing her unblinking stare on Frances.

'Malika and Aada, you will do as previously discussed. Farren and Griete, you will be going ashore to source new wood for repairs. Olitiana will be remaining on the ship with the rest of the crew – she will be in charge in my absence. We are on a tight schedule and the unfortunate incident with the kraken delayed us further after the impossible weather. We will be weighing anchor at midday, regardless of who is or isn't on the ship at that time, is that understood?'

A chorus of *Aye, Captain* passed round the assembled crew.

'And remember, Moroccan relations with the English and Spanish are somewhat strained at the moment. What with the British sacking Tangier and the Spanish being driven out of Larache we need to maintain a low profile. Speak French or Arabic, or else make sure you're not heard.' She looked seriously at Aleja and Frances. 'I trust you'll remain inconspicuous.'

'It'll be as if we were never there,' Frances said, grinning at Aleja, who was now captivated by the landmass inching closer. She still had a thousand and one questions rattling around in her head, but stepping on to another land for the first time in her life was a nice distraction.

After the captain had finished issuing orders, Malika stepped forward to prepare them on how to be culturally sensitive. They all wore sandy desert boots beneath light cotton djellabas: long, loose-fitting garments that dipped down to their ankles with long sleeves and a little hood. Light headscarves had been handed out to all those who were venturing deeper into the port city.

'Points to remember: greetings are more formal here, and any gestures or eating must be done with your right hand; the left one is considered impure,' Malika said, stalking up and down the deck in front of the assembled crew. 'If you're not Muslim, you are not allowed to enter the mosques; shoes should be removed if you go into someone's house, though none of you should have reason to do that; and make sure there is absolutely no drinking.' She narrowed her eyes at the captain, who arched an eyebrow in response. 'Any questions?'

There weren't any. 'Did you see the captain's face when Malika gave her that look?' Frances whispered to Aleja behind her hand. 'I bet she wished the kraken had eaten Malika for a moment there.'

Laughing quietly together, Aleja and Frances joined Griete in combing the deck, making sure there was nothing left to suggest that they were pirates. 'You invite all kinds of trouble if people know you're pirates,' Griete explained to Aleja in a low voice while Frances checked behind barrels for errant weapons. 'It's illegal in almost every country and there's only so much you can bribe yourself out of before you wind up on the wrong end of a rope.'

'She means they hang pirates,' Frances whispered loudly.

Aleja nodded. She already knew this. 'So you're pretending to be merchants? And . . . French?' she asked, squinting up to where a French merchant's flag had been hoisted.

'*Oui, oui,*' Frances said brightly.

Pistols and cutlasses had been whisked away out of sight in favour of daggers strapped to thighs and knives slipped into boots. Penumbra slept in the captain's quarters, Geoffrey had been heavily threatened to remain below decks, and Captain Quint had a hefty sum ready to bribe the harbour master into leaving their ship uninspected.

'Won't that invite suspicion, though?' Aleja asked Frances when she found out.

Frances flapped Aleja's concern away. 'Nah, the harbour masters are used to it. He'll just think we're avoiding taxes or bringing in banned goods or something.'

The Aftermath

Captain Quint stepped out of her quarters to survey them from the quarterdeck. 'Very well,' she said, speaking above the gentle slapping of the waves against the hull, her boot heels clicking together as she turned to address Olitiana at the helm. 'Let's make port.'

CHAPTER NINETEEN

Tangier

After Olitiana called out 'To your stations!', Frances jerked her head towards the mast and Aleja followed her, scrambling up the rope netting that led to the crow's nest. Her shadow trailed after her, shielding her from the worst of the sun. Up there, the view stretched further, the air shimmied through her pale-blue djellaba, and her excitement soared. Frances passed her a spyglass and she looked through it eagerly. Squat white buildings sat on tawny hills, running all the way up to the top where a complex of ruins was perched, staring back at the ship. The harbour was heaving with fishing boats and merchant ships, the water cluttered with rowing boats bobbing up and down on their ropes. An exceptionally shiny ship was being polished in the sunshine, its name proclaiming it as *La Promesse Lumineuse*, the radiant promise, which Aleja couldn't help smirking at, sure that the captain of that ship must be equally pretentious. A low wall ran round the edge of half the city, crafted from stone the colour of dust and crenellated along the top. Fat-nosed cannons poked through the gaps, prepared to defend the ancient centre of Tangier.

Morocco. *Africa.* Aleja drank it all in hungrily, her appetite for adventure rippling through her. Tangier had been greeting travellers to the northern tip of Africa for thousands of years, and now it was her turn.

Remembering how the *Ship of Shadows* had slunk into Sevilla still smoking and Velka's talk of their powerful enemy, Aleja guessed that Captain Quint was wary of being attacked again, which was why she and Frances were being sent into the streets of Tangier as lookouts. Aleja knew how to listen to the murmurs of a crowd, where the pulse of gossip lay, and her grasp of several languages made her an asset. She was determined that if there was danger she would find it, giving Captain Quint reason to look at her more seriously, to trust her with the secrets of their quest, which Aleja felt she had been infuriatingly close to being told before the business with the kraken.

Frances whooped with glee as the ocean breeze filled the mainsail and swept them into the harbour. Olitiana stood at the helm while the crew tended to the sails, guiding them past the anchored ships. Their shouted instructions to one another bounced into the general chaos of the city stretching out before them. Aleja couldn't help grinning; this, right here, right now, was what freedom tasted like. She copied Frances in spreading her arms wide, her knees hooked round the ropes, and, like that, the two of them flew above the ship, straight into a free berth. The anchor was dropped, the gangplank hoisted into position for the captain to stride down. She jumped down on to the dock to pay off the harbour master, while the rest of the crew scurried like ants beneath them, furling the sails and securing them in position.

Frances grinned. 'Are you ready for an adventure?'

Aleja stepped down on to the dock, Frances at her heels. Captain Quint raised an eyebrow at them in silent warning as she rolled her sleeves up, striding back up the rickety gangplank. Aleja caught movement from the corner of her eye: Malika and Aada were slinking into the city, their cream djellabas and headscarves instantly rendering them part of the crowd. When Aleja glanced back she saw her little shadow waiting next to the gangplank and realized something with a jolt: it couldn't leave the ship's magic. She hesitated, biting her lip, but gave it a wave, knowing she'd be back soon enough to comfort it. It flickered in response and Aleja let herself be pulled away by Frances.

'*Comment est ton français?*' Aleja asked Frances. *How is your French?*

'*Oui*,' Frances said, much to Aleja's amusement.

They walked out of port through the jumble of people, past the stink of a nearby fish stall, and up a set of wide white steps that led to the city wall.

'I don't know how you wore things like this every day,' Frances grumbled, yanking at the moss-green material covering her knees.

Aleja stopped still.

A large stone archway stood before them with a ring of half-moons dancing over the top of the curve. It marked the entrance to the ancient medina – the walled city. Camels were tied up just inside, their complacent faces visible above the streams of people wandering into the hectic market square. Through the horseshoe shape Aleja could see handwoven tribal rugs, babouche slippers with embroidered pointed toes, and hundreds of lanterns for sale, their detailed metalwork glimmering under the sun. Spices floated on the air, infusing it with cinnamon and saffron and other scents delightfully new to Aleja.

'What's wrong?' Frances hissed at her, tugging on her elbow to make her move.

'This is what I've always dreamed of,' Aleja whispered back to her. 'I wanted to explore the world more badly than I could tell you. And . . . and now I'm here. Doing it.' A hard lump appeared in her throat as she forced the words out.

Frances pushed her glasses back up her nose; she was sweating and they kept sliding down. She gently squeezed Aleja's arm. 'You're just like Captain Quint. Moments like these are the reason she captains a ship.'

Aleja could think of no higher compliment.

'Now, let's go. Standing here staring isn't going to make us blend in with the locals.' Frances flicked the edge of her headscarf round her neck for emphasis.

They wound their way through the maze of stalls, keeping their chatter to the lightest whispers to avoid being heard, and walking amid the local women to ensure they didn't stand out. It was hard for Aleja not to stop and stare. She dragged herself onwards, forcing herself past tiny glass teacups, mountains of spices in every shade of the sunset, wooden chests painted with golden swirls. She wished she could taste the dates stuffed with almond paste that sweetened the jumble of smells. Sellers called out to them, shoppers haggled and argued, cartwheels clattered by and lime-green parakeets squawked from perches above it all. The palm trees reminded Aleja of home, but she could feel the differences under her skin. And she loved every second of it – the chaos, colour and all.

Her eyes swivelling this way and that, trying to take in everything without pausing, Aleja caught sight of a familiar figure standing in a shadowed alleyway just off one of the frenzied market streets. She held her arm out to halt Frances. 'Isn't that the captain?' Aleja asked her in an undertone.

Frances frowned. 'Yes, it is.'

They immediately ducked out of sight. Captain Quint was talking eagerly to someone shorter who had their back to Aleja and Frances and was wearing a black djellaba.

'Who's she talking to?' Aleja asked. 'Let's get closer to see if we can hear anything.' She was about to sneak towards them, eyeing up the broken bits of stalls and old carts in the alleyway for cover, but Frances grabbed her arm.

'Leave it,' she said, pulling Aleja back into the bright street.

'You don't want to find out who she's talking to?' Aleja asked, amazed.

'Of course I do,' Frances whispered back at her, 'but I trust the captain and she'll tell us if it's important. Besides, didn't you want to gain her trust?' Frances gave Aleja a pointed look.

She was right. Aleja heaved a sigh. 'Fine.' Forcing herself to focus on the matter at hand, she began listening in to the chatter that streamed out of the stalls.

This northern tip of the great African continent spoke in Arabic, but Sevilla had once been ruled by the Moors, and Aleja was no stranger to the language.

'Let's sit here,' she said to Frances, pointing at a small café in the centre of the medina with little tables and chairs sitting under a great swoop of pale cloth. She gestured to the man hovering in the open doors. He vanished, returning swiftly with a silver tray on his arm. Placing two small glasses on the table, he then held a delicate teapot high above and poured a stream of hot, fragrant tea into each.

'*Shukran*,' Aleja said, her attention already roaming to their fellow tea-drinkers.

'Oh, it's minty,' Frances said in surprise, sipping her tea. 'And *very* sweet.'

A couple of fishermen were laughing heartily about another friend of theirs who had got in some trouble involving someone else's ship and a lost bag of fish the night before. Aleja ignored them and turned her attention to another table, where three sisters were swapping family secrets. Nothing there of use. She gazed at the throng of people weaving through the market square, picking out snippets of different conversations as they strode past the café. Frances, not understanding anything, sat happily drinking her tea.

'. . . good price on it.' One woman showed a bolt of turquoise material to another.

'Come and see all the ships sailing in . . .' a young boy exclaimed excitedly as a group of children ran past.

'. . . sailed in this morning,' said one man to another, speaking quietly in French. Aleja looked more closely at them. The breeches and white stockings they wore with their buttoned waistcoats marked them out as merchants.

Aleja picked up her tea, pretending not to listen. If Frances had slippery fingers, then Aleja had slippery ears, ones that trespassed outside doors and invited secrets.

'He's a lost cause. Lost his reputation years ago. Did you know he was once an admiral in the French navy?'

'Really?'

'Had the ear of the king himself. Or so they say. Who can put faith in idle rumours? Now he just sails from port to port, looking for a ship that doesn't exist. God knows how he gets the money for that.' The two men chortled before moving deeper into the medina.

Aleja's blood ran cold. *A ship that doesn't exist.* She had the feeling she knew exactly which ship they were talking about. It was only natural that the *Ship of Shadows* had enemies; they were pirates after all, and pirates tended to make enemies. She'd known that since she'd first spotted the smoking ship. She met Frances's eyes, willing the girl to understand the urgency. They had to hear more of this conversation.

'Shall we go?' Frances asked her quietly. When Aleja nodded she tossed a few coins on to the table.

'We need to follow them,' Aleja muttered under her breath, her eyes lingering on the backs of the men as they disappeared into a carpet shop near the souk's entrance. Rolls of carpets lined the entrance to the shop in deep reds and violets and burnt oranges. Inside it was dim, crammed with smaller rugs cascading down the walls and rolled carpets lined up like soldiers.

'The tribes make these carpets by hand up in the mountains,' a cheerful voice announced behind them. Aleja nodded politely, straining to hear the French merchants, who were now examining the rugs hanging down the walls. They needed to get closer.

'Feel the quality of the material.' The salesman appeared in front of them, thrusting a corner of carpet into Frances's hands.

'Na'am. Yes. Very nice,' Frances said in her halting Arabic, shooting Aleja a look of panic.

The salesman's grin widened, appearing beneath his moustache. 'I'll give you a good price, yes?'

'No, thank you,' Aleja said in her politest Arabic. 'We're just looking.'

The salesman's grin vanished at once. 'If you're not buying a carpet, then leave my shop,' he ordered.

'We'll buy one,' Aleja promised automatically. 'What about this one?' she asked, moving into the shadowy depths of the shop, as close to the two gossiping men as she dared. She pointed at a plum carpet that drew her in. She ran her fingers over it, wondering what it was that so intrigued her about it. It felt pleasantly fuzzy. A smattering of golden dots were embroidered across the centre of it and Aleja made a show of admiring them while she eavesdropped.

'. . . he chased that rumour all the way from Seville,' one of them was saying. The other hoisted a rug on to his shoulders and walked it over to the packing table on the other side of the shop, waiting for it to be tied securely. Aleja gritted her teeth; their voices had faded out of earshot. When she inched closer the salesman blocked her path, his eyes narrowed to slits.

'We'll take it,' Aleja said, eyeing the carpet in his arms with a forced smile. The salesman beamed and carried it across to the table. Aleja followed him, picking the thread of conversation between the two men back up.

'Long way to chase a rumour.'

'Not for the Fury – he'd hunt across oceans to take down the ship he staked his reputation on. I wonder when he'll admit he was bested by a legend.'

They'd sailed from Sevilla. From the very place she'd last heard mention of the Fury – the pirate hunter she suspected Velka had been talking about when she'd told Aleja they had a powerful enemy.

'Frances?'

'Yeah?'

'I think those French merchants are talking about the *Ship of Shadows*,' Aleja muttered under her breath.

Frances snapped to attention, turning her bespectacled gaze on to the men. 'Are you sure?'

Aleja winced. 'Nearly. But they mentioned someone else, a French sailor who made port this morning – they called him the Fury.'

'Get closer to them,' Frances said, paling. 'Find out for certain if they meant our ship.'

Aleja nodded. 'Then I need to borrow some pieces of eight.'

Frances stopped en route to the counter. 'Are you serious? I haven't been saving up for you to spend it all on a *carpet*,' she hissed under her breath, keeping a smile plastered on her face to maintain appearances.

'It's the only way to get closer; the salesman said we had to buy one or leave,' Aleja hissed back at her, mindful that they'd continued a conversation in English for too long now.

'No.' Frances crossed her arms.

Sensing the stiffening atmosphere, the salesman glanced up from securing the merchants' rug in a tight roll, his eyes narrowing again. The merchants hadn't noticed; they were standing to one side, the disagreement clearly of little interest to them. And every second Aleja spent bargaining with Frances was another bit of information sliding out of their fingers.

'I. Will. Pay. You. Back,' Aleja ground out from between her teeth.

'With what money?' Frances demanded.

'Frances!'

'Fine.' She threw a small bag of coins to Aleja, along with a lingering look of sadness.

Aleja ignored her guilt as she haggled on an agreeable price. She hoped her first set of wages would be enough to pay Frances back. While her carpet was being wrestled into a tighter roll and fastened with thick cords, she seized her chance to inch closer to the two men waiting their turn, under the pretence of admiring more rugs. Frances looked horrified as Aleja trailed a finger down a pine-green rug.

The first man laughed. 'Though, if anyone's going to catch a ship that doesn't exist, it would be François Levasseur. He's investigating every single ship in the harbour today in the hope of finding the *Ship of Shadows*.'

Aleja's finger froze. They had to warn Captain Quint. And then she turned and saw Frances's face.

'It's definitely him. The pirate hunter,' Frances whispered, her expression contorted with horror. 'We need to get out of here.' Her eyes darted around the carpet shop as if there was a faster way back to the ship.

'But why –'

'I'll tell you everything later,' Frances interrupted, flapping at her. 'Now, let's *go*.'

They left in a hurry.

'Shall we dump this?' Aleja asked, gesturing to the rolled carpet they'd hauled out of the shop, even though she felt a pang at the thought.

'No, we can't draw any attention to ourselves,' Frances said, panicking. 'And besides, I didn't pay a fortune for that thing only to leave it in some alley.' She glared at Aleja.

They picked their way back through the market square, the carpet heavier than either of them had thought it would be. This time Aleja didn't even look at the stalls. They had to get word to the captain as fast as they could. Frances had clammed up with panic, and Aleja hadn't had the chance to hear what she knew. It was driving her crazy.

Turning back towards the port, Aleja caught sight of Malika and Aada.

'What happened?' Malika asked them immediately. 'Did you hear something?' She glanced up, her gaze focusing on something behind Aleja.

And then Aleja saw the most terrifying thing she'd ever seen, worse than the kraken surging up from the ocean: Malika was afraid.

CHAPTER TWENTY

Pirate Hunters

'Get back to the ship. *Now*,' Malika said, her hand drifting towards her waistband, which was bulging with stashed weapons. Malika slept in a corner of the weapons room and never left it without sufficient weaponry. Aleja would have been surprised if she didn't sleep with at least a dagger beneath her pillow.

Frances cast a look at Aleja, beads of sweat dropping from her forehead on to the carpet rolled up between them.

'Run!' Malika snapped at them.

Huffing as they dragged the heavy roll along the docks, icy fingernails of fear raked the back of Aleja's neck. Malika hadn't hesitated before diving into the grey mass of ocean and fighting kraken just the day before. Aleja couldn't imagine what could scare her. Malika embodied Aleja's image of a deadly pirate, but she supposed everybody was afraid of something. She snatched a quick glance back to see exactly what Malika feared. To Aleja's great surprise it was just a man.

The ship loomed closer. Frances bounced up the gangplank, balancing on the narrow wood as she turned to pull the carpet up after her. Aleja chanced a second look back before stepping on to the gangplank. Malika was holding her sharpest dagger to the man's throat. He was blond, with a tri-cornered hat perched on top of his head and an eyepatch slung across his face, which was now snarling in fury. He wore black breeches over white stockings, with a long navy coat thrown over his white waistcoat. Gold buttons shone on every article of clothing, reflecting the sun. He and Malika glared at each other, locked in a silent battle. They had the attention of the busy docks, and a small group of sailors, also dressed in the French fashion, had circled them. As Aleja watched, her breath catching in her throat, Aada seized Malika's other arm and pulled her sharply back. With that the small group broke into action: the blond man raced in the opposite direction, on to another ship hidden in the far reaches of the harbour, the rest of his crew following, and Aada had to shove Malika towards the ship.

'Was he the pirate hunter?' she asked Frances as they sweated under their heavy load.

Frances pushed her glasses up her nose for the thousandth time that day. 'Yes,' she said. 'This won't be good,' she added unnecessarily. 'He'll be going to fetch –'

'How are you still here?' Malika's icy voice shattered their whispered exchange and both girls jumped guiltily.

'I – we –'

'Just *go*,' Malika said, picking up the carpet herself and shoving it the final few feet on to the ship's deck.

They scurried off, quick to get out from beneath her feet. 'Should I tell Captain Quint about what I heard?' Aleja quietly asked Frances, looking down to find the small shadow had reclaimed her the second she'd stepped back on board.

'I think she's about to find out anyway.' Frances jerked her head to the right, where Captain Quint was striding towards Aada and Malika.

'Did you send word ahead?' the captain said before catching Malika's murderous glint. 'Tell me,' she instructed.

'François Levasseur,' Aada answered instead.

Beside her, Aleja felt Frances stiffening with fear.

Captain Quint cursed. 'Again? How did he find us so fast?'

'Are you going to tell me how you know him?' Aleja turned to Frances.

'He's the pirate hunter.' Frances widened her amber eyes for emphasis.

'I gathered that,' Aleja said impatiently, 'but who *is* he? He's the one they call the Fury, isn't he?' she asked, remembering the stories she'd heard from sailors back in Sevilla.

'Aye. And he's the cruellest of the lot,' Olitiana said, appearing behind them and placing a hand on each of their shoulders. 'He captains *La Promesse Lumineuse*.' Aleja remembered the ship from when they'd passed it in the harbour. 'He's made the *Ship of Shadows* his personal target. After the captain and Malika bested him some years ago, he lost his position as admiral and was banished from the king's court, his reputation and wealth shredded. He became a laughing stock.' Olitiana looked graver than Aleja had ever seen her. 'Since then he's been constantly following us, haunting our steps around the globe, believing that if he captures us, it will restore him to his former glory. Even worse, since he's come to possess a certain artefact, his dark powers have the ability to strip away what makes our ship special, the power that lies at our core . . . our shadows.'

'He nearly sank us before we reached Seville,' Frances added seriously. 'We almost didn't get away.'

Remembering the state of their ship, Aleja suppressed a shudder. 'Is that why he ran back to his ship? To fetch the . . . artefact?'

Olitiana nodded grimly. 'Which is why we need to outrun him.'

Aleja looked down into her boot to see her shadow peeping back at her. She didn't want to lose it. She hoped the *Ship of Shadows* was as fast as the crew had boasted.

'Weigh the anchor and hoist the mainsail!' Captain Quint shouted, her boots clacking on the deck as she raced across to the helm. 'All hands prepare to set sail. Make speed!'

Chains creaked and rattled as the anchor was winched back up, and the huge mainsail was unfurled along with the rest of the sails as the crew scurried about, tugging on ropes and knotting them in place. Farren busied herself tying new planks of wood down with a length of rope as they crept out of the harbour.

'I heard it was the Fury who took Malika's hand . . . Is it true?' Frances asked, drawing Aleja's attention back to their conversation with Olitiana.

Olitiana sighed. 'Aye. He took her hand along with her shadow. And gave her those scars. He was angry at being thwarted by a woman, and a young, beautiful one at that. It made him want to steal her beauty for revenge. It didn't work. She wears those scars like some women might wear expensive jewellery, with pride. Don't pity her – they're a mark of her survival. She earned them. And then crept back to steal his eye that very same night.'

'Why didn't she kill him?' Aleja asked.

'She thinks death is too good, too easy, for him. She's sworn to take pieces of him, bit by bit, leaving him alive and dreading her next strike.' Olitiana paused. 'Or so she says. Personally I think she wanted to kill him in as cruel a manner as possible, but she was weak from losing her hand and didn't manage it before she had to flee from his men.'

'He deserves it all. He took Raven,' Frances said, her voice pooling with anger.

'Raven left to join his crew of her own volition,' Olitiana said, gently squeezing Frances's shoulder.

That was shocking news to Aleja. She hadn't imagined that the ship Raven had left them for had been their *enemy's* ship. No wonder Griete had been so upset. They'd all been betrayed. Aleja had uncovered another of the ship's little mysteries, but this time it didn't feel good.

'Well, I hope Malika gets him,' Frances said, crossing her arms.

Aleja eyed Malika. Her fear had firmed into a deadly resolve that evoked the stories whispered about the legendary ship. Fingering her blade, Malika was a nightmare made flesh. Standing at the bow, she stared out to sea as the harbour shrank in their wake. It chilled Aleja to see she cast no shadow. She gave her little one a worried glance. Another ship's sails puffed up with air as it also left the harbour in a hurry.

Captain Quint grabbed her spyglass and stared at it. 'It's him,' she said grimly.

Malika reached into a barrel for a hidden scimitar and drew it with relish. 'Let them come,' she said in a guttural growl.

'It would be better to evade them,' Captain Quint said, ignoring her first mate's fury. She nodded to Olitiana, who gave Aleja and Frances's shoulders one last squeeze before joining Captain Quint at the helm.

The hunters' ship edged nearer.

As the sea breeze filled their sails and the outline of Tangier started to fade into the distance, Aleja followed Frances up into the crow's nest where Frances passed her a rope.

'Tie yourself to the basket,' she instructed. 'Don't want you falling into the water.' She clamped a spyglass to her eye and pointed it behind them.

Aleja held on to the rope and glanced down to see an unsecured barrel bounce up with the motion of the deck, crash into Griete and pin her under it. No one else seemed to have noticed. Griete's yell had been lost amid the shouted instructions, screeches of gulls and creaking of the ship. In a panic Aleja dropped the rope and began to scramble back down the netting.

'They're gaining on us!' Frances shouted down to the deck.

The ship bucking under her, Aleja clung tighter to the netting, racing down it.

'Turn two notches starboard!' yelled Captain Quint below her. Hopping off the netting and on to the tilting deck, Aleja glanced up to see Farren tending to the rigging, Olitiana steering them into deeper water, the captain reigning over them all. Velka and Aada were adjusting the sails, angling the mainsail to catch the fastest winds. They skimmed over the waves, hurtling out to where the sky blurred into the sea, a bright blue strip of horizon.

Aleja ran towards Griete. When she got closer she noticed with a stab of panic that the girl's eyes were closed. She glanced up, but everyone was too busy saving the ship to help. It was down to her.

'They're turning,' Frances yelled. Aleja looked up to see the colossal ship slowly turning sideways in the water behind them. Aleja swallowed. *La Promesse Lumineuse* was huge. It made the *Ship of Shadows* feel like a toy ship. She wrenched her attention back to Griete and shoved the barrel, her feet slipping on the deck. It didn't move.

'Prepare for fire!' Captain Quint's shout was powerful enough to pierce the entire ship.

'Griete, Griete, wake up,' Aleja said, ramming her shoulder into the barrel. Griete opened her eyes, blinking at Aleja. 'Can you help push?' Aleja asked, relieved. Griete nodded, staring at the barrel on her legs with panic. 'It'll be all right – stay calm,' Aleja told her.

With Griete's help Aleja rolled the barrel off her legs. Griete rubbed her bruised legs and Aleja rushed to secure the barrel with a rope. She was tying it to the taffrail when the sound of cannon fire exploded across the water. Aleja held her breath as several black balls shot out from the open hatches on the hunters' ship and came hurtling towards them. Griete had just struggled to her feet when Aleja tackled her, knocking her back on to the deck as the cannon fire hit the patch of deck where Griete had been standing with a wrenching jolt. Aleja's breath left her body all at once and she and Griete were flung into the base of the netting in a painful jumble of arms and legs. Frances's spyglass smashed down, narrowly missing Aleja's head.

'Oops, sorry!' Frances yelled down.

Shaken, Aleja sat upright, pulling Griete to a seated position as the ship continued streaming away from the hunters.

The *Ship of Shadows* was engulfed in flames.

Aleja stared in horror before rushing to join the line that had quickly assembled. Farren and Velka filled buckets with seawater, passing them to Malika and Olitiana, who passed them to Ermtgen, the cook, and Aada to fling over the fires. Aleja joined them in time to collect the empty buckets and run them back to the start of the line. Captain Quint was at the wheel, guiding them away, Frances the lookout. After running buckets back and forth to the crackling wood, the flames grew smaller, fading to glowing embers, until the fires were vanquished.

'It's better they used cannons,' Velka explained to Aleja, rolling the sleeves of her djellaba up, revealing her vibrant tattoos. 'This way, we'll outrun them. Cannons weigh ships down and when they stop to use them it makes them even slower. He won't be able to board our ship now. Our shadows are safe for a little longer.'

Frances's triumphant yell came a few minutes later. 'We've lost them!'

Aleja let out a puff of relief. Once this would have been the kind of swashbuckling tale she would have craved. Now that she was in the story herself the stakes were more perilous than she could ever have imagined.

'Maintain this speed and set a new course,' Captain Quint instructed Olitiana. '*La Promesse Lumineuse* will assume we've charted a course across the Atlantic. Then, when we've put enough distance between us, we'll turn and sail back down the coast of Morocco.' She exhaled roughly. 'Hopefully we'll lose them for longer this time.' She turned to address everyone else. 'Good work, crew. That was some fine sailing and fast action,' she said, nodding at them. 'François can chase us around the seas all he likes; we're not going to let him best us,' she declared loudly.

Malika growled in assent, but Aleja noticed Velka chewing her lip, Farren moving to stand protectively next to her, and Olitiana's smile failing to reach her eyes. Since François Levasseur could steal their shadows – which would strip away the magic at the heart of the ship – Aleja knew he was a much bigger threat than the captain was letting on. Malika wasn't the only one who should fear his maniacal pursuit of them.

The crew divided neatly into two. A few made their way down to the galley, where the beginning notes of something spicy were already wafting up the ladder; Ermtgen was cooking again now that the fires had fizzled out. Aleja and the rest stayed up on deck, keeping the ship sailing smoothly. They would take their turn in an hour or so.

Aleja had had enough. She'd endured kraken attacks and pirate hunters and was desperate not to find out what other madness would stop her getting some answers. She'd been waiting to earn the captain's trust, to show her she could be patient, but if she didn't act soon she'd be back home in Sevilla before she knew it. She marched up to the captain, her desire to *know* thrumming through her bones. 'Where are we going?'

Captain Quint answered automatically. 'We'll be sailing further south. And then we'll be heading inland to the imperial city of Marrakesh.'

'And then?' Aleja pressed.

The captain looked at her. And then up at the crew.

'She's a tough little thing,' Malika said.

'And she rushed after me to help fight the kraken,' Aada added.

'She's been in the library most nights, puzzling over that book you want us to crack,' Olitiana called over from the helm.

'She saved me from getting hit by that cannon fire,' Griete limped over to say.

Frances scrambled down the netting in such a hurry it left her cheeks red. 'Even the ship thinks she belongs here – she's got another shadow, look!'

They all looked down at the shadow that was currently mimicking Aleja's own so that two long shadows slanted across the deck.

'It looks like you've made quite the impression,' Captain Quint said, scrutinizing Aleja for a long minute. Aleja held her breath. 'I think you'd better come into my quarters,' she said at last. 'It's time you heard the full story.'

CHAPTER TWENTY-ONE

Zerzura

Aleja followed the captain into her quarters. Captain Quint sat down heavily in her armchair, grabbed a bottle of rum and poured herself a big glass. Bright sunlight sparked off the rubies on the table. Penumbra fixed them with a baleful glare, his sleep disturbed. He shuffled around on his perch in the corner and ruffled his feathers before closing his lamp-like eyes once more.

'Where are we going after Marrakesh?' Aleja asked again.

'We will be seeking the lost city of Zerzura,' the captain said.

Zerzura. The mythical lost city, buried somewhere under desert sands and old legends.

Aleja frowned. 'Do you know where Zerzura is?'

'I have a vague idea,' Captain Quint said.

It was like being confronted with a sphinx. Aleja would receive the answers she so desperately wished for, but only if she asked the right questions.

'Why – *how* do you have Thomas James's journals? They were lost years ago. No one's ever read them.'

The captain gave Aleja a slow smile and Aleja's breathing quickened. There had to be some reason they were searching for the lost city, something as exciting as the city itself.

'My real name isn't Quint. It's James, and this ship belonged to my family. Thomas James was my great-grandfather,' Captain Quint said.

Aleja hadn't expected that.

'Can I see the journals?' Aleja asked, looking around the captain's quarters to see if she could spot them in one of the bookcases or lying on the messy table.

'Thomas James made our family rich,' Captain Quint said, ignoring her and taking a swig of rum. 'But those riches ran out long before I was born. I read his journals as a child, before a fire blazed through our family library, taking them with it.' Her expression turned fierce. Aleja understood; the thought of losing all those books made her wince. 'And his ship, which should always have been *my* ship, passed down to me through the generations of our family, was sold off. Still, I remembered enough. Enough to get back my ship and start investigating where my great-grandfather went.'

Aleja could practically taste the mystery unravelling. She leaned forward, hungry for more. 'What did he hide in the journals?'

Captain Quint took a long drink, watching Aleja steadily over the rim of her glass. Aleja felt she would burst with curiosity if the captain stopped now.

'He found something extremely rare. A map. A *magic* map. It's since been torn into pieces and hidden around the world. I believe the first piece is in Zerzura.'

'What is it a map of?' Aleja asked, thrilled. The more Aleja saw of the world, the more she desired to see. It was proving to be a more enchanting place than even she could have imagined.

'Once assembled, the map shows you where all the secrets of the world lie.' Captain Quint's eyes gleamed. 'Where jewels, treasure and riches have been hidden for hundreds of years. Where lost cities have been enveloped by jungles or deserts or ice. Imagine it – the world opening her secrets up to you like a flower.'

And Aleja could imagine it. The adventures she'd go on, the things she'd discover, the places she'd see . . . It was all she'd ever wanted for as long as she could remember. She wondered who could have wanted to tear up a map like that. It must have happened after

Thomas James had died. She opened her mouth to ask about it but the captain spoke first.

'But, of course, you'll be heading home again after we claim this first piece,' Captain Quint said, taking another long drink before setting her empty glass down. 'As per our agreement. Unless you've changed your mind.' She swung her boots down to the floor and turned her attention to one of the maps spread on the table.

Envy tasted bitter, like almonds plucked straight from the tree. It hit the back of Aleja's throat as she thought about all the things she wouldn't be doing. She knew her family must be worried sick about her and she couldn't abandon them. But thinking about all the adventure and magic that awaited the rest of the crew . . . it was almost too much to bear. Almost. 'At least I still have the desert to see,' she said, trying to distract herself.

The captain picked up another map. 'I'm afraid you won't be a member of the overland excursion. You'll be waiting on board with the rest of the crew, minding the ship.'

If envy was bitter, then disappointment was sour. 'But why? I would make myself useful,' Aleja protested.

'I'm sure you would. As will all the crew mates who were chosen.' Captain Quint slid the map to one side and stood up. She strolled back on to the deck. When Aleja trudged out behind her, Penumbra swooped overhead and up into the crow's nest. He perched there, majestically overlooking them as the captain took the helm.

Aleja let it go, but she wasn't done fighting yet. Staring out at the water as they sailed down the western coast of Africa, she was determined to see a larger slice of the world than her brief foray into Tangier. No, she wouldn't let that be the only exploring she did.

Aleja climbed a little way up the netting. Just far enough to feel like she was alone, surrounded by waves. She sat there, thinking. She wanted to be part of a real expedition, plotting her way across the desert by the stars. She wanted to tread on Saharan sand with her own boots, ride a camel and *explore*. Real, live exploring that would take her where no one else had been before. She wanted to wander around lost ruins and taste adventure.

So if the captain wouldn't let her on the expedition, then she would have to find another way.

It took a lot of sweating and shoving before Aleja and Frances managed to get the rolled carpet down the ladder and into Aleja's cabin.

'Remind me why we're doing this again?' Aleja grumbled.

'It'll make your cabin look homely,' Frances said, squashed in the passageway, her voice muffled.

'We're here now.' Aleja pulled on her end as she backed into her cabin. Frances pushed it in after her. They dropped the carpet on the floor and collapsed on top of it. When it was unrolled, it took up most of the room in the small cabin.

'The dots are in a funny pattern,' Frances said, squinting at the carpet.

Aleja came to stand next to her. 'They're in the shape of Cassiopeia,' she realized as she traced the constellation with her finger.

'I was right to make you keep it,' Frances said, nodding to herself as she looked at Aleja's wooden floors, the bunk, and the plain desk with the chamber pot shoved beneath it and the jug of water on top.

'Why? What's your cabin like?' Aleja asked eagerly, hoping she'd get a look inside it.

A few minutes later she had her wish.

Thick woollen blankets and sheepskins were piled up on Frances's bunk and across the floor. Cushions had been strewn about and there was a shelf crammed full of tatty books. Half-melted candles were dotted around the desk, along with a small animal skull, a huge ruby and a brass telescope. A carved mask scowled at Aleja twice, both from the wall it was nailed to and the antique mirror that reflected it. A ragged fishing net had been fixed above the mirror, hammered into the corner where two of the walls met to form a makeshift hammock, heavy with dyed silk pillows. Rough chunks of wood climbed up the wall towards the hammock like an awkward ladder. Frances's trunk was full to bursting and looked like it hadn't been closed in years. Aleja spotted trousers, boots and thick padded winter clothes poking out of it, as well as paper bags of sweets and more than a handful of precious stones. A pair of expensive-looking binoculars hung from a nail next to the porthole. There was even a tiny tree in its own pot sitting on top of the desk, leaning far over to the right in an attempt to drink up the precious sunlight spilling into the cabin.

'What do you think?' Frances asked, anxiously shoving her glasses up her nose. She was pink from dragging the carpet below decks and her hair stuck out oddly.

'I like it. It feels like a home,' Aleja told her honestly. She absent-mindedly touched the coin still strung round her neck and sat on Frances's bunk, curling her legs up beneath her. 'I can't believe Captain Quint had to steal her own family's ship back.' Her second shadow, girl-shaped, sat next to her. As Frances dug in her trunk Aleja looked around, spotting even more curiosities. A large, wickedly curved hook lay rusting in the corner, next to a wall of seashells making a rainbow of pretty pastels. A tiny statue of a dragon. A lump of pearly rock. Golden slippers curved at the toes. Aleja was entranced.

Frances pulled out two paper bags of sweets, handed one to Aleja and sat beside her, leaning back against the mountain of embroidered cushions. 'I know,' she said, rustling in the bag and pulling out a handful of sugared almonds. 'It's such a relief to be able to tell you everything now.'

'When did you find out about the map? Has Quint got any of the pieces already?' Aleja asked.

Frances crossed her legs, pushing her glasses higher up her nose. Aleja recognized the gleam of her friend's imagination and settled in to hear the story, sucking on a chunk of marzipan.

'Quint was raised on stories of her famous ancestor's explorations. She grew up in this huge mansion that was crumbling to pieces, but the library was still intact – then, at least – and she found his old, forgotten journals there.'

'Thomas James's,' Aleja interrupted.

'Yep. Well, he mentioned the map in there in a secret code. Quint spent years studying it before she cracked it. All riddles and puzzles – I'm useless at those things. You can look at a bunch of dots and order them into sense, but I only see the dots. That key to the ship that she desperately wants us to solve? It's nonsense to me.' Frances bit a nut in half. 'Anyway, she wasn't sure what to think, because, well, until you've seen magic with your own eyes, it's pretty hard to believe.' Frances shrugged, glancing down at Aleja's shadow. 'But she carried on researching.'

'What did she find?' Aleja asked, spellbound.

'It turns out that he suddenly became rich out of nowhere. Quint tried to track the money back to where he found it, but there wasn't anything. No inheritance from a forgotten relative, nothing. And here's where it gets interesting. When he grew older he began to panic about what would happen if the map fell into the wrong hands.'

'*He* was the one who hid the map,' Aleja realized, her mouth falling open.

Frances leaned in closer, excitement illuminating her eyes. 'He didn't just hide it, he tore it up into pieces and hid them in secret locations all over the world. Remote parts too. He made it near impossible to find a single piece of it, let alone all of them.'

'Why?' Aleja asked, unable to picture the famous explorer tearing up his own magic map.

Frances shrugged. 'No clue. But you need all the pieces, see, because the map will only show itself when it's been put back together again. So the captain's been trying to follow his steps from what she remembers of his journals, and his friend's journals. All the expeditions he's mentioned in. She's got a few ideas where we'll be going next, after Morocco, but she hasn't told us yet. She likes her mysteries and secrets.' Frances rolled her eyes, but there was affection in it. Aleja thought about how Frances had acted when they'd seen Quint meeting someone in Tangier. She always protected the captain's privacy.

'Are you going with them? To the desert?'

Frances nodded and popped another sugared almond into her mouth.

'*Qué suerte*. You're lucky,' Aleja moaned, flopping back on to the cushions. Her shadow melted down into a fox and tried to nudge her with its nose, as if sensing her disappointment. She rippled her fingers through the ink-black space it took up. 'What did you do to get a place?'

Frances grinned, showing the cracked nut between her teeth. 'I always get a place. The captain recruited me for my many talents.' She wiggled her fingers mysteriously. 'Though the desert is creepier than you'd think. Too many stories about what could be crawling underneath the sand.' She shuddered.

'Who else is going?' Aleja demanded, ignoring her talk of crawling things.

'Malika, Aada and Griete,' Frances said, ticking them off on her fingers. 'Olitiana, Farren and Ermtgen always stay with the ship. Malika, Aada and I always go with the captain. Griete and Velka sometimes go, sometimes stay, depending on what the captain needs. But Griete, much as she loves seeing new places, loves her creature comforts more.' Frances laughed. 'I give her a day before she starts wanting a bath or a proper bed! Now, what can we do to get her to let you come too?' Frances mused, plunging her hand back into her bag of sweets.

Aleja jerked upright with a gasp. 'I know what to do!'

CHAPTER TWENTY-TWO

An Explosive Lesson

Aleja's excitement propelled her down the passageway and into her own cabin, her shadow-fox bounding along eagerly in her wake. She was going to make sure the captain was impressed enough to let her go on the expedition. She snatched up Thomas James's book from her desk and opened it to the map and strange words.

Suye wepa thek aosk

Frances's words crept back into her head: *You can look at a bunch of dots and order them into sense.*

It was an anagram.

Staring at it, Aleja willed the letters to reorder themselves into sense. To find the pattern behind them, like she had with the carpet and its dots.

'Come on, come on,' she muttered to herself, staring at the thick parchment until the words went fuzzy.

And then it all slotted perfectly into place.

'*Speak what you seek?*' Captain Quint repeated, holding a lantern over the page. Penumbra's eyes were also fixed on the book from where he was perched on the captain's lap like a cat. Aleja's little shadow morphed from a fox into a huge owl that hopped around her feet. Penumbra watched it disdainfully.

'Yes,' Aleja said. 'First I figured out it was written in invisible ink, and then I thought it might be in another language, before I realized that it was an anagram.'

'I seek the first piece of Thomas James's map,' the captain said, her voice bouncing around the slanting wooden walls of her quarters.

Nothing.

'Ah.' Captain Quint set the lantern down. 'Perhaps there is something else to solve yet. Have you had any luck with the other pages?' she asked, flipping through the thin book. 'None of the others have so far.'

'No, but this shows I'm getting closer,' Aleja said, standing before the captain, ploughing on with determination. 'I need a place on the expedition. What if I cracked the code while you were in the desert? It could be the key to finding the map piece.'

'Perhaps, perhaps not.' Captain Quint buried her fingers in Penumbra's feathers and stroked the colossal owl again and again. Aleja waited for her to speak, but when she did Aleja was sorely disappointed. 'Either way,' she said, sliding the book across the table to where Aleja stood, 'stop bursting into my quarters.'

The next morning, Malika kicked a small trunk into the centre of the weapons room, her long sapphire skirt swishing as she did so. Her eyelids were painted blue, her eyes thickly lined with kohl, turning them luminous. Luminous and dangerous. She held her hand out towards the trunk. 'Farren, if you'd do the honours in assisting me with this class.'

Farren stalked to the front of the room, her auburn hair bobbing up and down as she walked, her mauve ankle boots clacking across the deck. 'It's got to be pistols then,' she said with a grin, shoving the lid of the trunk aside to reveal a gleaming collection of pistols, identical to the ones strapped to her hips. The length of Aleja's forearm, the pistols were silver and wooden and had a curled metal trigger. Farren picked one up, twirled it on her finger, then spun on the spot and shot at a straw-stuffed mannequin at the back of the room. Aleja and Griete jumped, expecting smoke and a loud noise, but none came.

Geoffrey materialized, perched on top of a longbow hanging on one of the bulkheads and watching the class with great interest. 'The pistol has yet to be loaded.' He cackled at them.

Farren ignored him. 'Take a pistol each, grab some black powder, lead balls and a brass funnel from over there carefully,' she said. 'That black powder is highly flammable,' she warned. 'One spark and bye-bye, ship.'

'In my day it was only honourable to engage in combat with swords,' Geoffrey intoned in the background as the girls picked up their pistols.

Aleja inspected hers with great interest; she'd never held one before.

Malika ignored Geoffrey too. 'You will have three to four rounds each time you load your pistol with gunpowder. You'll need to add a new lead ball each time you shoot. Who can tell me what the drawbacks are to fighting with a pistol?'

A sudden great clanging of swords and frenzied battle cries filled the weapons room.

Aleja and a few of the girls whipped round, almost expecting to see a charging attack of pointed swords headed their way. Had *La Promesse Lumineuse* caught their ship?

Malika rapped her pistol against the bulkhead. 'Calm yourselves,' she said, her voice slinking past the loud clashes of metal filling the room. 'It's an echo of a past battle, nothing more.'

Aleja saw Frances take advantage of the distraction and sneak half a biscuit into her mouth. Seconds later, Aleja felt something crumbly nudge against her hand – the other half. As she munched, Aleja wondered how long the invisible battle would last. She watched Malika prowl up and down the front of the room impatiently, before the sound vanished and left Aleja's ears ringing.

'You can only use them for short-range fighting,' Velka said, answering Malika's question as if nothing had interrupted them. She loaded her pistol with precision as Frances and Aleja fumbled to copy her, using the brass funnel to pour the black powder down the muzzle, then tamping it down.

'Good. What else?'

'The damp weather,' Aleja said, suddenly remembering an account she'd read on Thomas James, in which his guides through the jungle were outfitted with flintlock pistols that had failed them when they'd met with pumas.

'What about it?' Malika paused her pacing in front of Aleja.

'The powder won't work if it's wet,' she said, copying Farren and adding some wadding.

'Good. Always remember: keep your powder dry, ladies,' Malika said, plucking her own pistol free from the trunk and passing it to Farren. 'In pistols and in life two things have served me well. Being prepared for anything and always having an excellent back-up plan.' She looked at them all seriously. 'And, if it's raining or storming on the seas, use an oil-soaked scrap of leather over the lock area of the pistol to keep it dry.' She pointed at her pistol in Farren's hands, highlighting the lock area.

'Remember this will spark when you fire it, so don't fire a pistol around someone who's loading theirs,' Farren said, funnelling the black powder in after the lead ball.

The sulphurous odour bit at Aleja's nose as she watched Farren add wadding before handing the pistol back to Malika, who thanked her with a nod.

Malika didn't look right unless she was holding a weapon, Aleja thought, watching the pistol fit in her hand like it belonged there as much as her usual cutlass, scimitar or dagger. 'Now, what's the *advantage* of using a pistol?' she asked, looking around for the answer.

'Anyone can kill with a pistol,' Frances said with a wave of hers.

Aleja inched away.

'There's no honour in it,' Geoffrey muttered to himself.

'Clarify, please,' Malika called.

'You don't need to be strong to fire a pistol,' Frances continued, still casually gesturing. Aleja reached out to still her arm before she shot someone by accident. 'You just need good aim, which you can learn. If you're fighting against something or someone stronger than you, a pistol can give you more of an advantage.'

'Exactly.' Malika pointed at her. 'We practised fighting with pistols not too long ago, so this should be fairly fresh in your memories.' Aleja shuffled at this, knowing that they were covering the basics again for her benefit. 'But since we've been through three attacks in a short space of time, we'll be working on improving aim again. Those of you who can prove you have impeccable aim today will be allowed to carry a pistol and ammunition about your person for any future battles we may face.'

'Women carrying pistols.' Geoffrey sighed dramatically. 'No man shall ever care to wed you ladies now.'

Malika turned and shot Geoffrey. The explosion and shower of sparks was like a firework in a contained room. Aleja jumped, Velka yelped and Frances accidentally stepped on Aleja's foot. Geoffrey looked scandalized before abruptly disappearing, leaving a smoking hole in the wall behind him where the lead ball was lodged. 'Now Farren will show you how to shoot,' Malika continued calmly.

Farren turned out to be a natural teacher. She stood in front of them, a short distance before a mannequin with a target pinned to its body. She couldn't resist whirling the gun around as she spoke about aiming for the body (you had a greater chance of hitting something) and not the head (heads made for small targets and tended to move about more), and how the pistol would recoil, and which stance to shoot in. Then she assumed said stance, aimed and fired, quickly reloading another ball into her pistol and repeating the process until her gunpowder was spent. When she'd finished there were four smoking holes in the target, forming a diamond of shots directly over the mannequin's heart.

Aleja was suitably impressed. 'Where did you learn to shoot like that?'

Farren grinned at her. 'Oh, I can do a lot better than that,' she said.

'Another time, Farren,' Malika said.

'Right. Well, the short story is that before I came aboard the ship, I worked in a travelling carnival, shooting apples off volunteers' heads.'

'Amazing.' Aleja looked at Farren with admiration.

'Could you shoot an apple off my head?' Frances added.

'I think it's time we practised,' Malika said hastily.

A short while later, Aleja thought her head might explode with the smell of gunpowder and the noise that ricocheted around the walls of the ship. While Farren and Malika looked on, Aleja and Frances stood in a line with Griete and Velka, the four of them taking it in turns to shoot.

Already aiming by the time it was her turn to fire, Aleja lined up the target as best she could and shot, the pistol recoiling into her shoulder. Still, she was thrilled to see she'd hit the target on her first try. And relieved to discover she was better at shooting than she was with a cutlass.

Farren grinned at her. 'Nice aim.'

After she'd been complimented, Aleja started to relish the explosive force and piratical air that shooting gave her. Although she wasn't as good as Velka, she found she could hold her own against Griete and Frances. The odd round ended up embedded in the walls, trunks and even the floor, which smoked until Farren threw a bucket of water on it.

Aleja had got used to the pistol jumping in her hand and kept it steady, her body braced for the impact as she aimed and prepared for the fiery spark and bang that were to follow. She enjoyed how dramatic it felt, like she was the heroine in an adventure novel, executing heists and shooting her foes. She marked where her lead ball had punctured the target with a thrill of satisfaction; it was her closest yet.

'That's enough for now,' Malika called out. Aleja was disappointed. 'Velka, you've earned the right to carry a pistol when you wish. The rest of you, make sure you clean those out thoroughly before returning them to their trunk.' Malika tossed her pistol back to Farren before leaving the room.

Cleaning a pistol was a lot less fun than shooting one, Aleja discovered, smarting from not being allowed to carry one of her own yet. She scrubbed its awkward shape clean with oily rags, the metal greasy in her hands.

To her surprise, Griete stuck around, even after she'd finished her cleaning.

'Feeling better?' Velka asked her, dunking a sponge into a bucket of seawater as she cleaned gunpowder residue off the floor.

Griete gave her a slow smile. 'I'm getting there. Sorry for moping about.'

'Don't apologize,' Farren said, polishing the cleaned pistols extra hard, her long legs crossed in front of her. 'None of this is your fault. I never should have rescued Raven in the first place.'

Griete twisted one of her earrings round, but didn't disagree.

'You wouldn't have been *you* if you didn't,' Velka said, smiling at her. Farren flicked some suds from another bucket in her direction in response.

'You all have such adventurous stories,' Aleja said enviously.

Frances glanced away, scrubbing another pistol. Farren sent some sudsy water in Aleja's direction then, and Aleja laughed, scooping up a handful of water and throwing it back, half of it slopping over Frances's lap in the process.

'Hey, you soaked me!' Frances squealed, diving into Velka's bucket and splashing Aleja.

An infectious laugh bubbled out of Griete and she joined in, drenching Farren and Velka until Farren upended her bucket over Griete's head with a war cry.

'We'd better clean this up before Malika sees,' Velka panted, running her hands through her hair and chasing away the droplets that clung to it.

'Yeah, or we're dead for sure,' Frances said with feeling.

'I couldn't have said it better myself.' Malika's voice echoed icily across to them from where she stood in the doorway, surveying the scene.

'We were just . . . scrubbing the floors,' Farren said.

Aleja gave her best innocent smile.

Malika's eyes narrowed. 'And yet I don't see any brooms.'

'Oh, we just had them, but –' Frances began.

Malika snapped before Frances could launch into a story. 'Clean it up. Now.'

Aleja and Frances were determinedly avoiding each other's glances; Aleja knew one look at Frances and the laughter she was desperately trying to contain would fizz out of her.

Malika turned on her heel and strode out of the room, the door slamming behind her.

They waited until the last echoes of her footsteps had melted away before laughing until their ribs ached.

Chapter Twenty-Three

Making Port

'You know what will *really* cheer you up?' Captain Quint asked Griete the next day, bounding into the galley in a rustle of shadows and Penumbra's feathers. '*Diamonds.*'

'Diamonds?' Griete repeated, twizzling the sparkling stones in her ears.

Aleja looked up from her book, interested. The rest of the crew's ears perked up too. Captain Quint led them all up on deck and pointed out a small island. 'There.' She passed her spyglass to Griete, who looked through it eagerly.

'It's a smugglers' island,' Olitiana said, shielding her eyes from the sun to squint at it.

Aleja looked through the spyglass Frances offered her. The island was small and rocky, protruding from the ocean like a jagged tooth. It was directly in the path of the *Ship of Shadows*, and the sun bounced off something scattered across the rock. A burst trunk of jewels, glittering madly.

Malika's scars stretched across her face along with her smile. 'And it looks like someone was in a rush to drop their load off.'

Olitiana lowered the rowing boat. She and the captain vaulted over the taffrail into it, followed by Griete and Malika. Frances and Aleja looked at each other. 'Let's go,' Frances said, grinning before she jumped off board, Aleja scrambling to follow her into the boat.

Aleja gripped the side of the boat as Olitiana and the captain rowed fast towards the outcrop, her heart beating faster. Now *this* felt like being a pirate. When they reached the island and hauled the rowing boat up on to the shore, her heart thrummed even harder at seeing what lay in wait. The rock was damp and slimy, perforated with caves, plastered with errant seaweed and the odd curious seabird. Peering into the first cave, Aleja saw it was crammed with more trunks. She helped slide them out, the crew working fast together to raid the place. Olitiana hacked at the first lock with her cutlass and it burst open to reveal a fortune of diamonds nestled inside. Aleja let out a soft gasp.

'Help yourself,' Malika said wryly.

Griete dug up handfuls of diamonds. 'They're huge!' she squealed, stuffing her pockets.

'Grab everything you can carry,' Captain Quint instructed. 'We'll divvy it up back on board.' She and Malika heaved another trunk out for Olitiana to crack open to its sparkling wares; this one was stocked with rubies.

Aleja filled her pockets, Frances doing the same at her side. 'I can finally pay you back!' Aleja crowed, pawing through the jewels eagerly. *And a lot more besides*, she thought to herself, imagining all the ingredients she could buy for Miguel when she returned home. Perhaps a silk scarf for her abuela, too. And all the books she could carry.

Glancing back at the ship, Aleja noticed a smudge on the horizon. 'What's that?'

She pointed it out to Frances, who slid her cracked spyglass from her bulging pocket, tiny rubies skittering everywhere, and looked through it.

'There's a ship coming,' she said grimly. 'Looks like we're not the only pirates to discover this little island.'

Captain Quint whipped the spyglass out of Frances's hand to have a look herself. 'It's the Pirate Lord; I'd know his ship anywhere.'

'I've heard tales of him,' Aleja realized, adding a handful of diamonds to her loot.

'I'm not surprised,' Frances told her. 'He sails between Europe and Asia, looting and plundering treasure ships. Last we heard, his crew had set fire to half a dozen ships in the Mediterranean before you hopped aboard in Seville.'

Aleja remembered the talk of pirate attacks she'd overheard back home with a jolt. She'd never been entirely sure who had been responsible for those until now. 'Will he fight us for the treasure?' she asked, watching his ship inch closer on the horizon, nerves pattering up her spine.

'He would, but he's never been able to catch us,' Olitiana said smugly as the captain jerked her head towards the rowing boat.

'Everyone in!' Captain Quint called out.

They rowed back to the ship in a hurry, pockets clinking with riches, the small boat bouncing off the grey waves. They were sitting heavy in the churning water on the way back, the boat weighed down by a kingdom's worth of jewels.

Aleja and Frances clambered up the side of the ship to lessen the load, Captain Quint on their heels to help Farren, Velka and Aada winch the boat back up. Malika passed over fistfuls of the diamonds and rubies they'd thrown into the bottom of the boat, while Olitiana and the captain raced towards the helm.

With Farren and Velka trimming the sails, it didn't take long to race across the water and disappear over the horizon. Aleja stood at the bow, her shadow expanding into a lynx that kept the sun out of her eyes. She held her arms out and whooped as the wind rushed overhead, the *Ship of Shadows* the fastest ship on the seas.

The next port they sailed into was blue. It was a small harbour, and the crumbling houses that ran alongside it were all painted in rich shades of blue. Aleja felt like she was swimming in colour. Cerulean water, azure skies, cobalt houses. As they sailed in she stood on the ropes that clung to the mast, her bent knee clamping her in place. Her climbing had already improved from scurrying up and down the netting, and now she could stand on the netting the way Frances had when they'd first met.

Above her Frances was keeping a strict eye on the horizon through her cracked spyglass. As they gently sailed into port Frances shouted down the all-clear.

A small weight lifted from Aleja's heart. No pirate hunters in sight. No kraken bells ringing. It had been an easy sail down the western coast, one that had awarded each of them a glittering stash of jewels in the process. Aleja's allotment was stashed under a loose plank beneath her carpet, both because it made her feel more piratical and because her shadow was incapable of leaving it alone. The jewels had transfixed the little fox-shaped shadow, which had sat watching the reflected sparkles, immobilized, until Aleja had moved them away.

Now all she had to do was wrangle a place on the expedition.

'The captain's orders are final.' Olitiana looked down at Aleja, who stared back at her with imploring eyes. 'Now scurry off, I've got a crew to oversee.'

Aleja skulked along the deck, her shadow an unidentifiable blob plodding along behind her. Frances tutted sympathetically at her. 'The captain didn't say no,' she pointed out, repeating what Aleja had told her.

'No, but she didn't say yes either. Maybe I could sneak away inside one of the bags?' Aleja eyed the heap of supplies. Poles to assemble tents in the desert, blankets for when the temperature plummeted at night, compasses, spare clothes, medicines and bandages, food, faded old maps and many, many bulging skins of water.

'Cheer up, I'll teach you how to climb even faster when I get back.' Frances grinned at Aleja, whose scowl deepened. 'And then you can show me what you learned in weapons training with Olitiana.'

'I can't go to the desert *and* I have to carry on with weapons?' Aleja flung her arms over her head, blocking out the harsh southern sun winking down at them. 'Could this day get any worse?' she moaned dramatically.

It got worse.

A sudden commotion erupted on the dockside. Aleja ran to see, the rocking of the ship now second nature to her. It was the camels. The sense of being on a real adventure almost overpowered Aleja when she saw them there against the backdrop of blue. But then she remembered she wasn't allowed on the expedition and the excitement turned to ash in her mouth.

'We'll take them all,' Malika announced in Arabic, over the loud grunting of seven camels shuffling.

Aleja's little shadow stretched out into a camel, and she and Frances giggled at it. Its gangling walk round the deck cheered Aleja up a bit. Being on the *Ship of Shadows* was an adventure in itself.

'Let's watch,' Frances said, so she and Aleja climbed up on to the bow and sat there, dangling their legs over the side of the ship to watch the bartering from above. Aleja almost pitied the man selling the camels; she was still half scared of Malika's ferocity, which was now channelled into haggling the price down.

'I always forget not all camels have two humps.' Frances stared suspiciously down at the one-humped camels.

'Aleja,' Captain Quint barked behind the two girls, startling Aleja into almost losing her balance and falling on to the camels below. A thick lump of panic lodged itself in her throat as she jumped down on to the deck. Was she in trouble?

'In his time people called Thomas James the King of Explorers. Do you know what he said to those people?'

Aleja shook her head, Frances equally perplexed at her side.

'He said, "I certainly don't feel like a king when I've been trekking for weeks, unable to wash or rest. If only they knew what real exploring looked like." Real exploring isn't something to be taken lightly. It's hard work.'

'I'm not afraid of hard work,' Aleja said, raising her chin.

'Good. I've thought on what you said a few nights ago and I'm impressed you were the first to solve one of the pages. It seems I might have use for you on this expedition after all.' Captain Quint gave her a piercing look. 'I know you're enthusiastic, but this is serious business. You will work hard and behave yourself. Understood?'

'Yes, Captain,' Aleja said, hardly daring to breathe and burst this bubble of good luck.

The shadow of a smile flitted across the captain's face before she nodded and marched on, holding out her wrist for Penumbra to glide down on to. As soon as she was out of earshot Frances let out a high-pitched squeal. 'Now you won't have to sneak along!'

A grin spread across Aleja's face, one that refused to budge throughout the rest of the day, no matter what she was doing. Last-minute weapons class from Malika? Check. Helping Farren repair the wounded ship? Check.

Struggling over difficult translations of the endless maps Aada paraded under her nose? Check.

Her shadow darted in and out of the bag she packed in her cabin, flitting between new forms she hadn't seen it take before. An otter that dived off her bed, a seagull that flew round the porthole, and a small pony that sat next to her bag, watching her. 'I'll come back soon, I promise,' Aleja told it with a pang, wishing it could come with her. 'And when I do I'll give you a name.'

The rest of the crew shook their heads in amusement as she strutted around the deck followed by her camel shadow, each thought that popped into her head more fantastical than the last. She daydreamed her way through the day, picturing herself against a dramatic backdrop of dunes, cutlass in hand, as the sun set on a lost city of ruins rising before her.

Ermtgen laughed gently at Aleja's enthusiasm. 'Come and tell me how excited you are after you've been sitting on a camel for days,' she said, crumbling goat's cheese into a pan while Frances sneaked cake behind her back.

But Aleja didn't care. She was going to the desert. On a quest to find a magic map.

CHAPTER TWENTY-FOUR
The Expedition

Ermtgen was right: riding a camel was awful. The rolling, bucking movement as it moved from side to side was worse than a ship at sea, and the stench clinging to its straggly hair clawed its way up Aleja's nostrils. Her back and thighs ached, and it had only been a few hours since they'd left the blue port town behind. The air had been fresher there, salty and cool. Now, as they headed deeper inland, the sky wearing the sunset like a gigantic pink bruise, Aleja felt the heat descend on them. She was wearing her trousers and boots with a long cream tunic over the top and a headscarf to protect her from the brutal heat.

The stony roads that led inland from the coast were dry and dusty, speckled with the odd tree and bush. In front Captain Quint and Malika set a challenging pace. Their spines were straight as they expertly rode their camels. Frances and Aleja followed, Aleja struggling to steer her camel. Luckily it seemed quite content to follow the other three, but she'd bumped into Frances more than once. Behind them followed Aada and Griete, with the seventh camel bearing their tents and most of their water supply.

'Wrap your leg round the saddle post,' Aada called to Aleja. 'We have many more hours of riding ahead of us and that will be more comfortable.'

Aleja followed her instruction. Having one leg hooked over the saddle evened out her weight better as the animal carried on its curious pattern of movement. At least she now knew they got up with their back legs first, something that she hadn't been expecting when she'd first mounted. Aleja's face burned at the memory.

The second the saddlebags had been attached to her camel, Aleja had scrambled on to her saddle at once, not waiting for instructions, thrilled at setting off with the other members of the overland expedition.

'Your camel's name is Farasha,' Malika had told her, her lips twitching.

Butterfly. At the time Aleja had thought it a pretty name, if a bit odd. At least she hadn't got the camel called Al-Jafool, whose name meant a camel that is frightened by anything. Too skittish to take a passenger, it had been designated the supply camel instead. Aleja had sat there, waving at Velka and Farren who were sitting on the bow, Olitiana and Ermtgen standing beside them, ready to see them off.

Her little shadow had shifted into a silhouette of herself and it was lingering around the gangplank. Aleja had bitten her lip, wondering if it knew what was happening. She hoped it wouldn't spend the whole expedition waiting for her to come back.

At Captain Quint's command the camels had risen up. Aleja had been leaning forward, ready to compensate for the sudden lurch as Farasha stood up. But he'd lurched the other way instead. And Aleja had tumbled, head over heels, straight over the camel's neck and on to the dock. Dazed, she'd lain there sprawled in an untidy heap before she heard laughter. Farren was holding her side as she guffawed, Olitiana and Ermtgen laughing along with her, Velka hiding her smile. Her shadow, still in its Aleja shape, flickered round the edges. Even Penumbra had hooted.

It was going to take a while before the crew forgot that one.

Aleja noticed that Frances had her legs crossed on top of her saddle and looked as if she was reclining on the world's most comfortable chair.

'How are you doing that?' Aleja asked her incredulously.

Frances shrugged. 'Some people are brilliant at languages. Others at riding a camel.' She laughed at the face Aleja pulled.

'Don't worry, Aleja, on Frances's first trip on a camel, she was so nervous she made the camel nervous and it bit her every time she went near it,' Griete said, laughing.

Aada chuckled and Aleja felt better.

'And if you hadn't guessed from the smell of them, their spit isn't exactly pleasant either,' Frances said with a shudder.

They continued to ride. And ride. Deeper into Morocco they went, avoiding any traces of villages or towns, picking out their own route from the roll of maps and geographical charts Aada had stuffed into her tunic. The landscape was rocky and arid in shades of browns, oranges and reds, baked in heat every day. To make things more interesting Frances and Aleja raced their camels. Farasha was faster than Frances's camel, but to Aleja's increasing frustration he lived up to his name. Flitting and darting here and there, it was hard to keep him on course.

'Come on, Jamal!' Frances urged her camel, who huffed haughtily at her. Frances was first to pass their makeshift finishing line.

'No!' Aleja said. Farasha had stopped to chew something.

'There's no steering a camel,' Malika said as she and the captain sauntered past.

'What's your camel's name?' Aleja asked Frances when she'd caught her up. Frances gave her a blank look. 'You do know *jamal* is just Arabic for camel, don't you?' Aleja added, hiding her grin.

'Of course,' Frances said, looking put out.

The flatness gave way to hills, stubby ones at first that the camels tackled with ease, even as Aleja clung on to her saddle with each hill they descended. Then the hills grew into mountains, great earth-sculpted beasts that they skirted round in looping paths. They rode steadily into the night, following the lanterns Captain Quint and Aada were holding. The light they gave were pinpricks in the midnight hour. The sky hung heavily above them, the moon blotted out by clouds. Now and then, when the clouds parted, Aleja spotted a dizzying array of stars winking down at them, watching their slow progress across Morocco. The endless chatter that Aleja, Frances and Griete traded back and forth slowed to a crawl and, before she knew what was going on, they'd halted and Farasha was lowering Aleja to the dusty ground.

'We're making camp,' Aada told her, passing her a skin of water. 'Drink half of that each,' she instructed Aleja and Frances.

By the time they were inside their tent Aleja's eyes had already started closing. They could hear the low voices of the captain and Aada, still awake, discussing the location of the lost city of Zerzura over the crackle of the fire they'd lit.

'How does it feel?' Frances asked her, half buried under the sheet she'd cocooned herself in, away from any biting insects that might creep into the tent.

'How does what feel?' Aleja whispered back.

'Being out here, on the expedition. Travelling the world.'

No one could see Aleja's smile in the absolute darkness of the tent. It was a secret between her and the night. 'Like coming home.'

CHAPTER TWENTY-FIVE
The Imperial City

It turned out that riding a camel that first day wasn't the hardest part. Getting back on was. Aleja's muscles screamed at her as she shifted on her saddle, trying to get comfortable.

Captain Quint chuckled when she saw the expression on Aleja's face. 'It gets easier,' she promised, strapping the final sack of supplies on to a camel's back.

'I would sell my soul for a hot bath right about now,' Griete said, mounting her own camel. She let out a sad puff of air. Frances shot Aleja a triumphant look and Aleja had to look away before she giggled.

Aleja learned that Frances and Captain Quint had traversed this route across Morocco before, although

Frances had been years younger. It was Aada and Griete's first time, and Malika, who was Moroccan herself, knew it well.

'What's it like in the Arctic?' Aleja asked Aada, trying to find a way back into the conversation she'd been cheated out of back on the ship.

Aada looked at her, shielded under her white headscarf. 'Cold. Cold enough that the tears freeze in your eyes.'

'What is it with all these countries and extreme temperatures?' Frances grumbled, wiping off the sweat that was dripping down her neck.

'Ah, but the cold is worth it to see the beauty of the land,' Aada said as they rode their camels side by side, following Captain Quint and Malika at the head of the group, who were scoring a dusty path through the land. 'Fjords cutting the sea and sky apart into a thousand tiny islands. Waterfalls frozen mid-fall. Ice caves and whales. And the most spectacular phenomenon you'll ever witness: the aurora borealis.'

'The Northern Lights,' Aleja murmured, lost in a haze of wonder.

'Yes. Curtains of colour, greens, blues and purples, shifting and beaming down on us. Once you've seen the lights carve open the skies into their plaything, you've seen something truly wondrous.'

'I wish I could see them.'

'Perhaps one day you will.'

Aleja was mesmerized as she imagined icy landscapes and snowfall and glaciers, with the Northern Lights dancing above them all. Not to be outdone, it wasn't long until Frances began telling Aleja more and more dramatic recountings of their last visit to Morocco.

'. . . and then I grabbed the sack of amethysts and I launched myself back on to Cecil before the sultan's men could catch me –'

'Your camel was called *Cecil*?' Aleja interrupted.

'Yes, Cecil the camel. And then we raced back through the city gates with half a dozen soldiers at our backs –'

Captain Quint turned round with raised eyebrows.

'But Cecil and I outran them all,' Frances finished triumphantly.

The imperial city didn't look like much as they approached it. The roads widened into a larger thoroughfare framed by small crumbling buildings and tired camels. Donkeys pulled carts filled with people or piled high with fruits and vegetables.

'Let's split up. We'll be more inconspicuous that way,' Malika said, jerking her head to the side and ignoring the curious stares of the locals.

As Aleja fumbled with the reins, her camel followed the others over to a little cluster of argan trees. Aleja dismounted and patted Farasha on his large nose. 'I'll see you soon,' she told him.

'Aada and Frances, stay with the camels,' Captain Quint instructed. 'I'm going to find us a place to sleep tonight, then I'll come and collect you. Griete, you're coming with me. Malika and Aleja, head to Habiba's house. I'll meet you there.'

They dispersed.

Walking on foot into the city had Aleja wishing for the camel back. It wasn't far until the city walls loomed up in front of them, but the intense heat made each step harder than the last and Aleja found herself missing her little shadow more than ever.

'Who's Habiba? And why have we come to Marrakesh to meet her?'

'You'll find out shortly,' Malika said.

Aleja trudged along behind Malika, tired and grumpy. Until she looked up and saw the walls in all their splendour. Made of reddish-pink clay, the ramparts stretched imperiously above them, protecting the entire city within. Aleja stared in wonder.

'They close at night,' Malika said as Aleja noticed the huge wooden doors.

The city gate was crafted of limestone and sandstone and was beautifully decorated, curving above the doors in the traditional Arabian style Aleja recognized from the Moorish architecture in Sevilla. When land was traded and fought over like coins everyone wanted to put their own stamp on it.

Inside the walls the city was thriving. Aleja didn't know where to feast her eyes first, but she was momentarily distracted by how loud everything was. Donkeys braying, carriages clattering by, sellers shouting their wares and the chatter of old friends meeting in the street had the city buzzing.

'Stay close,' Malika murmured. 'And keep a watchful eye out for pickpockets.'

They wandered further in, following the flow of people. A sandy minaret pierced the cloudless sky next to a line of palm trees standing up like soldiers. Aleja marvelled at the little green-and-white patterned tiles on it before she felt Malika's sharp tug on her arm and they turned into the market.

Jemaa el-Fnaa was a large square, bigger than any Aleja had seen. Near the front a man dressed in white was sitting on the ground playing a Berber flute. Aleja gasped when she saw the hissing pile of snakes in front of him – cobras, known for their venomous bites. The man continued to play, entrancing the snakes to stand up on their coils, swaying like palm trees.

'Snake charmers,' Malika said, not the least bit surprised. 'No doubt those poor creatures have had their fangs removed anyway. It's a cruel practice. Come on, it's this way.'

They entered a narrow maze of streets and alleys, twisting and turning into the underbelly of the city. Little shop openings displayed heaps of spices in bright colours, carpets, slippers, food and lanterns. Most of the alleys had been covered by cloth strung above, rendering them dark, shadowy places.

'We have an ally in Marrakesh, one of our shadows,' Malika explained under her breath as she marched confidently through the maze, ignoring the stares her scars attracted. Sometimes it seemed onlookers were temped to comment, but Malika's glare was at its most terrifying and no one dared. 'She's expecting us; Aada and I sent word ahead in Tangier. Habiba has been researching how to locate Zerzura for us using her resources in this city. Here.' She stopped outside a tiny door in a quiet alley and rapped smartly on it. The knocks formed a pattern. *Two, one, two, three.* Then the door opened, and a pretty woman threw her arms round Malika and kissed her firmly on the lips.

'Come in, come in,' said Habiba, shutting the door behind them and bolting it before trading soft smiles with Malika.

They were standing in a courtyard in front of a little, squat house.

'Aleja, meet my partner, Habiba,' Malika said, the rare emotion she'd shown already tidied away.

Habiba offered Aleja a shy smile. Her eyes were light brown and filled with kindness.

Aleja smiled back, a burst of adrenalin perking her up. What had Habiba found on the lost city?

Inside the house Habiba poured them glasses of mint tea as she uncurled old scrolls. 'I thought these might be of interest. I've been researching Zerzura since your last message, and this was all I've found written down.'

'What can you tell us?' Malika asked, sipping her tea elegantly.

'It's deep in the Sahara Desert. I've found references to a city that's white as a dove, sometimes called the Oasis of Little Birds. In some sacred texts Zerzura is said to be a city filled with treasure, protected by a sleeping king and queen. Some say that the legend was started by Herodotus and his references to a lost city of Dionysus somewhere in the desert,' Habiba said, looking between the scrolls.

Aleja sipped her sugary sweet tea, remembering that Herodotus was an ancient Greek historian who had several shelves dedicated to him in the Sevilla university library. His work, *The Histories*, had been one of the last ones she'd picked up before fleeing aboard the *Ship of Shadows*. She wished she'd had a read of it now; perhaps it would have come in useful.

'There are also countless tales of the legends since, of course. Most are old stories passed through families.

You do know that it's generally believed to be much further east than Morocco, perhaps as far as Egypt?'

'I do.' Malika pursed her lips with displeasure. 'Anything else? I was hoping you'd found something more to do with the item I wrote to you about. The one we came to Marrakesh for.'

Aleja was listening intently, certain they were discussing the piece of magical map they were on a quest to find.

'Yes.' Habiba paused for a heartbeat. 'There are several accounts I've heard of a telescope that matches your descriptions. If it does what you claim, it should be able to lead you directly to the city itself – and therefore the map.'

Now, that's interesting, Aleja thought, taking another sip of tea to hide her surprise.

'What's the catch?' Malika asked, watching Habiba's forehead crease.

'It was gifted to the French consul from the sultan. He has it among his collections in his house. You're going to have to steal it.'

Chapter Twenty-Six

Al-Ssariqa

A knock sounded at the door. *Two, one, two, three.* Malika nodded to Habiba, who hurried to open it. Captain Quint stood there. Even without her captain's hat or battered, storm-stained boots on, she radiated authority, her presence filling the courtyard.

'Good job I brought Frances along,' she said after she'd been seated, poured a glass of mint tea and updated on everything. Habiba and Malika had switched to English for her benefit.

'If you get caught,' Habiba began, shuffling her gaze between the captain and Malika, 'the sentence will be severe.'

'We know the dangers,' Malika said, her eyes glittering.

In the shade Aleja shivered. If the dangers were anything like what she'd faced in Sevilla when she'd been accused of thieving, then they would be painful indeed. 'What does the telescope do?'

'It's an ancient artefact,' Captain Quint said, looking into her empty glass. 'Could I have another glass of tea?' she asked Habiba. 'I'm parched.'

'An ancient artefact?' Aleja prompted.

Captain Quint watched Habiba pour her mint tea with an expert flourish. 'Ah, lovely,' she said, picking it up and taking a long sip. 'Yes, an ancient artefact that, according to legend, was created to show you the way to the lost city.'

Aleja felt that would be worth the risk.

After leaving Habiba's little courtyard, Aleja followed the captain deep into the medina, the orange sand bright beneath their feet, the air spiced, the heat thick and the chaos ringing in their ears. They slipped down a narrow alley where a small door awaited them.

'We've got rooms here,' Captain Quint said, pushing the door open. 'Though Malika will be staying with Habiba, of course.'

Aleja couldn't comprehend how the riad had been concealed inside the tight maze of the medina. The traditional Moroccan house had been built round a courtyard with a shallow wading pool in the centre, tiled in every shade of green she could name, and many more she couldn't. Leafy plants and silver lanterns lined the square, thick cushions provided low seating areas, and all round the square curved archways led into the shaded interior of the building. Aleja followed the captain through one and up a flight of stone stairs on to the upper floor. Here the archways led to balconies overlooking the central courtyard. The walls and floor were creamy stone, and here and there perched a dark wooden table with a lantern on it, awaiting the night.

'You and Frances are sharing a room,' Captain Quint told Aleja, gesturing at a wooden door that curved at the top, nestling perfectly into the stone wall. 'I have the room next to yours, and Griete and Aada are just across there.' She gestured at where the walkway turned at a right angle to continue the square-shaped interior.

'Is Frances inside?' Aleja asked.

'She is. We'll see you both for dinner. Have a rest or explore the riad, but do not leave on any account.' the captain said over her shoulder as she disappeared into the next room along.

Aleja took a moment to look out over the balcony, unable to believe she was in Marrakesh. From the first floor the pool shimmered enticingly at her and Aleja longed to soak her feet in it. She pushed open her door, and was about to ask Frances to go with her, when she stopped still.

Frances wasn't there.

Wondering where she could be, Aleja slowly pivoted on the spot. The room was a riot of colour and textures. The beds were piled high with orange and yellow and saffron pillows, and there was a red-and-purple striped carpet on the floor. The walls were the same pale stone as the rest of the riad, but here there were embroidered wall hangings and latticed wooden headboards behind the beds. It reminded Aleja of what Frances's cabin looked like: a cave of riches. She was sad to have missed Frances's reaction when she'd first seen it. A low door went through into a small bathroom tiled in a colour as red as the sand Aleja had tracked through the medina. An ornate sink stood next to one wall, a mirror above it. Chamber pots and towels were stored neatly next to it. A large tiled alcove had space to be filled with water for bathing, and a bucket next to it. But Frances wasn't in this room either.

Tiptoeing past the captain's room, Aleja knocked softly on Aada and Griete's door. Griete opened it. She'd changed into a sky-blue djellaba, which painted her as vibrant as their surroundings.

'Hi, Aleja,' she said brightly. 'Lovely, isn't it? I had been dreaming of a bath.' Her eyes glazed over a little.

'Yes, I can't wait,' Aleja said. 'Have you seen Frances?' she asked in what she hoped was a nonchalant manner.

Griete's eyebrows pinched together. 'I thought she was with you. In your room?'

'No, she isn't. She must have gone to look for food in the kitchen, then,' Aleja said, thinking of all the times she'd caught her friend sneaking around Ermtgen's cupboards.

Griete's eyes rested on Aleja. 'If she isn't, come and find me and we'll look for her together, OK?' Glancing over her shoulder, Griete drew the door a little tighter against herself, lowering her voice. 'There's no need to alarm the others,' she said pointedly.

'You're right, thanks,' Aleja said, her nerves beginning to fizz on Frances's behalf. She didn't want to see her friend getting into trouble.

She found the kitchen empty too. Aleja was now certain that Frances wasn't in the riad.

Twining her headscarf back over her head, Aleja sneaked through the archways of the courtyard and left the riad undetected.

As she walked along, Aleja tried to memorize the bends and sharp twists of the medina. She supposed Frances might find her own way back, but since Aleja was already out she felt committed to finding her. When she reached the large market square again she still hadn't caught sight of Frances or the green headscarf she had been wearing. Not a flash of those wire-rimmed glasses either. She scoured the market for stalls that emitted mouth-watering scents of honey and almond and sugar, hoping to spot Frances filling a bag with cake. Suddenly she heard the distant strains of a shout. '*Ssariqa!*' Thief.

The word plunged her straight back to the pack of armed men who had chased her through the streets of Sevilla last month. Her suspicions flared. Aleja abandoned her sugary search and ran.

Racing around the narrow streets, trying not to skid where buckets of water had been tossed out on to the red sand, Aleja hurtled round a corner only to meet with a dead end. Gritting her teeth, she spiralled round and turned to another alleyway where a small huddle of people stood at the end. The commotion was louder here. Alcoves on each side of the alley sold an assortment of wares: bright bolts of fabric, a collection of pink, purple and gold lamps, silver trinkets and mountains of olives and oranges. Aleja scanned the scene, the shop owners all distracted as they craned their necks towards the end of the alleyway. A boy pushing a cart of scrawny chickens ran past Aleja and she jumped backwards to avoid him, the flat roofs above her catching her eye. Crammed together, they were ideal for climbing across. Smiling to herself, Aleja strolled past a distracted shop owner, his rows of baskets each holding a mountain of earthy spices, and into the dingy back room, where a steep flight of stairs led her up and then up again on to the roof. She looked down.

It was Frances.

She was being held by a ranting shop owner, who was being urged on by the crowd. *Not good.* This would be much harder to get out of than the situation in Sevilla. She was vastly outnumbered, with no time to fetch help. There was more than just Aleja's skin at stake this time. Frances needed her.

Aleja slunk along the rooftops as silent as a bird of prey. She wished that Penumbra was there to lash the man with his claws. But there was only Aleja and a panicked Frances down below. Skimming her eyes over the roof, Aleja noticed a patch of crumbling stone that had been left to fall into disrepair. She broke a chunk free, threw it high into the air and watched it arc down near the other side of the alleyway, where it plummeted into an arrangement of oranges. The crowd turned to stare just as Aleja sent another shard of stone in the same direction. She popped her head up over the roof just in time to see Frances curiously glance up in her direction. Aleja jerked her head to the side and gestured wildly at her friend before dipping down out of sight to ease another stone free.

The man who was anchoring Frances to the ground was Aleja's next target. Her stone hurtled into his chest and he doubled up at once, dropping Frances's arm and gasping for breath. Shouts broke out, but Frances had already vanished up a nearby wall. Rushing to meet her from above, Aleja reached down and yanked her over the top of the wall.

'Thanks for that,' Frances panted, beads of sweat dribbling down her face. 'I thought I was done for there.'

'There's still time for that,' Aleja pointed out. 'We need to get back to the riad before the captain notices we're gone.'

Frances paled a little and Aleja looked at her curiously, holding back the questions skittering around inside her head. 'This way,' she said instead, tugging on Frances's arm.

They ran and jumped over the rooftops together, their djellabas flowing behind them, strands of hair teased free in the breeze. A few streets away they scaled down another rough, half-broken wall, retracing their footsteps towards the riad.

'What did you steal?' Aleja asked, now that the immediate threat had disappeared.

Frances dug around in her headscarf and pulled out an ornate silver knife. 'To replace the dagger I gave you.'

'That was too risky,' Aleja said, running a finger down the engraved hilt. 'What if I hadn't found you?'

Frances went quiet as they trailed back through the medina. Aleja might have worried if her silence had lasted longer than a few minutes, but it was soon broken with a very Frances comment.

'I'm really hungry now,' she whispered as they stole back through the riad, hoping no one would spot them sneaking back in. 'Do you think it's nearly time for dinner? Or should we could go down to the kitchens and ask for some –'

She broke off as Aleja opened their room door to reveal Captain Quint standing there, lips pinched together, arms folded over her chest, glaring at them.

CHAPTER TWENTY-SEVEN

Frances Arthur Hedgewick

'And where, exactly, have you two been?' The captain's voice was icy. Aleja gripped a handful of her skirt as Frances cringed beside her. 'Well?'

'I, we, that is, Aleja . . . and then I . . .' Frances shuffled her feet.

The captain sighed, rubbing her brow. 'I explicitly gave you both instructions *not* to leave the riad.'

'I'm sorry,' Aleja said at the same time as Frances confessed.

'It was my fault. I sneaked out and . . . got into trouble and Aleja came to find me. She rescued me really,' Frances said, unable to stop a glow of pride infusing her words.

Captain Quint watched them both carefully. 'And why did you need rescuing?'

Frances flushed.

'Aleja, could you go and wait in the courtyard a moment, please? I'd like to have a word with Frances,' the captain said before Frances could open her mouth. 'And do not even think of leaving,' she snapped as Aleja stole out of the door, her worry and frustration swirling together.

Frances had never told her where she came from or why she was a thief. Aleja had respected her privacy so far, but now she wanted to know the truth.

Sometime later, when Aleja sat on the edge of the pool, cool, silky water lapping round her ankles, Frances reappeared, glummer than before.

'What happened?' Aleja asked instantly.

They were hidden from view by the rubbery leaves of the plants and trees framing the shallow pool. Tiled in emerald green and cobalt, the rectangular pool gleamed. Frances kicked off her shoes and sat beside Aleja to dip her feet in. 'She reminded me of her rules. The ones I promised to stick to when she took me on board,' Frances said.

Aleja opened her mouth but Frances carried on explaining, like she'd read her mind. 'We're pirates and pirates steal. But not from people trying to make an honest living,' Frances told her. 'It's all about picking your targets carefully, see. The captain doesn't care if I steal from a rich landowner who's a tyrant, or other pirates, or a merchant who makes his riches from cruel practices.' Frances circled her big toe in the water, drawing patterns that dissolved into tiny ripples.

Aleja remembered Frances telling her this before. *Like Robin Hood*, she'd said, back on the ship. 'Why steal at all?' Aleja wondered aloud, leaning back on her elbows to stare at the streaks of sunset ribboning across the sky above.

Frances sighed. 'Before I knew the captain, I had to steal to survive. And now, I guess, it's a hard habit to break. Being a pirate means a little stealing now and then, of course,' she said matter-of-factly. 'But sometimes I just . . . forget things are OK now.'

'It's all right, you don't have to talk about it if you don't want to,' Aleja said.

'No, I do want to. Plus you kind of deserve to hear it now after pulling that daring rescue earlier,' Frances said, grinning.

'Is this going to turn into another one of your stories?' Aleja shook her head dramatically. 'Because I'm still not convinced about that camel escape last time you were here.'

Frances's eyes widened as she gasped. 'You don't believe my story of Cecil the Camel and the Great Jewel Heist?'

'Nope. Not one bit.' Aleja smirked at her. 'Nor do I believe your story of the time you were sentenced to be a royal poison taster for the sultan.'

Frances clutched her heart. 'You wound me. And I thought we were friends.'

'Sorry to disappoint.' Aleja's smile lingered on her lips.

'So, I guess I'll have to tell you the story of Frances Arthur Hedgewick and the Accident instead then.'

'Your middle name is Arthur?'

Frances waved her hand vaguely. 'Not the point,' she said. 'I told you I was from London. I didn't tell you that, like the captain, I grew up in a lovely house. Nothing as fancy as her manor house, but then hers was in ruins. My parents were kind and caring and they loved me dearly.' She stopped talking and Aleja reached out to hold her hand. Frances nodded, blinked and continued. 'When I was about seven we were out shopping when there was a horrible accident. We were crossing the road when a horse got spooked and pulled a carriage over my parents.' Frances couldn't speak for a moment. Aleja had no words. Squeezing her hand, she waited while Frances took a shuddering breath and plunged on. 'I didn't have any other family or anyone to take me in when their house got sold to pay the debts they owed. So I made my own home in London instead.'

Aleja gave Frances's hand another gentle squeeze. 'That sounds hard.'

Frances nodded, rearranging her glasses. Aleja pretended not to notice her glistening eyes.

'It *was* hard. I had to steal to survive. Food and clothes and money. I climb so well because, well, I wasn't the only one trying to make a living off the streets, and sleeping in a tree or on someone's roof was better than keeping company with some of the others.' She fell silent after that. Aleja waited a few minutes in case Frances felt like sharing anything else, but she seemed to have come to a stop.

'Thank you for telling me,' she told Frances.

'You don't think less of me?' Frances looked up at her worriedly. Aleja felt a tug on her heart. 'I'm sure you've never stolen a day in your life.' Frances kicked the water morosely.

'I could never think less of you,' Aleja told her. 'I think you're brave and smart and funny.' Frances blushed. 'Besides, you never know what I might do now that I'm a pirate too,' she added, nudging Frances and wiggling her eyebrows to make her laugh.

Frances's laughter abruptly cut off as she leaned sideways to stare between two dark-blue plant pots. 'I wonder where the captain's going?'

Aleja peered out over Frances's head to see Captain Quint stalk through the archways, pause to cover her hair, glance behind her, then leave the riad. Aleja realized that the captain hadn't seen where she and Frances were sitting; the lush foliage had hidden them. 'Strange. Did she say anything to you earlier?'

'No, nothing.'

'Maybe she's going to get the telescope herself,' Aleja said, staring at the closed door as if she could see straight through it and into the captain's secrets.

'What telescope?' Frances asked. 'Did I miss something?'

Aleja filled her in on the story of the mysterious telescope, and then they took turns guessing how it might show the way to Zerzura.

'It's got to be something to do with the stars,' Aleja mused, looking up at the first pinpricks of light studding the sky.

'I bet it's magic,' Frances said, pushing up her glasses excitedly. 'Maybe the route to the lost city glows.'

'What do you think the city looks like?' Aleja asked, wondering how many other lost cities were buried around the world and wishing she could see them all on the magic map.

'Like a glittering golden palace filled with gold and jewels and treasure and –'

'A palace in the desert?' Aleja interrupted. 'I think it's more likely to be in ruins . . .'

They continued guessing about Zerzura as the evening meal was laid out, until Aada and Griete came downstairs for dinner in the courtyard and they turned their attention to the Moroccan feast instead. They were seated on plump cushions, and there was a spread of plates set on the low tables before them. Delicately spiced tagine, couscous with roasted vegetables and honey, and salad plump with sticky dates and feta. Aleja dug in with her fingers and scooped up mouthfuls with round, flat discs of bread. She was sitting between Frances and Griete, the pair of them enthusiastically discussing each dish in such detail that Aleja wished Miguel could have been there too. After hearing Frances's story, it had struck Aleja how different their lives had been – she had lost her mother as well, but that loss had been cushioned by her family. What if it hadn't been? Would she have turned to thievery too?

After eating until they couldn't manage another bite, Aleja and Frances clambered into their beds and slept until the captain came to find them, her arms stuffed with pastel ruffles.

'We've got a party to attend,' she said.

CHAPTER TWENTY-EIGHT

The Consul's Party

'How did she get an invitation at such short notice? The party's already started!' Griete was asking Aada when Aleja and Frances stumbled, half asleep, after the captain into her room.

'I have my ways,' Captain Quint answered. She passed the armload of ruffles to Griete.

'Is it wise to steal the telescope at the consul's own party?' Malika asked. She had reappeared and was sharpening her daggers in the corner of the room.

'The more people there, the less easily Frances will be noticed,' Captain Quint said.

Aleja felt a lurch of nerves on her friend's behalf. She went to sit next to Griete, who was attacking the gowns, half drowning in a sea of silk.

'Corsets won't get in the way of fighting; the whalebone inside will work like armour, deflecting the majority of sword blows,' Griete told Aleja, ripping the ornate sleeves off the captain's gown. 'It's the sleeves you've got to watch – you need to be able to move your shoulders easily.' Pulling a needle and thread through the jagged hems, Griete tidied up the gown until it was seamless once more. Aleja watched her nimble fingers at work. Next she went for Frances and Aleja's gowns. 'These full skirts are good,' Griete continued, holding out her hand for Aleja to pass her the scissors. 'Your feet and ankles will be clear; nothing will impede your footwork. Just don't run. You need to take small steps instead.' Griete chopped off the sleeves of Aleja's gown. 'Plus you can wear boots!' she added happily.

'Follow my instructions exactly,' Captain Quint told Malika and Aada after they'd all dressed hurriedly.

Frances shrugged when Aleja threw her a questioning look. Following the captain, the two of them rushed out into the night in a whisper of silk on stone.

A carriage was already waiting for them.

Frances looked even more miserable in her pale-pink gown than Aleja felt, dressed up in the blue equivalent.

Neither of them could disguise their sideways looks at Captain Quint, who ignored them, sitting opposite in a crimson damask gown that took up half the carriage. Her hair was curled and pinned up, and she wore a little star patch on her right cheek. Rubies glittered round her neck.

Frances would be posing as the captain's niece, Aleja as her charge, and translator if needed.

As they were whisked through a set of gates Aleja touched the coin hanging beneath her bodice for luck. A mysterious telescope leading to a piece of magic map hidden inside a lost city. What would that look like?

The horses pulled them up a long path thickly lined with trees, their hooves kicking up little puffs of reddish earth. The guards here were dressed in the breeches, stockings and wide-brimmed hats of Frenchmen.

They came to a stop at a set of gigantic bronze doors patterned with flowers in tight mathematical shapes. Captain Quint gathered her voluminous gown in her hands to hop down from the carriage. The carriage driver stumbled over his own feet as he rushed round to aid her.

'I think he fancies her,' Frances said, turning her snort into a cough when the captain frowned at her. Aleja hid her smile.

They were ushered into a courtyard. Low square pools tiled in rich indigo were dotted around trees that chirped with tropical birds. Water trickled down into hexagonal fountains and lantern light bounced off tiny marble tiles in turquoise, grass green and bright blues. Heat rose from the stone floors after a day soaking in the sunshine. Captain Quint produced an embossed invitation and they were escorted through an extravagant archway studded with green gems and blue glass into a long hallway. High ceilings had tiny slivers of windows cut into them. Too thin to allow moon- or starlight through, they plunged the hallway into darkness, and the floor and walls were tiled in dark green, making it feel even cooler. As they walked down the hallway Captain Quint stopped fanning herself and sighed in relief.

'Thank goodness for that,' she said.

Aleja agreed – suddenly the amount of silk, satin and lace she was wearing wasn't as unbearable.

A set of tall wooden doors carved with large petals swung open for them. The melody of a lute spilled out to greet their ears as they strolled into the main receiving room. By the light of chandeliers, men and women milled around the room wearing elaborate wigs and powder, loudly discussing politics, dancing or drinking champagne. Candle wax dripped down on to the mosaic floor from the chandeliers, shadowy recesses in the walls were filled with benches piled with tasselled plum-coloured cushions and women gossiping in clouds of perfume, and servers wandered the edges of the room with silver trays bearing flutes of champagne or dainty confections of spun sugar that Frances was eyeing greedily. Couples dancing a minuet carved out a large space in the centre of the room, their lavish outfits a shimmering rainbow of flounces and ruffles that looked cumbersome to dance in.

'I feel like I've got lost and walked into Paris.' Aleja stared at the scene in front of them.

'I believe,' Captain Quint said, taking a flute of champagne, 'that's the general idea.'

'Huh,' Aleja said, turning to whisper something into Frances's ear, only to find her friend missing. Aleja's heartbeat quickened. She hoped Frances wouldn't run into trouble stealing the telescope. Judging by the size of the place, there were a lot of rooms she had to hunt through: a labyrinth of cool mosaics, dark wood and tinkling fountains. Aleja reached out to confidently take a flute of champagne. She managed one rather large swallow that bubbled up her nose before she could choke it down. Captain Quint turned at her spluttering and arched an eyebrow, her lips twitching. Aleja put the champagne back on the next passing tray in a hurry.

A man in a pale-grey suit with lace ruffles and gold buttons appeared at Captain Quint's side.

'Louis Chénier, at your service, *mesdemoiselles*,' the consul introduced himself in English as he leisurely surveyed Captain Quint's face. *He knows her*, Aleja realized as she bobbed a quick curtsy. At least that solved the mystery of how the captain had got invitations at short notice. 'I have not seen you for some years, Madame Quint,' he said in a lower voice as a gaggle of young women in elaborate brocaded gowns strutted by with feathers bouncing in their hair. The consul ignored them, sipping his flute of champagne. 'But then the British have not been well received in Morocco since you sacked Tangier, isn't that right?'

Captain Quint surveyed the consul over her glass. 'Then it's a good thing I sail for my own interests. I bear no allegiances to the British crown.'

Aleja stood awkwardly to the side, hoping Frances would return soon. She felt far more at home on the haunted, kraken-nibbled pirate ship than at this party.

The consul tapped a long finger on the stem of his glass. His many rings clinked against it. 'Some call you pirates. Tell me, do you know what they do to pirates in this kingdom?'

Aleja suppressed a shudder; she really hoped they'd lost the pirate hunters stalking the *Ship of Shadows*. She thought about the Fury, and Malika's stolen shadow. Since she'd gained a little shadow of her own, the thought chilled Aleja to the bone. She now understood why the others feared François: they couldn't hide behind rumours and magic around him, not when he could rob them of all that and then hand them over to the authorities to face a death sentence for piracy.

Captain Quint gave him a smile that leaked danger. 'Some also call me wife material, but everyone is entitled to their own delusions.'

The consul looked delighted. He bent closer and whispered in the captain's ear, 'Isn't that your *niece*?'

Aleja whirled round, horrified to see a guard shove Frances to the floor. 'I caught this girl stealing jewels,' the guard announced, holding a large ruby up to the crowd. The laughter and chatter and even the lute player all paused to watch the developing scene. Frances stayed down. Aleja's jaw tightened with the effort of not rushing to her side. *Why had Frances been stealing rubies?*

'Really, *Captain* Quint? Stealing from me?' The consul waved his hand. 'Take her away. We'll deal with her in the morning,' he said in a louder voice, addressing the guard.

Aleja momentarily lost the ability to breathe. Her fingers twitched restlessly at her sides. She felt useless.

'That's not necessary,' Captain Quint said quickly. 'I'm sure we can come to some arrangement . . .'

'You're shameless.' The consul shook his head. 'Seize these two,' he announced. Seconds later, large hands clamped down on Aleja's and Captain Quint's shoulders. The consul waved his hand. 'They can share her fate,' he said, turning to pluck another flute of champagne.

Dizzy with fear, Aleja was marched towards the same exit Frances had been dragged through, Captain Quint suffering the same indignity at her side.

'Stay calm,' the captain murmured, sounding more irritated than anything else.

They were led down another marble hallway and a short flight of steps to where a thick door stared back at them, rough wood with a large bolt slung across it. The guards unbolted it, revealing the shadowy cell they were thrown into, before the door was slammed shut and the bolt clicked back, leaving them prisoners locked in darkness.

Frances sighed from the shadows behind them. 'Well, that didn't go as planned.'

CHAPTER TWENTY-NINE

Midnight Climbing

'There's a window up there,' Aleja said, looking up. A sad beam of lantern light flickered through it.

'I can't climb that wall,' Frances said before Aleja could ask. She placed a hand to it. 'It's too smooth.'

'At least tell me you got the telescope,' Captain Quint said over her shoulder, from where she was inspecting the bolted door.

Aleja saw the white of Frances's teeth as she grinned, holding out her arm to the captain. 'Of course.'

'I don't understand, if you hadn't stolen the ruby –' Aleja began, but Frances interrupted her.

'First rule of thieving: always have a brilliant distraction ready in case you get caught. Just after I took the telescope, a couple of guards burst in on me. I snatched up the ruby and a handful of emeralds to distract them with and they thought they'd caught me in the act and didn't bother searching me for anything else.' She turned to the captain. 'How long until help is on the way?'

'An hour at most.'

'Excellent.'

'You knew we were going to get captured?' Aleja asked Captain Quint.

'Well, I rather hoped we wouldn't,' she said mildly. 'But I left instructions in case we didn't return at the appointed hour.'

Aleja remembered her telling Malika, Aada and Griete to follow her instructions exactly. She also remembered something Malika had said back when she'd been teaching them to keep their gunpowder dry, about always having *an excellent back-up plan*.

Frances rummaged around in her dress. 'Cake, anyone?'

Sometime later, a whisper shattered the tense silence the three of them had been sitting in since the last of the cake had been eaten.

'Captain? Are you down there?' Aada's voice trailed down into the gloom.

Captain Quint stood up, her gown swishing against the cell floor. 'We're here.'

Minutes later, they heard the click of the bolt easing up before the door opened. Malika was standing in the doorway, the candlelight flickering at her back illuminating both her and the wicked curve of her scimitar. It gleamed. Something dark was dripping down it.

'Fabulous,' Frances breathed.

They ran softly through the long hallways, each one stretching out further than Aleja remembered.

'Prepare yourselves,' Captain Quint whispered at Aleja and Frances. 'If we get caught escaping, they won't wait to sentence us. We'll be killed on sight.'

Concentrating on making her feet soundless, Aleja tried not to panic. She tugged her dagger out of its sheath in her boot and clenched it. She'd fought off a kraken with her dagger; she could face whatever came next with it too.

'I took out the guards patrolling this section,' Malika told the captain, 'but we can't leave through the main gate. And the city gates are locked at night.'

Captain Quint cursed. 'And the camels?'

'They're already loaded with our supplies. Griete went ahead to prepare them for our departure. We were right to leave them outside the city gates.'

It seemed they'd be leaving the imperial city faster than Aleja had expected.

Down another hallway they found Aada waiting for them, her pale hair ghostlike in the shafts of moonlight cutting through the windows. She indicated the coils of rope slung over her shoulders. 'Fancy a bit of midnight climbing?'

There's nothing like the threat of execution to get you moving quickly up a wall, Aleja thought. Even if the wall was slippery smooth and the rope tied round your waist was trying to squeeze you in half. After making it to the top, Aleja allowed herself a moment's rest before pulling the rope up after herself and throwing it down the other side. Frances scrambled to tie it round the trunk of a palm tree before darting back out of sight again.

Seeing the silhouettes of two guards strolling along the path beneath her, Aleja lay flat on the top of the wall until they'd gone. The moon was lazing about in the clear, starry skies, the imperial city glowing beneath it. The rose-coloured buildings and decorative mosaics preened in the night and the air was scented with cinnamon and other spices. She held on to the rope, testing her weight, before running down the wall in small leaps and bursts of adrenalin. Captain Quint reached out to slow her fall when she neared the ground.

Aleja untied the rope, rolled it up swiftly and handed it to Aada. Then she hesitated. 'But how will Frances get down?'

No sooner had she said the words than Frances appeared, jumping down from the branches of a nearby tree. 'Never doubt my climbing abilities,' she said, pushing her glasses up her nose. Aleja took one look at her proud smile and tactfully decided not to spoil it by mentioning the cell wall she hadn't been able to climb.

A hurried dash through the shadowed back alleyways and then there was another climb before them, longer this time, the city walls higher and much more visible. Captain Quint climbed up first, testing the strength of the rope as she dug her boots into the wall before scrambling up its height. Then it was Malika's turn to scale it, the rope tied round her waist. Resting her wrist against the wall for balance, she used her hand to grip on to the rope and pushed herself up with her legs. Aleja was anxiously waiting her turn when she felt the icy bite of steel at her neck, freezing her in place.

'Got you,' the guard said.

Aleja, thinking fast, debated whether she could duck and roll faster than his sword arm could move. She heard him inhale. But before he could shout out his findings, the blade vanished and there was a muffled squawk and a scuffle of boots on the stony ground. Aleja could breathe again; Aada had got him. With a zing of metal the guard's sword swung wildly round, trying to fend off Aada's attack. Instead it nearly cut Aleja's head off.

At once she dropped to the ground, catlike, the blade passing over the space where her head had been seconds before.

The guard quickly regained his wits. He and Aada eyed each other warily. Aleja slipped her dagger back out from her boot and gripped it tightly, tracking the arc of the guard's sword. Aada's dagger was blocking its blows, but they were making too much noise. Blades clanking, grunts of exertion, scuffed boots against the ground. It needed to end, quickly. Before they drew more guards on to them. Aleja swept out her leg, kicking the back of the guard's knee as hard as she could. It buckled and sent him sprawling to the ground, where Aada quickly used the hilt of her dagger to knock him out. Tearing a strip of gauzy fabric from the bottom of her skirts, Aleja gagged him and bound him to a tree with another strip of silk.

'So he can't sound the alarm when he wakes up,' Aleja explained.

'It appears we'll make a pirate of you yet,' Aada said, and Aleja felt herself flush with pride.

Aada hoisted her up on to the rope and Aleja climbed up, her palms burning against the rope and hot sandy wall. Droplets of sweat dripped down the neckline of her dress as she dragged it up the wall, cringing to think what the puffy skirts looked like from below. She hoped no one could see up them. When Aleja's feet touched the ground, her dress flouncing out around her, she smiled with relief. Griete was standing in a cluster with the captain and Malika, and was looking extremely put out to have been left with the camels.

Captain Quint ripped her gown off to reveal her trousers tucked into boots. She slipped on a longer tunic, like the one Malika wore, and wrapped her head and face more tightly in material until only her eyes were showing. Aleja hurried to change as well. Aada skimmed down the final bit of the wall, untying herself from the rope and giving it a sharp tug before it shot back over the wall.

A horn sounded, sending a group of nesting storks flapping away from the wall. 'We've been found missing,' Malika said wryly. 'Let's go.'

'Where's Frances?' Griete asked.

They all stared up at the wall. 'She's still on the other side,' Captain Quint said. 'She was tying and untying the ropes for us.'

'*Dios*. Can she climb that without a rope?' Aleja looked at the wall towering over them, blotting out the moon.

Captain Quint mounted her camel. 'It doesn't look like she can, or she'd be here by now. Habiba's house is a short walk away. She knows to wait there.'

But the thought of the guards patrolling between the wall and Habiba's house, buried in the medina, gave Aleja a wave of panic.

'We don't have long,' Griete said, twirling a curl between her fingers. Again and again.

'No. We don't.' Malika leaped on to her own camel from behind.

'We can't leave without her,' Aleja said, running towards the wall, desperation snatching at her.

Aada caught her arm. 'She'll be OK, Aleja. I promise you,' she said.

The horn sounded again, closer this time. A few shouts accompanied it. Aleja swallowed roughly, thinking of Frances on her own with just her stolen knife, fighting against all those guards. 'She has the telescope,' Aleja said, suddenly realizing that the key to finding the lost city still lay in Frances's hands. She sighed in relief. 'Now we have to go back for her.'

But the captain pulled out a shiny gold telescope that twinkled of its own accord and held it up. 'I'm sorry, Aleja, but we really must leave now.' She kicked her heels into the camel, propelling it into a sprint.

Aleja climbed on to her own camel, frustration prickling her tear ducts. If *she* was too slow, would she be left behind as well? Griete offered her a small smile, then took her own reins, sprinting after the captain. Aleja followed, her heart sinking lower into her stomach with each step of the camel's hooves.

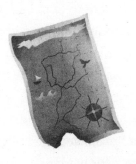

CHAPTER THIRTY

The Sahara Desert

The desert wasn't the same without Frances.

Aleja hoped she'd made it back to Habiba's house safely and wasn't locked away in the cell again. Or worse. She had worried every day they rode their camels towards the desert. At night the tent felt too big and empty. She hadn't realized quite how much she'd got used to Frances's mischievous grin, constant stories and ability to procure cake at the worst of times. She hadn't realized how quickly Frances's friendship had burrowed into her heart. Now, as she stood on the brink of a sand dune, the Sahara Desert spread out before her, caramelized in the sun, she had only one thought: *Frances should be here.*

'We should continue south-east,' Captain Quint said, shielding her eyes with a hand to look at the telescope. It was dazzling. Flecked with precious stones that glittered ferociously, it opened out to the length of Aleja's forearm and could collapse down to the size of her hand. 'Go deeper into the desert, until someone can figure this thing out.' The captain tossed the telescope back to Aada, who peered through it.

Aleja knew what Aada would see: nothing. The telescope that had promised them the route to the lost city of Zerzura, to their map piece, showed . . . nothing. It was terribly frustrating.

'Perhaps under certain night skies,' Aada mused.

'We've tried looking through it by night. By day, by night, it doesn't make a difference. The thing is a fraud. A nice bit of legend and nothing else,' Malika snapped, glaring at the telescope.

Aada silently passed it to Griete, who examined it, extending and collapsing it several times in a row. 'Maybe if I took it apart . . .' she began.

'No,' said Captain Quint, quickly taking it off her and handing it to Aleja. She looked through it out of habit; Aleja knew there was nothing to be seen. Nothing but hot sand.

But Griete had given her an idea. Maybe it wasn't to be looked through, maybe it was more like one of Griete's tools. She looked over every inch of its shiny surface. Then she ran her fingers over the telescope. It felt like sand had got stuck to the bottom of it; it was gritty under her fingertips. She brushed it with the hem of her headscarf and tried again. It still felt gritty. With a small burst of excitement Aleja turned it over and squinted at the bottom of it. It didn't look like anything was there. She flashed it back and forth in the sunlight. *There.* 'There are letters on it,' she said suddenly.

'What?' Captain Quint appeared at her side at once. 'Where?'

'Here.' Aleja pointed to them, turning the telescope back and forth again to make the sun flash over the tiny engravings.

'Someone write these down,' Captain Quint barked.

Griete scrambled for her spanner. 'Read them out.'

'They're written in Arabic,' Aleja told her, her finger tracing the elegant swirl of the letters, trying to work out what they spelled. 'Oh, they're *numbers*: 14761232.'

Griete dug her spanner into the sand, writing out the numbers. Aleja, Aada, Malika and Captain Quint all stared at them over her shoulder. 'What do they mean?' Captain Quint said, repeating the numbers out loud. 'How do they point to the lost city?' She let out a rough sigh.

Aleja turned to Aada. 'Can I see your maps? Your oldest map?' she said, thinking of the age of the telescope.

Aada rummaged in the saddlebag slung over her camel, bringing back a sheaf of ageing parchment. 'This one is my oldest,' she said.

The others looked on curiously as Aleja spread out the huge map on the sand. Farasha, also interested, tried to nibble it before Aleja shooed him away. The map showed the entire country of Morocco in detail. And there were the numbers Aleja remembered along the top and side, back from when she'd sneaked into the navigator's room.

'If I'm right, then the numbers are coordinates,' Aleja said, running her finger along the top to the tiny square marked 1476. Next she trailed her other finger down the left-hand side of the map, all the way down to the square where the tiny 1232 was written. She joined her fingers in the spot where they met deep in the south-east of Morocco, a specific point in the Sahara Desert. 'They lead here,' she said.

Captain Quint almost fell over Aleja in her eagerness to see. 'Brilliant work,' she said, clapping Aleja hard on the back. 'Back on the camels!'

The wind grew, the sand billowed around them, and they continued trekking through the desert in their quest for the map piece, guided by Aada's navigation. The temperature climbed and climbed, until Aleja's throat dusted over and she didn't think it was possible to sweat any more. Until her lips cracked and her nose burned and her head began to pound. The day melted into night as they rested, roasting dinner over a fire and slowly drinking their ration of water. But they didn't sleep. Now they'd reached the desert they'd sleep during the hottest part of the day, as the nights were the coolest time to travel.

But they weren't the only ones who were crossing the sands by starlight.

It began with a whisper.

'What is that?' Griete asked, spinning round to look behind her.

'Al-jinn,' Malika said, one hand clasped round her scimitar as she rode.

'What's that?' Aleja asked.

'Jinn are supernatural creatures.' Malika's eyes kept roving the desert, following the whisper as she spoke. 'They come from fire and have free minds.'

The whispers circled round them and Aleja saw shadows creeping alongside the camels. She held on to the coin at her neck, patting Farasha with her other hand. 'Are they dangerous?'

Malika shrugged. 'Are men dangerous? Jinn have the potential to be good . . . or evil.'

The shadows brushed against them and the camels began grunting loudly, rearing their heads back. Here the presence of shadows set Aleja on edge; they were worlds apart from her own little shadow. She thought of it waiting for her with a pang. Everything Frances had told Aleja about monstrous things lurking beneath the sand suddenly crowded into her head.

'Keep your reins tight,' Captain Quint warned. Aleja stroked Farasha's neck, whispering to the camel to calm him down.

'I just need to – No, *wait*!' Aada said, shouting the last word as Al-Jafool, the supply camel, suddenly spooked and bolted, snapping its ties.

Malika closed her eyes, massaging her temples. 'Tell me that didn't have any water on it.'

It was taking longer than anticipated to trek across the desert, and water was running lower by the mouthful.

Aada winced. 'I'll get it back.'

'It's long gone now. Leave it,' Captain Quint said. She took a pistol out from her saddlebag and shot it into the shadows.

'What exactly are you hoping to achieve with that?' Malika asked her icily.

'I'm not going to risk the expedition because a few demons decided to interfere.' Captain Quint reloaded the pistol and shot again.

'Al-jinn can be demons?' Aleja asked, horrified.

The shadows hissed and reared back.

Malika glanced at Aleja. 'What were you expecting – kittens?'

Aleja swallowed and held on tighter to Farasha's reins.

'There,' the captain said in a satisfied tone, tucking her pistol away again. 'Onwards we go.'

'You'll pay for that later,' Malika warned her.

When the sun finished clawing its way back up the sky the next day, Aleja was faint from exhaustion, and still deeply worried about Frances. She crawled into the tent and fell into a deep sleep. Her dreams were filled with shadows that had teeth and claws and eyes which looked back at her when she peered into them. Griete shook her awake to another flaming sunset and many more hours of riding. She had been sleeping in Griete and Aada's tent since the supply camel had fled with hers and most of their water. Luckily, Frances's camel had been carting the other tents and the rest of the water.

'But why did we leave Frances behind?' Aleja stared at Captain Quint's back, her anger stirring.

'We had no choice. I think you know that,' Griete said gently. 'She'll be fine. We'll stop at nothing to get her back.'

'We could have waited another day before we left for the map piece. For the desert,' Aleja said stubbornly.

'We could have,' Griete acknowledged, 'but that would have been even more dangerous if we'd been found. Sometimes you have to make hard choices. You know that as well as anyone, Aleja, after leaving your family.'

'I'm going home to my family.' Aleja's fingers grazed the coin at her neck. But now when she thought of home she thought of the ship.

'Are you?' Griete asked, but Aleja didn't reply.

They tracked their way across the dunes, and still there stretched out more dunes in front of them, as relentless as waves across the sea. A sea of sand that kept coming, scorching them by day, billowing in the cold moonlight by night. They travelled until Aleja's head began to throb. She helped assemble the tent before morning arrived, gasped her water down, and collapsed on to the simple bedding that moved each time she shifted. Closing her eyes, she waited for sleep to reach out and claim her. It didn't. After twisting about, she gave up and opened her tent flap. Aada was still sitting outside, watching the crackle of the fire they'd lit before dawn had arrived.

'Can you not sleep either?' Aleja asked.

Aada turned to look at her, seemingly surprised by Aleja's appearance. 'It always takes me a long time to sleep. First, I like to relax.'

Aleja sat down opposite her, the dying flames flickering between them.

'I prefer to gaze at stars, but fire can be soothing too,' Aada said, her voice melodious as her eyes unfocused once more.

Trying to clear her mind, Aleja looked deep into the flames rippling against the desert backdrop. It was hypnotic. And calming. It took Aleja a moment to register that Aada had spoken once more.

'Why can't you sleep?'

Aleja shrugged, wrapping her arms round her knees, not sure she wanted to explain.

'Is it because you're missing Frances?' Aada asked gently.

It came bursting out of her then, whether she liked it or not. 'It isn't right. She should be here,' Aleja said.

'She should. It was unfortunate timing. Although having a friend to miss is a treasure more valuable than any jewel. Friendship is a comfort to keep your heart warm at night.' Aada smiled.

Aleja's throat felt even drier. Before she could answer, she caught a flicker of movement behind Aada. Darker than the flames that danced before her, its movement a strange shifting beneath the sand. 'There's something there,' Aleja said, chilled despite the fire and the dawn bright around them.

Aada turned to look. 'Get the captain,' she said.

Aleja scrambled backwards, turned and fled into the captain and Malika's tent. Malika lay asleep but Captain Quint was poring over a book by candlelight. 'What is it?' she asked, snapping it shut.

'There's some kind of beast outside,' Aleja said.

Malika suddenly shot awake, whipping out a dagger from beneath her pillow as she leaped up.

'You're going to be the death of me one day,' Captain Quint muttered under her breath.

A snarl pierced the air, echoing around the dunes and gathering more snarls.

All the hairs on Aleja's arms stood up.

Chapter Thirty-One

Twisting Stars

Captain Quint dug through her sack and pulled out two pistols. She handed one to Aleja, along with a few extra lead balls. 'It's already loaded. Stay inside the tent – take this just in case.' She opened the tent flaps and disappeared. Malika stalked out after her, twirling her dagger.

The tent flapped shut. Aleja heard shots fired and a string of snarls and hisses. She wasn't sure whether to follow the captain and Malika or not. She wanted to prove that she was every bit as brave as them, but she was scared to disobey the captain's orders. Trying to decide, she shuffled her weight from foot to foot until a growl skulking around the back of the tent made her freeze. Something unnaturally large scuttled by, its body pressed against the material of the tent. Tracking its path along the back of the tent, Aleja held the pistol out in front of her. The beast stopped and Aleja heard it sniffing. Then it let out a guttural snarl that sent fear crawling through Aleja's bones. Running out of the tent, she saw Captain Quint firing into the air to frighten the beast away. And now that dawn had melted into the bright blue sky of morning Aleja could see the beast clearly. It was horrific.

Covered in thick sand-coloured scales, it was the width of four large horses, supported on stubby legs thick with muscle. Five heads were perched on top of the immense beast, each one bearing the tapered snout of a crocodile, with low beady eyes and rows and rows of dagger-sharp teeth.

It was heading towards Malika, and Aleja saw the problem at once: the captain couldn't risk shooting one of her crew. Malika and Aada were braced with their backs against each other, blades bared at the beast creeping closer to them.

'What *is* it?' Aleja gasped.

'I have no idea,' Captain Quint said grimly. 'Some kind of desert beast.'

Gulping, her hands slick against the pistol, Aleja realized she was in a better position than the captain and shot at it. The bullet just bounced off the beast's scales, but it did distract it. With a bolt of relief, Aleja watched the beast rear one of its snapping heads and back away from Malika and Aada. Until she realized the heads were turning to size her up instead.

'Aleja, run!' Aada called out.

Running backwards to keep an eye on the hideous beast charging towards her, Aleja fumbled for another lead ball and popped it down the muzzle of her pistol with shaking hands. Remembering Penumbra's attack on the kraken's eyes, she shot at the closest head to her.

She missed. The lead ball thudded into the sand.

Malika, dagger in hand, was racing after the beast, Captain Quint and Aada on her heels, both brandishing blades. Throwing herself down on the sand, Malika tore her dagger along the beast's unscaled stomach. All five heads reared and screeched. Frustrated at her miss, Aleja took advantage of the moment to reload her pistol and shoot a third time. This time her shot buried itself in the beast's closest head with a spurt of sticky dark-green blood. It gave a high-pitched whine and inched backwards to where Captain Quint stood. The captain had stuffed her pistol back into her belt and was holding her cutlass instead. With both hands she raised the cutlass, bringing it swooshing down in a heavy arc that lopped one of the beast's heads off.

Unbalanced, the beast screeched again, tottering away from them towards a sand dune. Malika gave chase, her dagger coated in dark-green sludge, but the beast was remarkably fast. It began burrowing into the sand. Aleja realized with a sickening awareness that it had appeared from beneath the sand in the first place, which made her wonder what other *things* were down there. She cast a look down, horrified at the thought. Malika stopped running and threw her dagger at the beast, now half submerged. The dagger soared across the sand and pierced the beast's vulnerable underside. It stopped at once. Three of the heads were still visible, though its massive scaly bulk was shrouded by sand.

They all stared at it. Aleja held her breath, waiting to see if it would lurch in anger and rush back at them, like the kraken had. Her pistol was useless now without any more ammunition, so she found herself clutching her trusty dagger once more, the weight of it in her hand comforting. But nothing happened.

'Dead,' Malika announced in satisfaction.

'Let's ride. We need to set up camp far away – before something else scents that blood,' Captain Quint said, nodding at the streaks of green sludge smeared across the sand. 'Pack up your tents.'

Aleja held her pistol out to the captain.

'Keep it, you've earned that. That was some nice shooting,' Captain Quint said.

'Thanks,' Aleja said, a smile creeping across her face as she tucked the pistol into her belt like she'd seen the captain do.

'Where's Griete?' Captain Quint asked, raising a hand to her forehead to squint at the desert around them.

Aleja's heart lurched as she turned on top of the dune, half expecting to see Griete's mangled body lying on the sand somewhere.

Aada strode to her and Griete's tent and peered inside. She opened the flap to reveal Griete in the deepest sleep Aleja had ever seen, her hair fanned out about her, arms tangled. Aleja giggled.

The captain let out a short laugh. 'That may be one of the most impressive things I've seen,' she said, still chortling as she headed off to help Malika disassemble their tent.

Another week later and Aleja was beginning to think that some legends were just that – legends. Perhaps they'd never find the lost city of Zerzura and the magical map piece hidden there. Perhaps she'd been away from home for so long and Frances had been left behind for nothing. They were following the map, Aada navigating by the stars and her sextant, but it was taking far longer than anticipated and Aleja was worried they were lost.

Tempers brewed in the heat, helped along by the dwindling water, and the sweat, sand and dust coating everything. Even Aleja's thoughts were sticky and clumped together. It wasn't long before arguments bubbled to the surface.

'I give up!' Griete yelled, tugging her headscarf. 'I can't keep going in this ... this *desert*.' She said the word like it was the worst curse she could think of. Aleja secretly agreed.

'We're nearly there,' Captain Quint said automatically.

Griete laughed hysterically. 'You've been saying that for *days*. When are you going to accept that this lost city of yours just doesn't exist? For all you know we could have been going round in circles all this time!'

Aleja swivelled round on Farasha to look at Griete, surprised. But when she saw Griete's unfocused eyes she understood: it was the effect of the heat. The captain seemed to reach the same conclusion and didn't say anything.

Malika frowned and opened her mouth to reprimand. Aleja winced on Griete's behalf. Instead Malika shrugged, closed her mouth, then said, 'She's right.'

That caught the captain's attention. 'Excuse me?' She halted her camel.

'We're running dangerously low on water. We should have turned back a day ago. If we don't find the lost city soon, chances are we're not *going* to find it.' Malika pointed at the map tucked under Aada's arm. 'How do we even know that's the right map?'

They all looked at the map.

'We've been changing directions trying to find the location – why would we need to do that?'

'The sands are always shifting; you were born near here, you know that.'

'I do know that. I also know they don't shift *that* much. Are you trying to tell me that we're following a moving map?' Malika's voice lowered in pitch as she glared at the captain. Captain Quint stared back at her, stony-faced.

'This is not good,' Aada muttered beneath her breath, turning her face up to the early morning sky.

'Not now, Aada,' Captain Quint snapped, not breaking eye contact with Malika.

Aleja shuffled closer to Griete, who was quietly crying now. She handed the girl a dusty cloth to mop her eyes with.

'Malika's right,' Aada announced, ignoring the captain. 'We have been travelling in circles.' She traced imaginary lines in the sky, connecting invisible constellations. 'The stars have been twisting round us and I never noticed,' she said in a dreamier voice.

Malika frowned and turned to Aada. 'So it wasn't the map – it was you? You didn't notice? All you ever do is stare at the stars. How did you not notice you were leading us in circles?'

Aada slid off her camel so gracefully that Aleja didn't realize she'd fainted until she puddled on to the sand at their feet.

'That's it,' Captain Quint said, hopping off her own camel. 'We're making camp.'

'Captain,' Malika said suddenly. She was ignored. '*Elizabeth*. Look.'

Aleja looked where she was pointing. The sand was roiling like the ocean, churning and frothing and spitting. She took a step backwards, remembering the beast that had crawled up out of the sand.

The desert erupted, throwing sand in all directions and half blinding them. Aleja blinked furiously.

There, rising from the sands, was the lost city of Zerzura.

Chapter Thirty-Two

The Lost City

'Well, will you look at that?' Captain Quint said in a single breath.

The sand continued to roll over the desert, revealing a lush oasis springing up out of nowhere. And buried within it were glimpses of the lost city, shining like a jewel. Sparkly golden domes, glittering emerald spires and tropical gardens. A lazy stream of water circled it all. The air tasted thick with magic, a heady, spicy scent that tingled when Aleja breathed. The sands settled. But however much Aleja blinked in disbelief, the vision didn't melt away.

Captain Quint walked towards it. Aleja followed, stumbling as the sand gave way beneath her boots. She felt a pull towards the lost city, an insistent longing to explore, to discover. It was deeper than excitement – she *needed* to go. After all they'd been through to fight their way to Zerzura – escaping Marrakesh, leaving Frances behind, and battling the desert and its beast – Aleja couldn't believe she was finally setting eyes on it. Was this what it felt like to be an explorer discovering a fresh piece of the world? With a jolt she realized the adventure wasn't over; they still had to find the map piece.

'Wait,' Malika said behind them, her hand resting on the scimitar tucked into the sash round her waist. 'We can't all go down there. What if it disappears again?'

The captain nodded. 'I'm not asking anyone to take that risk.'

'I'll go,' Griete blurted out. She stood up.

'Very well,' Malika said. 'Then I shall stay with Aada and watch over the camp.' She looked suspiciously at Zerzura. 'I don't trust this magic.'

'I'm coming,' Aleja said, ignoring Malika and pulling her dagger free from her boot. She was determined not to be left behind.

After whispering a quick goodbye to Farasha, who nuzzled his nose into Aleja's arms in return, Aleja walked down the sand dune after Captain Quint and Griete. The lost city of Zerzura glistened under the hot sun. They were presented with a large archway, taller than ten camels, coated in a patchwork of green precious stones and flanked with palm trees. Stepping through, Aleja tasted the wild spiciness of the air again, which was stronger inside the city, and shivered with anticipation. They were closer than ever to the magical map piece now.

Once they were through the archway, the lost city opened up for them like a storybook. A wide stream stretched out ahead. Large stones nestled in it, polished smooth by the water lapping around them. They formed a stepping-stone path through the city. The water was lilac and scented, bubbling up seemingly out of nowhere. Thick undergrowth, bushy and studded with bright flowers, crept up everywhere, punctuated by tropical trees. Here and there tiny waterfalls formed by themselves and tinkled prettily. It made a nice change from the harsh hot winds blowing across the sand dunes. Aleja jumped on to the first stone; the water bore the same wild spice she'd tasted on the air. She led the way deeper into the oasis, Captain Quint at her side. The captain's excitement mirrored her own, as thick as the magic in the air.

They leaped from stone to stone through the stream, until the trees and undergrowth suddenly parted with a heaving rustling to reveal the city itself. Pale stone buildings were nestled low among the greenery, topped with dazzling golden domes. Water trickled down the walls like oversized fountains that bubbled back into the system of magical streams. And in the centre of it all was a palace.

The palace was also capped by huge golden domes, and ornate metal doors patterned with flowers loomed up before their eyes. The doors were framed by two enormous statues, each carved in white marble. And either side of the pale stone palace were sparkling green towers decorated in emeralds and peridot and jade and edged in gold leaf. Aleja's heart beat faster as she gazed around.

'Let's try through here first,' Captain Quint said, leading the way. Just as she reached the doors the statues' arms lowered, barring them from entry.

Aleja studied the statues. Both wore crowns, but one had a more delicate face than the other, and the suggestion of longer hair. 'They're the sleeping king and queen,' she realized, remembering what Habiba had told them.

'How do we get past them?' Griete asked, hopping on to the large stone on which Aleja and the captain both stood, staring.

Captain Quint drew her sword.

'Who dares seek entry to our land?' one of the statues boomed in an echoing voice.

'Thieves and plunderers are not welcome here,' the king said, the words grating out of his stony mouth.

'We don't want your treasure,' Aleja shouted up to them, making Griete jump. 'We seek only something left here by one of our own, many years ago.'

Both statues tilted their heads down to look at Aleja. She cringed at the sound of the grinding stone and one of her hands found its way to her dagger. Little stones and flecks of dust spat down at them.

'It's a piece of a map. Have you seen it?' she added, thinking they had nothing to lose.

Captain Quint gave her a sharp look but said nothing and instead looked back up at the statues curiously.

'Do you think the young one speaks the truth?' the king asked the queen.

'I believe her to be honest,' the queen replied.

It was only when Griete whispered to Aleja, 'What are they saying?' that Aleja realized the statues had been conversing with her in Arabic. And Captain Quint had understood, too.

'Very well,' the statues spoke as one, their voices deep and scraping. 'You may ask us two questions.'

'Ask them carefully,' Captain Quint told Aleja, her knuckles tightening round her sword hilt. 'Don't let them trick you into wasting them.'

Aleja thought for a moment. 'Where is the piece of the map we're searching for?' she shouted up.

'That which you seek sounds like treasure,' the king said.

'Does that mean –' Aleja began before falling quiet. She had too many questions but just one left. *Sounds like treasure* . . . Was that a clue? It must have been.

'Careful,' Captain Quint murmured again.

'Where is the treasure hidden in Zerzura?' she asked instead.

The three of them looked up at the statues. Aleja held her breath.

After a long stare down at them, the queen responded. 'What has a mouth yet not a tongue? Compared to this, the city is young.' Their arms snapped back into place and the heavy doors to the palace swung open of their own accord.

Aleja repeated the words in English.

'It's a riddle,' Griete said, whispering it again to herself.

Captain Quint strode through into the palace. Aleja and Griete hopped off the last stepping stone after her into the cool marble hall. Pink blossoms bloomed out of nowhere, dangling down in the spiced air, and turquoise fountains trickled down the walls, but there was no treasure. Carved archways led into other rooms and halls, each as empty as the last.

'Compared to this, the city is young,' Aleja said. 'The city has to be Zerzura.'

'Agreed,' said Griete, 'but Zerzura itself is beyond hundreds of years old; it's remarkable it's not all in ruins.' She looked up at the domed roof they stood under, its intricate carvings of golden swirls and shapes in perfect condition.

What was older than it? The desert and the sky, certainly, but how the treasure could be hidden there Aleja didn't know. She thought back to the first part of the riddle. *What has a mouth yet not a tongue?* She very much doubted it was referring to an animal or a person; you couldn't hide treasure there. It had to be about a place. But what place had a *mouth*? She scrunched her face up with the effort of puzzling it through.

'Let's look in the other buildings,' Captain Quint said, striding back out through the palace and on to the stream again. It split and curved round the palace, visiting each of the green towers before wandering off to the other smaller buildings further away.

Aleja, distracted by her own thoughts, almost slipped off the stone. Rivers had mouths, but this stream's origin was magical. Rebalancing herself, she suddenly stood up, looking at the ground between the streams and lush greenery. The rocky ground. Surely it had been there before Zerzura. And where the land was rocky or mountainous, there were . . .

'Caves,' she said triumphantly. 'It's a cave!' Griete and the captain turned to look at her. '*What has a mouth yet not a tongue?* We have to find a cave mouth! The treasure is *underground*.'

'*Excellent.*' Captain Quint's blue eyes shone brighter than the sky. 'Now, let's find my map.'

They split up to look for an entrance that would take them underground. Aleja headed straight for the tower to the right of the palace, Griete went back into the palace to explore the rest of it, and Captain Quint leaped on to the stepping stones that led to the left-hand tower. Jumping on the stones along the stream, Aleja felt grateful for the lilac water splashing around her boots and keeping her cool. She couldn't help the wild grin spreading across her face. Exploring felt *good*.

The tower glittered in the sunlight, its emerald walls as lush as the tropical plants that surrounded it, sneaking higher as Aleja watched. It had no doors; pointed archways led straight into the tower and Aleja stepped confidently inside.

But the centre of the tower had no floor. Instead she dropped straight into a pool of sapphire water. And Aleja couldn't swim. Spluttering and panicking, she tried to remember what she'd read about swimming, how to move through water. She kicked out and her foot made contact with the bottom of the pool. She realized with a great rush of relief that she could stand up. The water came just up to her nose. She kept her head tilted back so she could breathe and was trying to climb back out of the side of the tower when she heard a piercing whistle screech through the air.

Griete's head suddenly appeared in Aleja's line of sight. 'What happened?' she asked, trying not to laugh. Aleja scowled at her. 'That was the captain's whistle. She must have found the entrance to the cave,' Griete said, grasping Aleja's upper arms and hauling her out of the water. Aleja followed Griete to the other tower, wringing the water from her hair and sopping clothes.

Captain Quint, now holding a lantern, beamed at them when they neared, oblivious to Aleja's soaked appearance. 'Look.'

The tower housed a long line of steps carved from stone, which plunged straight down into the bowels of the earth. The rest of the tower was hollow, like the water-filled one Aleja had fallen into. Something was scrawled on one of the walls.

'Wait!' Aleja said before anyone could step inside.

'What is it now?' Captain Quint asked impatiently.

Aleja pointed at the Arabic script. 'That says *danger*.' She picked up a nearby rock and threw it inside. It lay on the stony floor in front of the steps for a moment. Seconds later, a dull creaking sounded and lines of sharpened stakes suddenly fell from above, impaling the floor.

'Huh. Well, let's be careful from here on then,' Captain Quint said.

Griete exchanged a look with Aleja.

Aleja tossed another handful of stones down the steps. Nothing happened. Captain Quint slowly trod on the first step, then the second, holding up a hand for Aleja and Griete to wait before they followed. She stepped down again, then again, melting out of sight. Griete stepped down next, before a loud clicking noise caused her to shoot back up.

She gasped. 'What was *that*?'

'The steps are disappearing,' Captain Quint shouted up to them. 'They take it in turns to move into the wall. First, it's the even-numbered steps, then the odd ones. You need to jump!'

'I don't like the sound of that,' Griete moaned, but she jumped anyway, and Aleja followed her.

The lantern that Captain Quint was carrying swayed as she jumped down the stairs, sending flares of light shooting up. The steps were long and thick, and jumping over the missing ones as well as trying not to land on one that was about to hurtle into the wall was exhausting work. Each time Aleja jumped down, her boots squelched. She was getting tired fast, her eagerness to find the map piece the only thing propelling her onwards and deeper underground.

At the bottom was a low archway. Hanging from it was a huge hourglass. Griete unlaced her boots and kicked them into the dark cave beyond. Nothing happened. They all peered into the cave.

Aleja caught movement out of the corner of her eye and nudged Griete. 'Look.'

The hourglass was slowly flipping upside down.

'It looks like we're being timed,' Captain Quint said darkly.

Griete stared up, watching as the first grains of reddish sand fell to the glass bottom of the hourglass. She whispered under her breath, calculating.

'How long do we have?' Captain Quint asked.

'I'd say about an hour until the city sinks back into the sand. But without my instruments my calculations are rough. Very rough,' Griete warned them. 'We need to keep an eye on it.'

'Come on,' Aleja said, impatiently ducking through the archway. She heard the others follow her, and when Captain Quint held the lantern high Aleja gasped at the sight that awaited them.

They were standing in a gigantic cave burrowed into the depths of the earth. She could see that where it ended another cave began through a low arch and so on, continuing until Aleja's eyes couldn't keep up with them. The air was curiously chilled and tingling with magic. Stalactites hung from the high rocky ceiling and stalagmites launched up from the ground, their tips interlacing round the edges of the cave. And the spaces in-between glittered. Mounds of emeralds, sapphires and rubies. Heaps of gold, coins, necklaces and jewelled goblets. Old rusted trunks sat half rotting, packed with a dizzying array of treasure. Empty fountains were decorated with gold and precious stones, and there was a stairway descending even deeper into the earth. Into what, Aleja couldn't begin to imagine.

They'd stepped into a cave of wonders.

CHAPTER THIRTY-THREE

The King of Explorers

'How are we going to find the map piece in all of this?' Aleja slowly pivoted, greedy to take it all in. With a loud rush of air, light flared behind her and the treasure gleamed; Captain Quint had used the lantern to light an old fire pit.

'Let's get moving,' the captain said. 'Remember what we're looking for. Leave everything else,' she said pointedly at Griete, who was already wearing a diamond-encrusted tiara. Griete put it down reluctantly.

'But how –' Aleja began, unable to imagine finding a single scrap of paper in the mountains of treasure heaped around them.

'We'll find it,' Captain Quint said, pacing towards the north of the cave.

'We need to hurry,' Griete said to Aleja, nodding back at the hourglass.

Aleja was alarmed to see a mound of sand at the bottom already. They didn't want to be in the city when it sank beneath the sands once more. She headed to the right side of the cave, scanning each pile of treasure as she picked her way through the stalagmites, slipping on loose coins. Goosebumps dotted her arms beneath the sleeves of her tunic. Aleja wrung the water from her headscarf and wrapped it tighter round her neck to stop her hair dribbling water down her back as she pressed on. Something crunched beneath her foot. It was a bony arm. Jumping backwards, she saw it was an entire skeleton half buried under an avalanche of gold and jewels, a crown still on its head. Aleja gulped and hurried past.

The cave was swimming in treasure. Diving into piles of jewels and digging through hoards of golden coins, Aleja wasn't sure where to look first. She opened trunks, peered under statues, looked inside golden cups dotted with diamonds. Nothing, nothing and yet more nothing. Judging by the dull clunks and thuds of Griete ploughing through the other side of the cave, she hadn't found anything yet either.

Time was slipping through their fingers.

'It's got to be here somewhere – keep looking!' Captain Quint shouted back to them, the echoes of her voice bouncing off the cave walls.

Aleja looked around in a panic. A stack of books rested near her, their spines mouldering. She clambered over to them, flipping through and shaking them upside down to see if anything fell out. It didn't.

'We're running out of time,' Griete said.

The hourglass was filling faster and faster.

'No!' Captain Quint glanced back at the system of caves they hadn't even stepped in yet. The stairs leading deeper into the earth. 'We need more time.' Snatching up her lantern, she marched over to the stairs and ran down them out of sight. Griete ran over to the caves buried behind them, smaller and labyrinthine.

Aleja frowned, stepping into an empty fountain crafted from a gigantic slab of marble. She climbed up the central statue to get a better view. They had to be missing something obvious. Thomas James hadn't wanted the map found, which was why he'd hidden it here in the lost city. She doubted he'd seen it as treasure, so it wouldn't be among sapphires or gold, where someone filling their sack with riches would accidentally stumble upon it. *Where would he have hidden it?*

Aleja screwed up her eyes, shutting out Captain Quint thundering back up the stairs, calling out, 'Nothing but tombs down there!' and Griete rushing back in.

She ignored the noises and curses that came from the captain and Griete racing through the treasure at an increasing pace, shoving piles of jewels aside and tipping chests upside down until it rained coins and rings. She ignored the falling sand in the hourglass too. She ignored everything that wasn't the crucial question on her mind: where would someone *not* think to look?

Aleja opened her eyes, and her gaze fell on the skeleton she'd stepped on before. Something Captain Quint had told her back on the ship popped into her head. *People called Thomas James the king of explorers . . .* 'I certainly don't feel like a king when I've been trekking for weeks, unable to clean or rest . . .' Aleja stared at the crown perched jauntily on top of the skeleton's head. *Someone put that there after he died*, she realized, scrabbling back down the statue and over to it.

The skeleton stared back at her. One of its eye sockets was broken. '*Lo siento*,' she whispered to the skeleton, *sorry*, then gritted her teeth and poked her fingers through the broken eye socket. It was dusty and creepy and she closed her eyes as she poked deeper. Her fingers rustled against something and she yanked them out quickly with a yelp. Then, steeling herself, she pulled out the thing she'd touched. 'You'd better not be an insect,' she muttered under her breath.

It wasn't. It was a thin scroll of parchment, yellowed and coated in dust, but still intact. Aleja unrolled it with shaky fingers. The bottom-left chunk of the world looked back at her.

'I've got it,' she said, hardly daring to believe it. Then louder. 'I've got it!' She held it up higher, laughing with delight.

'You found it?' Griete asked, her mouth hanging open.

Captain Quint let out a very uncharacteristic whoop of joy.

Then the fire pit and lantern extinguished themselves, plunging them into darkness.

CHAPTER THIRTY-FOUR

Desert Magic

'What was that?' Griete's voice was hushed.

Aleja's fingers closed on her dagger. The darkness was absolute, darker than the blackest night. She couldn't see her own hand when she waved it in front of her face. *What's happening?*

'We've got what we came for. Let's go.'

Aleja heard Captain Quint crunching across a carpet of golden coins and gems as she gave the order.

There was a whisper. Not in any language Aleja recognized, more like a dull hiss. It crept along the corners of the caves, collecting more hisses as it moved, until it whispered over their heads, engulfing them. Fingers of fear stroked Aleja's spine. This wasn't the spicy wildness of the air shimmering through Zerzura – this was something *else*. She felt the hisses moving around them, the scratching of magic against her skin. She whirled round in the pitch black, clutching her dagger. Whatever it was, it was toying with them.

Flames roared into life, sparking along the cave walls as the mounted torches lit by themselves. Illuminated in the sudden glow, Aleja saw the horror she felt mirrored on Griete's face.

The hisses rippled through the caves, building and deepening until they shifted into howls that bounced around, echoing and sneaking up behind them.

Aleja ran. Ducking round low-hanging stalactites, skidding on gemstones, she ran across the centre of the main cave, Griete and the captain at her heels. In front of them the hourglass was still measuring out time in grains of sand.

'I don't understand,' Aleja said, staring at it. 'We didn't run out of time.'

Griete snatched her arm. 'Do you hear that?'

It was a dull thudding in the distance, the noise eerily rising up towards them.

'It's coming from the stairs. Something's coming up them,' Captain Quint said, drawing her cutlass and spinning round.

The thudding was marching. It grew closer and closer, the sound of hundreds of feet pounding up the stairs.

Aleja didn't want to see what would emerge from the top of the stairwell, but she couldn't look away. Griete seemed to be having the same trouble. 'It's the jinn,' she moaned, her eyes huge in her pale face. 'It's the same hissing that we heard, that we *felt*, in the desert. Malika warned us we'd pay for disrespecting them!'

The marching grew louder.

'Why are you still standing there? Run!' Captain Quint shouted.

They ran. Out of the stairwell burst a stream of skeletons, their joints juddering as they marched, the bones in their feet clicking on the cave floor. Griete let out a shriek. Aleja ran faster, her heart hammering inside her chest. The skeletons were everywhere, moving unnaturally fast through the cave. Aleja was running, but they moved swiftly after her, their blank faces turning to stare at her, hunting her through the cave. Bony hands reached out towards her and she ran harder, faster, dodging piles of treasure and stalagmites. Her breath ripped out of her lungs in jagged pants but she kept running towards the hourglass, dangling over the gates to freedom, trying not to look back at the hordes of the dead at her back. Then something brushed against her. She glanced back, horrified to see a group of skeletons almost upon her. *She wasn't going to make it.* Finger bones tangled in Aleja's hair and pulled at her wet clothes, tugging her back towards the pack of skeletons, their empty eye sockets staring at her. Aleja screamed.

'I can't get to you,' Griete yelled. She was hacking away at the skeletons that surrounded her, but as fast as she slashed her sword through the air, splintering through bone and beheading them, the skeletons kept coming. More and more of them poured into the cave.

'There are too many to fight,' Captain Quint shouted across from where she was wielding her cutlass. As fast as she felled them, more rose to take their place.

Aleja spun to face the skeleton that was pulling her hair. She jabbed it with her dagger until its hand fell off. She looked down at it, nauseous. The hand skittered along the cave floor towards her. She screamed again.

This time Griete materialized before her, stamping on the hand and attacking the rest of the skeletons that scrabbled at Aleja's clothes.

Captain Quint glanced at the hourglass. It had nearly run out. 'We really don't want to be here when that empties. I'll hold them off.' Brandishing her cutlass, she inched towards Griete and Aleja, allowing them to run out of the arch first.

Half climbing, half jumping up the vanishing stairs was a challenge. A few seconds later, Aleja heard Captain Quint run through the arch, the unstoppable torrent of skeletons at her heels. A few tumbled down the gaping holes between steps, landing deep below with a series of sickening cracks that chilled Aleja's blood. The rest were still leaping forward and reaching for them with their clawing bony fingers.

The first tendrils of daylight appeared, stroking the top steps and revealing the archway they'd come in through. Weaving through the stakes that still filled the tower, they burst out into the dazzling midday sun and ran along the stepping stones, through the lost city and out into the desert, the howls of the dead at their backs.

Aleja fell to her hands and knees to scramble up the steep dune, the sand burning her palms. With each crawl forward the sand pulled her down again and she cried out with frustration.

'Keep going,' Captain Quint said behind her, but Aleja couldn't see; with her hands plunging into the sand to propel her up the dune she couldn't shield her eyes from the sun, and after being in complete darkness the light was blinding. She felt a sharp, unexpected longing for her little shadow. A hand closed over her wrist and she yelped in surprise. But it was warm and real, and followed by another hand reaching for her other wrist. She was yanked up the remainder of the dune and on to her feet, to stare into the faces of Malika and Aada. Griete was already at their side. She wheeled round to see the captain ascending the dune. Behind her the desert yawned open.

'Mount the camels,' Malika said, eerily calm as ever, even as cracks in the desert rippled towards them.

Still half blind, Aleja found her way to Farasha, who butted her shoulder affectionately. She pulled herself on to his saddle.

Malika turned to the captain. 'I warned that you would pay for disrespecting the jinn.'

Captain Quint hesitated, resting her hand on the hilt of her cutlass. 'You were right. I apologize,' she said eventually.

Malika nodded and the moment between them passed, the tension scattering like sand in the wind.

They paused at the top of the dune to watch the lost city sink back down into the sand.

'Why does it appear and disappear?' Aleja wondered aloud, wishing she could have explored a little more, intrigued by the dark secrets Zerzura was concealing.

No one could answer her.

'I suppose it's harder to find that way,' Captain Quint said at last. 'How it works? I have no idea. But after living for so many years on a magical ship I find I am more and more difficult to surprise these days.' She snapped back to attention and leaped on to her camel. 'Now go, go, *go*,' she urged, leading them away at a gallop, racing against the desert that was tearing itself apart at their backs.

Aleja stole a final glance back at Zerzura. Sand was pouring like a waterfall into the huge cracks cutting through the desert. The last echo of magic whispered across the sands, and the lost city lay sunken once more.

CHAPTER THIRTY-FIVE

The Golden Telescope

They all took turns looking at the piece of the map. When Aleja examined it the parchment curled its edges, letting out tiny puffs that whispered ominously.

'Probably a defensive measure,' Captain Quint said, looking at it with starry eyes before tucking it into a glass vial. She strung it on a chain round her neck beneath her tunic. Aleja couldn't stop thinking about the other pieces of the map. It was hard to think of the crew setting sail for other destinations as thrilling as Zerzura without her.

'What now?' asked Griete. Her face was sunburned, every inch of her covered with sand, dust and the kind of dirt that only comes with battling cursed skeletons.

'Now we go home,' said Captain Quint, and Aleja felt a pang of longing for the *Ship of Shadows*. She couldn't wait to tell Farren and Velka everything, stack her plate high with Ermtgen's griddle cakes, see if her little shadow came back to her . . . She'd even found herself missing Geoffrey's ghostly complainings. But more than anything she was longing for those midnight hours spent unlocking the magical ship's secrets with Frances, sneaking cake, or just sitting side by side on the deck as the world rushed by one wave at a time.

'And Frances?' Aleja asked.

'We'll be picking up Frances along the way.'

Now that there wasn't an army of skeletons after them and the first piece of the map had been retrieved, Aleja dwelt on Frances, fresh worries sinking into her skin.

Griete fell into step beside Aleja, their camels walking side by side. 'Don't worry,' she said, breaking into Aleja's thoughts. 'Remember what I told you before? About the *Ship of Shadows*? The name has another meaning. Your shadow's always got your back, protecting you from anyone who might sneak up on you. This ship, this crew, it's our shadow. It will stand behind you, as it does with Frances. She'll be safe, Aleja. And you'll always have a home with us.'

The way back through the desert was faster now that they weren't chasing round in circles, searching for a lost city beneath the sands. Aada, having regained her senses, plotted their directions by starlight. The golden telescope was of no use since Aleja had cracked its code, and one night Captain Quint rode her camel alongside Farasha and passed it to Aleja.

'This is for you.'

'You don't want it?' Aleja asked, tracing the delicate swirls in the gold.

'It's served its purpose. Consider it a token of my gratitude. You kept your head under immense pressure and used your brain. You're one of the smartest girls I've met and I do hope you will change your mind about joining my crew on a more permanent basis.'

Aleja blinked hard as Captain Quint gave her a searching look, dug her heels into her camel and cantered off, leading them through the desert.

Over the next few days the sand firmed beneath the camels' hooves, the ground grew rockier, and the first trees appeared. They stopped at a small Berber village, where the houses were built with red clay, to refill their water skins and swap coins for a hot meal before they continued on their way. They halted frequently to drink and eat, for Malika to pray, for them to take turns going to the bathroom while hiding behind a camel.

'Still find the desert exciting?' Griete asked Aleja, giggling at her expression.

Aleja sighed, regretting the days she'd spent telling anyone who'd listen that she didn't care how long it would take to cross the desert. They'd left Marrakesh three weeks ago. Three weeks of riding camels every day. 'I still want to travel the world,' she said.

'But?' Griete pressed.

'But I'd be perfectly happy never to set foot in a desert again,' Aleja admitted, using the side of her headscarf to mop up the sweat from her face for the thousandth time that day.

They didn't venture back into the imperial city. 'I'll go in alone,' Malika announced as they watered their camels outside the gates. 'I fit in the most after all,' she said wryly. 'Besides, I want to say goodbye.'

Malika didn't need to say to whom. Captain Quint nodded her assent and Aleja knew that, like the others on the ship, Malika's history was long and personal. Habiba didn't seem to mind that Malika spent most of her time away, judging by the brief time Aleja had seen them together. Guilt seized her thoughts as she thought about her own family; did they fear the worst? She nibbled her lip, trying to imagine what returning home would be like. What her father and abuela would say. What Miguel had thought when she'd gone. She even found herself missing Pablo.

All of that hurtled from her mind, however, the second Malika reappeared some hours later, a smaller figure at her side.

Aleja flung herself on Frances. 'I was so worried you'd been caught,' she said, feeling Frances hugging her tightly back.

'Nah, I'm impossible to catch,' Frances bragged.

Aleja hid her smile as her memories of Frances getting caught – twice – popped into her head. 'I can't believe you missed out on the lost city,' she said instead.

Frances pulled a face and threw her leg over her camel, who was staring at her balefully. 'Yes. Me either. Days upon days of riding camels in an unbearable desert, where cursed skeletons chased you out. Meanwhile, I got to eat cake with Habiba every day,' Frances said with a grin.

Aleja groaned, her stomach snarling at the mention of cake. Frances cast her eyes over the rest of the group, who were leading the camels back to the coast. 'Want to keep a secret?' Frances whispered.

'Always,' Aleja said at once.

Frances ferreted around in the sack between her crossed legs. 'I saved you some,' she said, reaching out to pass Aleja a small bundle.

She opened it to find little squares of honey-soaked sponge green with pistachios and drizzled with flaked almonds. Aleja thought she might die of happiness as she nibbled on one, the sweet stickiness coating her tongue and distracting her from the ache of another day's riding.

It took the rest of the journey to exchange their stories of everything that had happened to each of them since they'd last been together. Frances had narrowly escaped detection by the city watchmen as she'd hidden up a tree nearby until the sun rose and the city filled once more. Then she'd hopped down and made her way back to Habiba. 'Luckily she'd been asked to wait at her house in case one of us needed her.' Frances laughed. 'Can you imagine if I was left outside? In that dress? They would have found me straight away!'

Aleja could imagine and it didn't bear thinking about, but in the safety of the day, another cake in hand, she laughed along with Frances. As did Frances when Aleja told her about reaching her hand into the skeleton's eye socket, along with a dramatic re-enactment that had Frances squealing in horrified glee.

'I'm definitely going to have to teach you how to swim, though,' Frances said when Aleja had finished telling her story, complete with falling into the pool of water. 'Pirates *definitely* need to know how to swim, and you're as pirate as the rest of us now.'

At that Aleja's grin was every bit as wide as Frances's.

Before they knew it they'd reached the coast. The little blue port town was waiting for them just as they'd left it. The horizon beckoned, and there, in the harbour, was the *Ship of Shadows*.

Captain Quint feasted her eyes on it. 'Welcome home.'

Malika and Griete were dispatched to sell the camels. Before they went, Aleja patted Farasha on the nose, not minding the smell now that she smelled as bad as them. 'I'll miss you, you funny animal,' she told him, much to Frances's amusement.

The ship smelled of fresh wood. Its gaping holes had been patched over with new planks and everything was immaculately scrubbed, basking in the sunlight on the smooth-as-glass harbour water. Captain Quint strode up the gangplank, a sack of supplies over her shoulder. Aleja and Frances brought up what was left – they'd lost half their clothes and one of the tents after the supply camel had bolted. Aleja hadn't minded squeezing in with Griete and Aada, but she had minded the rationing of food and water.

'It feels good to be home,' Frances said before looking around and frowning.

'What is it?' Aleja asked, glancing down to where her little shadow had rushed over the deck and dived into her boot, shaking.

'It's too quiet,' Captain Quint answered, drawing her cutlass and dropping her load in one smooth movement. 'Something's wrong.'

Chapter Thirty-Six

Forked Horizons

'Aleja. Fetch me Malika and Griete. Now,' Captain Quint ordered.

Aleja dropped her sacks, turning to run back down the gangplank. But her way was barred by a man bearing two swords. She backed away, thinking of her empty pistol and her small dagger, which were no match for him. Stepping back on to the ship, she realized they were surrounded by figures with drawn swords, hemming them in. It was a trap they hadn't seen coming.

'Where's my crew?' Captain Quint demanded. Aleja was proud to see that her chin was raised high and she held her own head higher.

'They are no longer your crew. They are my prisoners.' François Levasseur strode forward, his eye blazing, his polished boots tapping smartly on the deck, his sword bloodied.

Aleja tried not to panic, unable to believe he'd tracked their whereabouts. Her skin crawled. She made to edge closer to Frances, but realized the girl was gone. Blinking, Aleja couldn't see where she'd vanished to. Surrounded by pirate hunters, with only the captain at her side, Aleja hadn't envisaged their welcome back this way. She glanced at the bright splash of blood on François's shining sword and a sickening feeling crept down to the pit of her stomach. *Where was Malika?*

'Where are they?' Captain Quint stared stonily back at him.

Ignoring her question, François Levasseur smiled slowly. 'They are awaiting their sentence.' He beckoned to one of his crew. 'Read the captain what happens to captured pirates.'

The man opened a small book and began reading in a monotone. Panicking, looking for Frances but trying not to be obvious about it, Aleja caught the odd word that mangled her thoughts with fear. Words like *sentenced to death* and *hanging.*

'I'll surrender to you,' Captain Quint said, stepping closer to François, 'in exchange for their lives.'

François's lip curled into a sneer. 'I don't think so. You are vastly outnumbered and you and your little urchin here –' Aleja realized with a start that he was referring to her – 'will be following your other *pirates* to your death. Seize them!' he yelled.

Captain Quint balled her hand up into a fist and punched François Levasseur in his remaining eye. Drawing her sword, she said, 'Get behind me,' to Aleja, who clenched her trusty dagger, glaring. The men surrounded them in a ring, Aleja and the captain back to back in the centre.

Aleja looked around, expecting to see Raven, the girl who had abandoned the *Ship of Shadows* for the pirate hunter's crew, but there was no one who could be her. Just a mob of pirate hunters. They inched closer, swords snapping like crocodile teeth at their ankles, making Aleja jump as they laughed cruelly at her. She spat at them and the laughs hardened into jeers.

'Not yet.' Captain Quint's whisper sneaked into Aleja's ear.

What was the captain waiting for? Hope sparked in Aleja's heart. But seconds later François recovered. He gestured to one of his men, who scurried forward with a charcoal-coloured stone urn.

'I was waiting for you to be here to watch when I strip the shadows from your ship,' he said to Aleja's horror.

She watched the marbled veins criss-crossing the stone begin to glow. François twisted the lid off and Aleja felt the deck shudder beneath them, like the ship had gasped. Aleja shook her boot. '*Sal de aquí*,' she whispered down to her shadow. *Get out of here.* 'Go. Hide.' The tiny inky bloom darted away to Aleja's immense relief.

Seconds later, the shadows clustered round the edges of the deck began to rustle. Aleja's mouth fell open as the first shadow was dragged towards the urn. It formed long human hands that reached out as if it could claw its way free. Aleja looked down to see both her and the captain's ordinary shadows were distorted – the urn was sucking the nearest shadows into it.

'No!' Captain Quint screamed. She launched forward, her sword pointed at François. She broke through the men surrounding them, forcing François to drop the urn to defend himself. He batted the captain's sword away with his own, and they were off, fighting across the deck in a frenzied blur of sword thrusts and parries, the ringing clashes of metal deafening as they whirled and fought their way around the ship.

A few bright droplets of blood splashed on to the deck, but Aleja couldn't tell whose they were. Or who was winning – they moved too fast for her to see. She looked down to see the shadows rush away from the urn – it had stopped glowing now that it had been picked up by a different pirate hunter. Only François seemed to possess the dark power to make it work. Snapping back to attention, she saw a couple of François's crew had stopped watching the sword fight and were slinking closer to her.

Aleja put her dagger between her teeth and ran up the ropes, climbing up to the crow's nest. Clambering faster than ever, she flew up the ropes ahead of the two boys who were chasing her. She leaped into the basket at the top and spat out her dagger to point it at them. The boys paused.

A battle cry below stole their attention. Leaning over the rim of the basket, Aleja watched as Malika and Griete vaulted on to the ship, scimitar and cutlass in hand. Seconds later, the captured crew charged up the ladder from below decks, screaming their anger, flinging severed ropes off themselves, followed by Frances. François had been bluffing; the crew had never left the ship. Aleja grinned, awash with relief that Frances had found and liberated them. The two boys rushed back down the ropes to their shipmates' aid.

Before Aleja could follow she noticed something.

François wasn't the only one who kept looking at the captain. At first, she'd thought it was because she'd been the greatest target, now she realized they were looking at something specific: her neck. And the piece of map in the vial she'd strung round it. Which meant . . . *they knew about the map.*

It gave her an idea. She tore off a patch of her white tunic and rolled it up to resemble parchment. Then she began to climb out across a yard. Shimmying along the supporting beam, Aleja shouted, 'Is this what you're looking for?' She waved the scroll in her hand.

Half of the crew froze, glancing between her and the captain, confused. She was right.

'What are you waiting for? Seize her!' François snapped at his men, between the clashes of his sword against Captain Quint's.

A large group of pirate hunters ran and leaped up at the netting, scaling it fast, swords between teeth. When they'd passed the halfway point, Aleja launched into action. Using her dagger, she began to saw at the ropes. They frayed and split, one by one popping free of the netting. The pirate hunters noticed the ropes beneath them slackening and started to shout, clambering back down again. But they were too late. Sawing as fast as she could, Aleja freed the last of the ropes and the entire group of pirate hunters hurtled down to the deck in a tangle of ropes. Half of them were knocked out, the other half hopelessly ensnared in netting. She'd taken out more of them than she'd expected. Climbing back into the crow's nest with a thrill of satisfaction, Aleja peered down to see what else was happening.

Griete arced her cutlass high above her; Farren stood balanced on the furthest point of the bow with a pistol in each hand to pick off the men who rushed towards her; Velka stood below Farren's feet, holding her sword threateningly. Still clutching her dagger, Aleja scoured the deck for Frances, until Malika stole her attention.

Malika was a whirlwind of devastating deadliness as she tunnelled straight through the sword fights, aiming directly for the man who'd taken her hand and her shadow. Aleja rushed to the other side of the basket to watch. François blanched when he spotted her, crashed into Captain Quint and grabbed at her to steady himself, then shoved past Frances and Aada, his sword slashing at her before he dived overboard. When his first mate noticed, shouting the alarm, the rest of his crew halted, uncertain whether to continue fighting without their captain. Aleja frowned – she hadn't expected him to flee so easily. She noticed Olitiana and Malika exchange a look at his odd behaviour and her suspicions grew.

Captain Quint straightened to her full height. 'I will take no prisoners. No man alive,' she growled, plucking her tri-cornered captain's hat from atop the steering wheel and setting it back on her head. Penumbra streaked down from the sky with a blood-curdling shriek and settled on her wrist with his wings spread fully.

The pirate hunters fled.

'Nicely done, Captain,' Olitiana said, letting her sword arm droop now the threat had passed. 'It's good to have you back.'

Aleja skimmed back down the ropes. 'What are they doing?' she asked, watching the pirate hunters. Aleja and Frances ran to the taffrail to look.

François Levasseur had climbed back on to his own ship, *La Promesse Lumineuse*, which was moored a short distance down the harbour. His crew were running back and weighing anchor, preparing to sail away in a hurry. A small figure was standing on the deck. She had long black hair, almost black eyes and a sulky expression that was twisted into a frown. She was wearing a shapeless black dress that fell to her sharp knees, and knee-high lace-up black boots. And she was staring back at the *Ship of Shadows*. Frances gasped.

'Raven?' Aleja guessed.

Malika stuck her scimitar in her sash and pulled out what looked like twin blades, throwing knives. 'She betrayed us,' she said, arcing her arm back. Aleja and Frances were now gaping at Malika instead.

'Malika, no!' Captain Quint said in alarm, rushing over and knocking the knives out of her hand.

Malika stared at the captain like she'd lost her mind. 'She knows our secrets. She's undoubtedly the reason why that *man* –' she spat the word out like it was poison – 'knows about the map.' She plucked her knives off the deck.

'She's got a point,' Frances muttered to Aleja, who privately agreed. It didn't stop either of them looking anxiously at Malika and her knives, though.

Captain Quint threw a look back over her shoulder. 'It wasn't her that told him.'

Malika continued to stare at the captain. 'Is this some kind of sentimentality?' she asked warily, still holding on to her blade.

Captain Quint exhaled roughly. 'Raven is there on my orders,' she said, her voice low and urgent. 'She's my spy.'

Frances's mouth fell open. '*What?*'

Captain Quint gave her a fierce glare. 'This goes no further than the four of us, understood?'

Malika reluctantly sheathed her throwing knives. 'Surely you don't believe one of us would betray your secret?'

'I don't. But every additional crew member who knows is an extra person who could be caught and interrogated. Mark my words, François has a vendetta against us and this won't be the last time we find him lying in wait. Since we have yet to seize the source of his power, we might not be so lucky next time, and the fewer people who know, the safer she is,' Captain Quint said.

'That's who you met in Tangier,' Aleja said, shocked.

The captain nodded. 'Aye.'

They watched the pirate hunters' ship inch out of the harbour when Captain Quint suddenly cursed, scrabbling at her neck. 'He took it!'

'What?' Malika wheeled round to look at her, whipping her scimitar out.

'The map! He took it!' Captain Quint raced to the helm, her knuckles whitening round the wheel. 'Chase that ship!'

Now that the captain was no longer wearing a headscarf, Aleja saw that the glass vial round her neck was missing. The first piece of the map was gone. That was why François had fled so easily then – he'd got what he wanted.

'Erm, Captain?' Frances asked timidly.

Sails were unfurled, the ship bloomed in white, and shouts were relayed across the deck as orders were carried out and the anchor was weighed on its creaking chains.

'Captain Quint?' Frances asked again, louder this time.

'What's wrong?' Aleja asked, noting the determined set of Frances's jawline.

Frances sighed dramatically. 'So I guess no one's interested in this then?' she said, pulling the glass vial out of her pocket and waving it in the air. That drew Captain Quint's attention.

'How did you get that?' She relinquished the wheel to Olitiana and strode towards Frances and the curl of parchment nestled inside the glass vial.

'A thief can always spot another thief. I swapped the vial for something of equal weight in his pocket before he jumped.' Frances's grin was mischievous.

'You are *brilliant*.' Captain Quint took the vial back, holding it tightly.

'What did you swap it with?' Aleja asked, pride filling her up until she was sure she'd burst.

Frances looked mournful. 'My last pastry.'

Aleja watched the Moroccan coastline melt into the horizon behind them. Standing on the tip of the stern, between her shadow, now in the form of a girl, and Frances, it was hard to believe that her adventure was coming to an end. Pirate hunters, terrifying monsters, lost cities sinking into the desert and caves crammed with jewels had been a pretty good run, though, she considered.

'Aleja?' Frances spoke up, her eyes still fixed on the little blue town vanishing into the endless horizon of sea and sky.

The creaking of the ship, flapping of the sails and screeching of gulls swooping above them felt natural to Aleja now, as did the salty breeze rushing through her hair and ruffling her trousers.

'Yes?'

'I don't want you to leave. You're the best friend I've ever had. But . . . if I still had a family, I'd want to go home to them too.' Frances hopped down on to the deck, pushing her glasses back up her nose. 'I just thought you should know that.'

She left before Aleja could open her mouth to speak.

Sometimes friends became family too. The family you chose to have when your lives cosied up against each other's as if you'd always been there.

Farren had given her a quick fierce hug when the chaos had ended. Velka's smile had been wider than she'd ever seen it. Ermtgen had pressed cake into her hand, Olitiana had praised her for finding the map, and her shadow had danced beside her. Everyone had celebrated being reunited again. Just like a family. Aleja went down to her cabin, trailed by her shadow, which had adopted its fox shape. Sitting on her plum carpet, she stroked it. Her fingers passed straight through it on to the carpet below, but the shadow-fox preened anyway. 'I've decided on a name,' she told it. 'How do you feel about Tinta? It's Spanish for ink, because you're ink-black and because ink stays – like I want you to.' Her shadow swished its tail and leaped up at her, slinking out into its girl shape to fold its arms round Aleja in a whispery embrace. 'I'll take that as a yes, then,' she said, laughing.

She was going to miss magic. In Sevilla magic had been just an exciting seafaring tale that echoed in dark tavern corners. Nobody but Aleja and the odd mad sailor had believed it existed, glittering under the surface of the everyday. Being aboard the *Ship of Shadows* had taught her how magical the world really was.

*

A little later, Aleja wandered into the library to find Thomas James's book. It had been left on the wooden table.

'Speak what you seek,' she whispered to herself, running her fingers over the blank map she'd opened it to. Looking around to check the library was definitely empty, Aleja said, 'I seek the second piece of the map,' feeling a little foolish.

She didn't expect a response.

The map engraved on the table began to warm, forcing Aleja to yank her arms away from it. She placed a hand on the engraving of Africa. Nothing but cool wood. The same for all the other continents . . . except Europe.

Minutes later, Aleja repeated her actions for the captain. 'This is why it didn't work the first time in your cabin; the book is *physically* a key to the ship – you have to use the right page in the right place to unlock the hidden information!' she told her excitedly as Captain Quint pressed a hand to the table.

'Of course, why else would he have called it the key?' Captain Quint marvelled, Penumbra perched on her shoulder. Taking the book, Captain Quint re-examined the other, unsolved, puzzles. 'These must all unlock other places around the ship. There are four left, one for each piece of the map.' Aleja, who had been bouncing on her toes with the thrill of her discovery, suddenly stilled. She would not be the one to solve those other puzzles. She would never know where the other pieces of the map were hidden.

The *Ship of Shadows* sailed closer to Sevilla each day. And each day Aleja stood at the bow, watching their progress, feeling her choices colliding against each other. Her horizons were forked, tearing her in two different directions. She couldn't leave her family, especially Miguel. But she was finding it harder and harder to imagine leaving the *Ship of Shadows* too.

This wasn't an answer she could find in a book. For this she would have to follow her heart. And in her heart she wanted to be a pirate.

Acknowledgements

A huge thank you to my fabulous agent, Thérèse Coen, for being the first to come aboard and always being here for me, guiding me through the seven seas with endless kindness and enthusiasm. I couldn't have wished for a better agent!

To my wonderful editor, Emma Jones, I feel incredibly lucky to have you onboard. Your advice is always insightful and inspiring, and I've loved working with you. Thank you for taking both Aleja and me under your wing – we're both a million (nautical) miles better off for it.

I couldn't be happier that *The Ship of Shadows* found a home at Puffin. I owe all of you my endless gratitude and appreciation for being the best crew on this journey.

Acknowledgements

Special thanks to Ruth Knowles for believing in me and my story from the start, and Shreeta Shah and Michelle Nathan for all their hard work and brilliance. A big thank you to Eliza Walsh, Jane Seery, Katy Finch and Sophia Watts in Production and Design, and to Jennie Roman, Claire Davis, Petra Bryce and Leena Lane for your superb eagle eyes!

Thank you Karl James Mountford for the most gorgeous cover art – you've made my story look like proper pirate bounty!

A barrel of love and thanks to my best friend, Christine Spoors, who's been there for me from the very beginning of my writing adventure and every single day since.

Thank you to all my amazing friends and fellow authors who've cheered me on and offered endless encouragement, especially Alex McGahan, Sarah Hackmann (mother of ferns), my Shakespearean Sisters (you know who you are!) and Rachel Rowlands. Huge thanks to C. G. Drews, whose advice, motivation and shared flailing has kept me buoyant. A bottle of Captain Quint's finest rum to Vic James and L. D. Lapinski for all the DMs, and one of Frances's best cakes for Abi Elphinstone and Alex Bell for reading my manuscript and saying such lovely things about it.

For Jenny and everyone at The Dance Studios, thank you for all the support and getting me off the sofa and away from my laptop!

Acknowledgements

For Sarah, Mercedes and all my past students and friends in Puente Genil, thank you for making my time in Spain some of my favourite memories. *¡Te echo de menos!*

Thank you to my parents for taking me to the library every week as I was growing up and always encouraging me to follow my dreams. Thanks to my brother Paul for de-stressing me with all the cute animal videos, and Babcia for supplying me with lots of lovely books and endless pierogi. For Dziadzio, who I miss every single day. For my Uncle Joe, Aunt Marion and my cousin Hannah, thanks for all the constant enthusiasm and support. Thank you to Jane and Chris Brothwood for being the best in-laws ever and forever cheering me on, Chelsea Brothwood for being such a lovely sister, and Gill and John Biddulph for being another set of grandparents to me.

Thanks with all my heart to Michael Brothwood. For always listening (including in that hotel room in Marrakesh when I ranted about the lack of female pirates!), celebrating my successes, calming my panics and loving my pirates as much as I do. Our travels around the world inspired this book, and I couldn't have done it without you.

And lastly, to whoever's holding this book in their hands, a huge welcome aboard *The Ship of Shadows* and thank you for joining Aleja and me on this adventure!

ABOUT THE AUTHOR

Maria Kuzniar spent six years living
in Spain, teaching English and travelling
the world, which inspired her debut novel
The Ship of Shadows. Now she lives in
Nottingham with her husband, where she
reads and writes as much as she can and
bookstagrams at @cosyreads. She is always
planning her next adventure.